The Angel's Final Charge

Part III

of

The Real Vampires

The Angel's Final Charge, The Real Vampires Trilogy, © 2003, Paul Beach

All rights reserved, including the right to reproduce this book or portions thereof in any form whatsoever.

This book is a work of fiction. Names, characters, places and incidents are products of the author's imagination or are used fictitiously. Any resemblance to actual events or locales or persons living or dead is entirely coincidental.

Acknowledgements

For Beverly, the love of my life; she is my reason for breathing. For my best friend Shawn; you will find him throughout this book. For Brenda; this work was completed only with her encouragement. For Marie; my deepest gratitude and appreciation.

Table of Contents

I – Chad the Vampire 1

II – The Story of Scott 6

III – The IRS Agent and the Drug Dealer 15

IV – Janet and Gerald Discuss Poop 23

V – Jamie and the Vampire 30

VI – Chad's Close Call 37

VII – Profiling a Killer 41

VIII – Officer Nader and the Vampire 52

IX – Marcus Asks a Favor of Tina 60

X – Detective Work 66

XI – Noonan's Big Moment 73

XII – An Eventful Night 78

XIII – The Framing of Jensen 94

XIV – Marcus Meets Tim the Vampire Slayer 101

XV – Death with Dignity 111

XVI – Marcus and Sarah 130

XVII – Henderson Works the Phone 136

XVIII – Marcus Gets Some Recon 142

XIX – Jensen Sings 148

XX – Marcus Confronts the Slayer 152

XXI – The Real Vampire 165

XXII – A New Day 194

CHAPTER I

The white and yellow lines of the dark road seemed to stand out from the recent rain. There were just enough cars passing by to be severely irritating. Chad preferred the quiet peace of the night, but every time the annoying noise of one car had finally faded into oblivion there would be another pair of headlights appearing on the rise. And because of the foggy, wet conditions none of the motorists could see Chad until they were right on top of him, which meant he had to give way – step off the pavement and into the dripping ferns. It was either that or receive a road-grime shower from the passing vehicle. Trucks were the worst.

But even in the midst of this nuisance, Chad had a larger, more powerful discomfort to alleviate. It wasn't fatigue or infirmity. Chad had freed himself of the weakness that was the result of his AIDS. He had made a choice, and had traded in that inevitable death for a dark life; a life without light; a life that promised to be steeped in the misery and death of innocent others! And a chance for vengeance. He had become a vampire. Now he had the hunger, and despite all of the power that vampirism afforded him, the discomfort of this hunger was strangely stronger than the discomfort of infirmity.

The decision to become a vampire had been an easy one for Chad. Getting his hands on some of Marcus's blood had taken some cunning, some ingenuity, and a lot of luck. Hell! The whole episode had been one huge stroke of luck. Even the girls had unwittingly helped him to be turned.

Learning that Marcus was a real-life vampire had indeed been shocking, but from the first moment that Marcus had sucked blood out of Chad's wrist, Chad had been entertaining thoughts of what he would be able to do himself, as a vampire. Of course, it had become quite clear from the beginning that Marcus wasn't going to make anyone a vampire, but after hearing how Marcus himself had become a vampire, Chad knew that that didn't matter. Being away from the hospital environment had done wonders for Chad's general condition. He had

had the strength and energy to take action when the opportunity presented itself.

Marcus slept during the day in a cellar under the cabin. The vampire kept the door locked at night, and barred from the inside during the day, as Chad had learned after fate allowed him entry to the room's interior. Not even Scott, the caretaker of the cabin, had a key to the cellar door. Nor had he ever seen the inside of it, until that one night when Marcus had staggered back to the cabin after his 'night-walk' with two bullet wounds. Everyone had seen the inside of the chamber then.

The girls, being girls, had insisted on pampering and fawning over the wounded vampire, and he had probably needed it. The wounds were ghastly and looked worse than mortal. That Marcus had even been moving under his own power seemed amazing to Chad. The .38 caliber bullets had entered squarely into his stomach, and left messy exit wounds on his back.

Scott and the girls had helped Marcus down into his cellar room. The chamber was far from plush or lavish, but it was very clean. It was rather narrow but went in a fair distance. They had laid him down in a functional little bed, the room's only furnishing located as far from the door as possible. Marcus had been on the edge of consciousness.

As they exited the room to give Marcus peace for his regenerative sleep, Chad had so helpfully turned out the low-watt lamplight that was the room's only lighting. He made a show of turning the lock on the cellar doorknob, but there was, of course, no way to lock the bolt or hang the bar. It would be okay this one time.

That had been only nine days into the 'vacation.' The next morning as Scott was in town buying food and supplies, and the girls were busy doing whatever, Chad had emptied the gas out of one of the dirt bikes, and filled the tank on the other. Then he had re-entered the cellar through the unsecured door.

Direct light from the outside did not make it from the open door to the far end of the room where Marcus lay in the bed. Chad crept in quietly, remembering the story of Humayun, and approached the bed. His heart raced with fear and excitement. What could he say if Marcus woke up right at that moment? *'Oh, hi. I was just checking on you. How are you?'* It was weak. Did he really have the balls to do what he was about to do? Chad steeled himself. He *had* to do it. Too much depended on it. He was not going to die without getting revenge.

He grabbed Marcus's limp hand and bit down hard on the fleshy bit between his thumb and forefinger. The hand became rigid and jerked

I – Chad the Vampire

away, but not before Chad's teeth had bitten through the flesh. Like Marcus and Viviana so many centuries before, Chad now had the same little chunk of Marcus's hand in his mouth.

Marcus's eyes flew open. As fast as lightning the vampire's injured hand shot up and caught Chad by the wrist. "What have you done, Chad? What have you done?" Marcus's voice held as much fear in it as Chad's would have if he had tried to speak.

With all of the strength that he could muster, Chad brought his free hand down on the vampire's injured stomach. The blow wasn't much to the vampire, but it was just enough to make Marcus let go, and Chad scrambled toward the door. Marcus could only watch him go.

Chad had then jumped onto the freshly fueled dirt-bike and cut through the woods in the direction of the highway. He had done it. He had duplicated Marcus's steps to becoming a real vampire and gotten away.

Typical Oregon weather, (that is, a cool, depressing drizzle) had plagued Chad all afternoon as he covered as much ground as possible on the dirt-bike. Eventually, it ran out of gas and Chad abandoned it. Finally, as daylight faded he had made it to the highway. He turned in the direction of Portland. He had absolutely no money.

Picking up hitchhikers can be very dangerous. Chad did not expect anyone to stop for him, even though he feverishly hoped that someone would. There could be no doubt that the terrible hunger he now felt was for fresh human blood. Whoever did stop for him would die, there was no question. Chad didn't like it, but shit happens; that's just the way it is. Picking up hitchhikers can be very, very dangerous.

So what kind of foolhardy person stops for a hitchhiker?

Barry Woodside drove an '89 Lincoln Continental. He was fifty-four years old with four ex-wives. He worked as a real estate agent, mostly brokering time-shares at resort cabins on lakesides all around the mountainous region. Barry was a heavy man with a full head of wavy, grey hair, and not without his share of health problems. He was between wives right now so his life was terminally boring. Barry was not always honest in his everyday dealings with his fellow man, but he could be big-hearted and sympathetic, especially to a poor wretch out walking down the highway on a cold, wet night. "Hey, pal! Do you need a ride?" he called after slowing his bulky vehicle.

"Thank god you stopped," said Chad as he opened the heavy car door. "I crashed my dirt-bike in the woods."

"Are you okay?" asked Barry.

It would be best to take this hairy-eared man before he got the car moving. Chad wasted no time. He had only a jack-knife, which he now thrust into Barry Woodside's shoulder. The older man was caught completely unaware by the sudden move, and he screamed in pain as Chad turned the blade. Blood oozed onto the thin material of Barry's sweater.

With his victim's right arm incapacitated Chad removed the blade and fought to arrest the flailing defensive movements of the panicking man.

Barry tried first to push Chad away and then to unlatch his seatbelt. He was successful at neither. He screamed and yelled, hit the car horn, finally gunned the engine in a kicking paroxysm causing the car to lurch forward. His left hand instinctively gripped the wheel trying to right the direction of the moving vehicle.

The young vampire took the opportunity to jab the jack-knife deep into his victim's throat. Barry now jammed the brakes and groped with his one good hand trying to remove the paralyzing blade.

Chad quickly managed to throw the shift lever into PARK bringing the large car to a gently skidding stop on the slick pavement. Then, batting his victim's flailing hand away, he pulled the blade back out with a quick jerk. The exiting blade was followed immediately by a steady, pulsing stream of blood, and Chad sealed his hungry lips over the wound. A weak hand now pushed against Chad's head in a last-ditch effort to rid the victim of this parasite. But Chad, without looking, drove the knife once again into his victim, this time into the poor man's leg. His victim was now sufficiently subdued and the vampire finished bleeding him out with comparative ease. The victim smelled greasy, and the blood left a coat of film inside Chad's mouth.

At length, the flow of blood abated and Chad's lips pulled away from the wound. He said with mock sympathy to the dying man, "Aw! Did you accidentally get pricked by an AIDS infected hypodermic needle? How sad! How tragic! I guess you'll die."

Tim and Desperado watched in silence, each man bored out of his skull, as the strange, white-haired man walked purposefully along a narrow country road. The smelly van was currently parked and the Vampire Slayer and his invisible friend sat in it waiting for their quarry to get a little further ahead. Presently, Tim would start the van again, drive a short distance ahead of the walking man, then stop again and wait some more. It was in this tedious fashion that Tim and Desperado had followed the strange man in a seemingly random course around the

I – Chad the Vampire

United States for the last several years. It was only the strange man's proven track record for leading them to vampires and other adventures that kept them going.

It was dawn of the eleventh day since they had left the Portland metro area. Tim had been kicking himself for not storming the house where they had seen the vampire. Now the two of them watched as the wizard stopped momentarily to check his amazing tracking device. Tim and Desperado gaped as the tall man turned around and walked back toward them.

"What's this?" Tim wondered aloud. Was the funky dude coming back to ask Tim for a speedy conveyance in the van?

But the man walked methodically by the van and its occupant.

"He's going back," Tim stated in disbelief. "He's going back! Oh my god!! He's going back to Portland!! What the fuck?!"

"Hey now, Mister Pottymouth!" Desperado chastised. But then he quickly turned frustrated as well. "I've had it with tailin' this geek! I say we go back to that house in town and do our own raid. We know the vampires are there. After we take care of 'em, we can catch back up with this dude if we want. We've lost him before and found him easy enough!"

Tim was indeed frustrated, and it wasn't the first time that they had struck out on their own to initiate an action. Still, something, he wasn't sure what it was, urged him to stay on the strange man for just a bit longer.

CHAPTER II

"Now that Miriam is feeling better, can we finally do something about Chad?" Janet asked. After four weeks at the cabin Mimi was at last getting over the symptoms of withdrawal.

There had been some worry from the girls after Chad had disappeared. Everybody knew exactly what had happened. Of course, Janet had been the most upset of the group. If Marcus had been troubled by the incident he did not show it.

"Chad has made his choice," Marcus had said. "And he will now reap all of the effects of that cause which he has set in motion. No amount of worry or stress from you at this time is going to help the situation. It will only dis-empower you."

"But we've got to do something," Janet had protested. "We can't just sit up here and let this happen!"

"Would you have tried to interfere at my own turning, child? Undo all that has happened since? Would you endeavor to stop the tide?"

And so Marcus had simply gone on as before. He did not feel responsible for creating Chad, since the young man had done it of his own volition. There was nothing to be done. The old vampire tried to instill some peace in the worrisome Janet. "The situation will most likely resolve itself without any interference from us."

Marcus hadn't meant to go out and get shot. The vampire had been doing most of his feeding from his friend Scott and the girls. But feeding must be done with utmost care, even with three donors, and so it was that Marcus had gone out hunting one night. His donors had needed some time to recuperate.

Initially he had come across a small encampment of three poachers. He was about to make a victim of one of them from the shadows when a single Fish and Wildlife officer came on the scene with the intention of making a grand and heroic bust. Marcus decided to feed on the law officer because, as he explained later to the girls when telling the story of how he had gotten shot, "While killing bears solely for the purpose of harvesting their gall bladders can be a grossly inhuman activity in which to engage, enforcing arbitrary, statutory law is far more despicable and damaging."

II – The Story of Scott

It was simply a pity that Chad had bolted before Marcus had had a chance to tell much of his wisdom and experience on surviving as a vampire in the age of the communication revolution. Not that Chad would have been able to stay after having done what he had. The old vampire would certainly have killed him.

Besides, Marcus was also scheming. He was pretty sure that Chad was on his way back to Portland to exact his revenge upon those persons that he felt were to blame for ruining his life. If Chad should be so foolish as to be found out and destroyed, the authorities might be quick to credit him with many or perhaps even all of the late murders and disappearances around town. With some careful planning such a scenario could be orchestrated.

And so it was that as the sky began to darken over the mountain on the twenty-third day at the cabin, Marcus arose and found the girls anxious to get back to Portland; back to their lives – their new lives, as Mimi was now living drug-free, and Janet would most likely be looking for a new career.

Even Marcus was to have business waiting for him. The annular report for Bradley Holdings was waiting at home for his analysis. Receipt of that report was one of the only things that kept the old vampire abreast of the passing years anymore. This report would contain a summary of the business, including an update on the pending IRS action against the company. If the news was bad, he would have to have another meeting with Ms. Goulier.

They loaded up the SUV, gave their hugs and good-byes to Scott, and Marcus piloted the vehicle down the twisting, rutted mountain trail to the road. Shortly after they had gotten underway, Mimi asked, "Marcus, you never told us about your friend Scott. I know that he was in the army and fought in Vietnam, but he never told us how you two met."

"Shucks," said Marcus modestly. The girls had come to really enjoy his story-telling. "I caught up with Scott once when I was trailing a certain army colonel whose duty it was to track down deserters. I have been known to hang near the airport after dark. I can find victims there who are in town on business or whatever, and I have methods for finding out how much these travelers might be missed.

"So it was 1969, and I was sitting at one of the terminal gates. When I saw the pompous, straight-backed walk of the young army colonel, I just knew that I had to have him. He walked with the air of someone who felt indemnified by some imaginary government for any action that he might take. It was clear that he fancied himself above the law, and maybe he *was* above the law of the land; that weak statutory law written by weak men to serve their political and financial ends. But he was certainly not above the Law of Nature, and I was hungry enough to teach him that final lesson seconds before he was to die.

"First, I picked his pocket, stole his wallet, and after finding no pictures of wife and children, I felt pretty fine about making him disappear. I noticed that the young man did not seem well-traveled or experienced, and I even managed to return his wallet without him finding out. All this I did as he was talking on a pay telephone, engaged in a discussion where he requested, rather forcefully, immediate assistance at a certain address in northeast. 'Do not approach until I get there,' he commanded. I watched him as he rented a car, which was perfect since I always parked near the rental lot myself just for this purpose. It was a cinch to follow him as he drove off in his rental car."

"Oh my god, that is so clever!" Janet said, musing. Only a month earlier she would have been abhorrent over the idea of someone hunting another person with such a murderous purpose. Now, after listening to the story of Marcus, her mind had opened up to the idea that such ugliness might actually have a small purpose in the workings of the world.

"Yes, isn't it?" continued Marcus. "So, anyway, I followed the colonel to a lovely neighborhood. He was staking out a house that I was soon to learn was the home of the Hinckley residents. Scott Hinckley had gone AWOL, as it is called, in Vietnam and had somehow managed to get back to the states. This colonel's mission was to collect Scott and bring him before a court martial, and he was hoping and expecting to find Scott trying to hide at his own home. And as it turned out, the young colonel's hunch was, in fact, correct."

"Presently, another vehicle arrived, and a muscular man wearing a uniform with the markings of the military police alighted from it. I watched and listened from my car as the young colonel, my would-be victim, met the other man, the MP, at the front walk of the house. 'I requested two MP's!' snapped the colonel. To which the imposing fellow replied, 'I'm all that was available on such short notice. I can handle him.' It was interesting to note that the junior officer didn't regard the superior with any of the anticipated respect. That should have been his first clue that something was amiss.

"The colonel knocked on the door of the house and confronted the middle-aged man that answered. A very heated debate ensued. Basically, the deluded soldier's position was that he had every right to enter the premises and take delivery of the deserter. The man at the door said that it would require the force of a larger 'army' than the one present for the young colonel and the MP to gain entry. And it was at that moment that the muscular MP officer, with stunning efficiency ushered the other two surprised men back into the house. I could tell that both the older man and the colonel were under the control of the MP, though I could not see any kind of a weapon from where I was.

"I was not sure what exactly had happened myself, and being the curious cat that I am, I felt compelled to look into it further. You see, the darkness of night is my domain, I fancy, and if something is going to 'go down on my turf,' so to speak, I feel that it is my prerogative as a being damned to the night to know about it and involve myself, if I should feel so inclined."

The girls listened breathlessly as the vampire continued.

"I lit from my vehicle and ran to the doorstep of the house. The door had been bolted, probably by the muscular man in an effort to slow down any escape attempt by his prisoners. As I set about picking the lock I could hear voices from inside the house. Someone was demanding that Scott show himself or there would be dire consequences. Moments later I heard the muffled report of a gun, and then the horrified yell of a man. I quietly opened the door a crack and heard another male voice from further back in the house saying that he was coming out! 'Please don't shoot!'

"A wide hallway ran from the entryway, past a staircase on the right and into what was probably a kitchen. Immediately to the left was a doorway that led into a front room, where I could just see the backside of the terrified army colonel. Suddenly the back of my would-be victim's head exploded exactly at the same time as the sound of another muffled gunshot registered in my ears, and his body fell heavily to the floor in the doorway. I remember feeling a little disappointed that I had not had the chance to feed on the pompous ass.

"Coming down the stairs was another young man, the man that was soon to become my friend. Alarm showed on his face as he caught sight of me and he asked 'what do you want?' assuming that it was I that had demanded his appearance.

"A burley voice from the next room said for him to 'get yer butt in here, before I waste yer old man!'"

"So that was when you first met Scott?" asked Mimi.

"Yes. Confusing isn't it?" said Marcus.

"Yes. Very." Both girls nodded.

"Yes, well, I guess it would be. Scott was most confused and fearful when he heard the other voice while I stood there silently with my finger on my lips. He called out asking if this was about his deserting in Vietnam.

"The faceless voice from the next room answered, 'I don't give a rat's ass about that.'

"'Please don't hurt my parents,' said Scott, and he quietly continued the rest of his descent down the stairs.

"'Then you'd better hurry up, junior,' said the voice.

"I watched Scott walk to the far end of the hall and enter the front room from another doorway that was located there. I heard the gruff voice say 'good' right before I heard a third gunshot. I sprang into the room myself, jumping over the crumpled body of the colonel, and I daresay that what I saw then was quite haunting, and that is saying a lot.

"There were two other dead bodies on the floor in addition to the dead army officer. One was a middle-aged woman, Scott's mother, and the other was the older man, Scott's father, just now coming to rest from where he had fallen from the clutch of the man that had just shot him. The man with the smoking gun was the muscular officer that I had seen so proficiently escort the other two men inside. Now I could see his slightly weathered features and his jet-black hair cut in a flattop. He was powerfully built and he exhibited the kind of fallacious, detached confidence that only comes from much killing. I recognized that look of satisfaction and pleasure on his face; I had seen it before, in the mirror. He greatly enjoyed killing. Without a doubt, he was a professional.

"I imagine that the only thing that saved Scott's life was the start that the shooter got from my sudden appearance at the other end of the room. As I advanced, the large man fired a hasty shot that was intended to hit Scott squarely in the head, but instead, grazed his shoulder, spinning him around. That gave me just enough time to cross the room and disarm the man with a blow to his wrist. I surely broke it, but the man had an astounding tolerance for pain, probably even a love for it, though I am certain he was not expecting such a forceful blow. As is most often the case, notwithstanding my excellent first strike, his threat assessment of me came in low; perhaps one my biggest advantages in a melee. He assumed an attack stance and tried to take me, probably assuming that he would defeat me with ease. Alas, he was a comparative novice. I ended up breaking his neck, carefully so as not to kill him."

"So that you could suck his blood?" said Mimi.

II – The Story of Scott

"Smart girl," said Marcus. "Yes. And by that time I was 'working up quite an appetite,' to borrow the phrase."

"So, who was the man with the gun?" asked Janet.

"We were never totally sure," said Marcus. "I tried to question the man, but he was tight-lipped and I really did not have the methods or the patience to torture him for information – distasteful activity! It was only after hearing Scott's amazing story that I deduced that the man's mission had been to eliminate Scott and anyone that he might have confided with about what he had seen in Vietnam."

"Was he a witness to war-crimes?" asked Janet.

"War is a crime in and of itself," said Marcus. "But to answer your question, 'yes.' He witnessed an incredible atrocity.

"By 1968, there was already a lot of anti-war sentiment even among the American troops in Vietnam. They were only vaguely aware of all that was going on over here, but the general consensus among the troops was that they did not belong in Vietnam. Scott had heard rumors that the CIA was smuggling opium out of Thailand and selling it to finance the war, but it was considered conspiracy theory bullshit. Until one day he witnessed certain American troops wasting an entire village near the Mekong River. Scott had filmed it! Men, women, and children, all slaughtered.

"Being a low ranking intelligence officer, he investigated the incident for his own satisfaction, and uncovered proof of the drug smuggling. It had been necessary to wipe out the village in order to facilitate the drug trafficking. In addition to that appalling footage of the massacre, Scott also captured on film and audio tape two of the kingpins of the operation handling contraband and issuing orders for its disbursement! It was not the CIA as an agency per say, but it was several individuals within the CIA, Navy, Air Force, and Congress, using their positions to coordinate and execute the entire operation. The heroin was produced in Thailand, and smuggled through Vietnam down the Mekong River by American troops who had absolutely no idea of what they were really transporting. They just believed that they were fighting the good fight against communism for their country and president. The drugs were actually retailed on the streets and campuses of America.

"Understand, I do not personally see anything inherently evil in drugs. They are a resource like anything else in this world. Depending upon their application they can be both harmful and beneficial. But because of the regulation of drugs, they have become like the gold of India.

"So, the true purpose of all actions taken in Indochina was to protect this drug smuggling operation from certain Asian military leaders who would liked to have taken control of this cash cow for themselves. You see, American agents have been growing opium in Asian soil and using American resources to 'export' it since World War II. The profits from this enterprise have been ungodly. When the 'powers that be' in Washington eventually stopped funding the Vietnam War, without reducing the burden upon the American taxpayers I might add, these war-time profiteers continued using the American troops and resources to carry on the operation, paying for all of it out of their own over-flowing pockets, effectively prolonging the so-called 'war.'

"And this is the kicker – most of the individuals behind this horrendous business are still in Washington today, entrenched in positions of great power, and running this 'country!' They are the real vampires. They suck the blood not only out of this country, but of the whole world! They have made lifetime careers of destroying and stealing, and they are responsible for much suffering and death. They are the true Bringers of War. Their behavior has only worsened since Vietnam."

Mimi said, "I think I'm going to be sick." Normally she would have been slow to take the word of just anyone about something so incredibly atrocious, but she believed the vampire. He had seen so much of the world in his life. His perception of the world and reality must be infinitely truer than hers or anyone else she might know.

The sweet, emotional Janet sat quietly, wiping her wet eyes.

Marcus continued. "It was obvious to both of us that Scott's life as he knew it was over. He would require the ultimate in witness protection if he expected to live, so Bradley Holdings bought the cabin and the surrounding mountain property and there he has had as comfortable a life in secret as he could have. Because Scott already carried with him such a terrible secret, and the physical proof, I felt reasonably comfortable in exposing my own secret to him. He was never so imprudent as to ask me to turn him. He probably fears that I would simply kill him if he ever did, and he is mostly correct in such a fear. Vampirism also scares him immensely; he is far too sentimental. Scott is a tender child, and being sent to Vietnam at nineteen was for him an enormous travesty in itself. He spends his time writing and now for the past few years he has been authoring an internet website that dispenses valuable and empowering educational information.

"Anti-government?" asked Mimi without any disdain.

II – The Story of Scott

"Anti-external authority," answered Marcus.

For a time the three of them rode silently on into the night, each in deep contemplation of all that they had seen and heard in their respective lifetimes, slowly getting closer to the lights of the metro.

Finally, Janet broke the silence. "Marcus, are you going to hunt Chad down and kill him?" It was obvious that the question had been difficult for her to get out.

The vampire took in a deep breath and let it out slowly. "I won't have to hunt him down."

Detective Darrel Hutchinson hated stereotypes. It irked him to no end when someone engaged in profiling. He glared at the snickering young punk with the multi-colored hair, then exited the café with his morning coffee, and a donut. How had the little punk been able to tell that he was a cop in the first place? It's not like he was wearing a uniform or something! Maybe he'd caught a glimpse of the badge attached to the detective's belt underneath his overcoat.

Hutchinson had just reached his official detective car when the cell phone attached to his belt chimed the old theme song to the seventies hit TV show SWAT. "Hutchinson, get down to the Skidmore Fountain. We gotta John Doe suicide." It was Rahal.

"Another one?!" Hutchinson asked in disbelief. God! This was the third apparent suicide this week. Hutchinson didn't want to suspect anything like a trend.

"Yeah. If we get any more wrist-slashers like this, we'll have to dedicate an investigation to it," said Rahal with some fatigue in his voice. "But for now, just get down there and keep a lid on it. We don't need any more attention right now."

Hutchinson sped through the crowded lunch hour streets. It would have been faster to hoof it! He fought the temptation to flash the emergency lights hidden behind the front grill. Right now it would be prudent to not call attention.

Blessedly, the scene at the Skidmore Fountain, when he finally arrived, was subdued. Only two other patrol cars were there, along with a pair of bicycle patrolmen. There were only two other people hanging about. The dead body was actually a fair distance from the fountain itself, laying slightly propped up against some garbage behind a dumpster in an alley just off a bit from the main plaza.

One of the cops turned to Hutchinson as the detective approached. "Hey, lieutenant. It's cool. It's a suicide. The guy was obviously homeless. You don't have to worry about it."

Hutchinson frowned seriously at the underling. "I'm not here for that," he said. "I'm here for damage control. Cap'n Rahal wants to keep this under wraps for a while. So no press, and do something to placate those onlookers over there."

"They're the ones that found the body and called it in," said the cop.

"Fine," said Hutchinson coldly. "Make yourself useful; get a statement, and get rid of 'em."

The homicide detective stepped down the alley and looked over the lifeless form. You know, it just didn't look that bad. The face of the pathetic bastard actually looked more at peace dead than it would have alive. His arms were held out as if to display the deep gashes on the wrists. The left hand still loosely held the bloody razor blade that had done the job. It was a perfectly convincing looking suicide.

But where was all the blood? There should have been more blood…

CHAPTER III

It was another beautiful, cool sunset over the city. Sunset had been coming a bit earlier these days. Shannon Goulier exited the Federal Building through the grand glass door. After the day she'd had, tonight was a night for the Clover.

She didn't have the energy to fake a sociable smile as she entered the busy nightclub. The real reason for her being there was something that Shannon wanted to drown with alcohol. She wasn't there to pick anybody up. She ordered a wine cooler from the bar; shortly, she would be graduating to White Russians. The area around the bar was crowded, and normally, Shannon would have been happy to seat herself right in the middle of it. But tonight she wanted seclusion, and she scanned the room for an available table. She quickly noticed that the unlit corner booth was unoccupied.

Shannon looked into the darkness of the booth from her location at the bar, feeling an exhilarating déjà vu. Immediately, she knew why. There was Mark, sitting exactly as he had been three months ago. Why hadn't she seen him before? The memory of that wonderful night flooded into the forefront of her brain. What a night!! It had been the last happy time in her life. In a blink, the memory replayed itself.

Shannon knew that despite the pain, all that the young man had said that night was exactly what she had needed to hear. And she had had every intention of giving her whole life a shakedown. But it had been less than a week later when her routine blood test came back positive for HIV. Understandably, the news had turned her life upside down.

After some quick investigating, it was discovered that she had contracted the AIDS virus from a past lover – ironically, it had been the first man she'd slept with after her husband left her. It had been a fling, and one quite foolish, she had thought, even before she had found out about the HIV. Even before the divorce had been final, Shannon had been haunted by the thought that twelve years of marriage had killed her sex appeal. In a futile attempt to prove to herself that she was still sexy, she had jumped in the sack with the first willing male. The first willing male had turned out to be a young naval officer that she had met at a nightclub. The sex had been utterly forgettable.

Since that rather horrid night, Shannon had had about twenty other one night stands, and ten more week-long relationships. With the revelation of her impending slow and painful death, her life became consumed with trying to inform as many of her past lovers as she could. The task of calling up men that she hardly knew, men that probably didn't want to hear from her even if it had been good news, was a chore that she was loath to perform. Reactions had varied all the way from a quiet 'damn', to weeping, to 'You fucking bitch!! *Click!*' She had succeeded at contacting only about half of them. She couldn't even remember the names of some of them.

And so the glorious night that she had spent with Mark had been the last happy day in her life. To say that her life had sucked profusely since that night would be a masterful understatement. She continued her job at the IRS, as something about carrying out her duties there gave her a feeling of vindication. About the only behavior that she had changed was her sleeping around, for obvious reasons.

So now here she was, back in the Four Leaf Clover, and there was Mark, checking in on her just as he had promised. She was very glad to see him, but her heart broke with the knowledge of the task that lay before her.

Shannon Goulier, aka Suzanne Gold, stood up from her bar stool, exactly as she had done two months earlier, and walked over to the dark booth where sat Mark, aka Marcus the Vampire. He took her hands in his from across the table and said, "Shannon, my dear, how have you been?"

Shannon managed only, "Hello, Mark," before she lost her composure, bowed her head and started sobbing.

The vampire said nothing, but secretly used his amazing powers to calm the distraught woman and help give her a sense of well-being.

"I have something terrible…" her sentence trailed off into sobs.

The ancient night walker paused for a moment, waiting to see if she would recover; continue. When she didn't, he said, "Come now, Shannon dear, get yourself together. Tell me what is the matter. I am no good at guessing games." In truth, Marcus knew all about her late diagnosis. He'd been keeping tabs on her personal life for months.

With teary eyes and cracking voice, Shannon said, "I don't know exactly how to tell you this, and I'll understand if you hate me…" She averted her eyes from his again. To Shannon, those beautiful light brown eyes seemed so pure and innocent. And she would be the instrument of their defilement, and death!

If she only knew the truth…

"Come now, Shannon," Marcus coaxed, gently squeezing her fingers.

Sobbing, she said, "I'm HIV positive."

Marcus didn't drop his smile; just maintained a gaze that reflected ages of wisdom and perspective. "It is alright, dear."

The beleaguered woman continued to carry on, "You need to go get tested. God, I hope you've been practicing safe sex. You may need to…"

"Shannon," he interrupted. "Shannon!" She stopped finally. Her red-rimmed eyes looked sadly into his and she realized for the first time that there was no distress there. "It is okay, Shannon dear. Everything will be okay."

Needless to say, the poor woman was confused, but very relieved that the young man had taken the news so well. For the moment she didn't care why. She said, "Oh Mark, I'm so sorry," and the sobs began again.

"Shhh, my dear, shhhh," said Marcus. "This should not be your most pressing health concern."

Still confused and crying, Shannon asked, "Wha-what do you mean?"

Marcus, aka the young man named Mark, just smiled and said, "Come, my dear. Let us go get a room at the San Teresa."

The suggestion brought flooding back again to Shannon the memory of that night and the out-of-this-world sex that they had shared. She had put out of her head the idea of ever feeling that way again after she had received her dreadful diagnosis, and now the thought of it filled her with such joy that the tears began flowing again.

The lovers exited the Four Leaf Clover, and Marcus escorted Shannon the IRS agent down Fifth Avenue. They walked in silence, Shannon unknowingly holding the arm of a vampire. She looked down, her gaze fixed on the red-brick sidewalk while he gazed longingly out at the glow that lingered atop the west hills.

Presently, they arrived, and Marcus stopped just down the street from the entrance. "I shall be right along," he said, pressing a key into the hand of the cheerless woman. "You head up and make yourself comfortable. Room 202. I am just going to fetch a little something." And the far too trusting Shannon did exactly as she was told.

This time, Marcus hadn't even paid for the room, he just happened to have the key, and earlier he had made sure that the room was not currently occupied. It would not be good for Fast Eddie to see them walking in together. Rather, the vampire walked around the block, stepped into an alley to the side of an old office building, jumped and grabbed a metal fire-escape rail, and climbed up with the grace of a spider. Like a shadow he ascended the three flights to the roof, crossed the rooftop to its edge and jumped the twelve feet over to a fire escape on the Hotel San Teresa. Down the fire escape to the second floor, he entered and stepped down the hallway to room 202. The door had been left just barely unlatched, and Marcus pushed it open.

Shannon lay on the bed, already undressed to her bra and panties. She had been able to regain her composure. And she had had just a minute to reason things through. She was now suspecting that Mark had already had AIDS. Why else would he have taken the news so calmly? And that thought made her just a little upset. Not so upset, mind you, that she was going to turn down a glorious night of sex with the world's most amazing lover. But how could he have not cared enough to tell her? How could he have knowingly put her at risk like that? Why, if she hadn't already had the AIDS virus, he might have given it to her! It was just a little upsetting.

What had she been thinking, after all, sleeping with a drug dealer?! It didn't matter much now, but it had definitely been the crowning point of all the many foolish things that she had done in her life. Of course, how could she regret it, when none of it mattered anymore? Especially when she was fixing to go do it again right this second. She was perfectly willing to have sex with this man right up until she died. Shannon could only hope that her daughter would make better choices in her own life.

Too late...

Marcus removed his trench coat, shoes, and shirt and joined Shannon on the bed. "I'm so glad to see you are feeling a little better," he said.

"Thank you," Shannon replied. "I'm so sorry I made a spectacle of myself back at the club."

The vampire was of course very grateful that she hadn't really made a spectacle of herself. Thankfully, their entire conversation had gone unnoticed by everyone else.

"That is all right," said Marcus. "It is easy to get upset when you lose proper perspective."

Shannon's suspicion flared. "Is that how you were able to take the news so well?" she asked.

"Exactly," he said, smiling.

"Level with me, mister," she said, letting anger leak just so slightly. "You've already got AIDS, haven't you?"

Marcus chuckled but said nothing, letting her go on thinking like that for just another moment.

"It's true," she asserted when he didn't immediately deny it.

"No, dear, I do not have AIDS. And I can not get it."

"How?" she asked.

Marcus ignored that question and went on. "And I am not a drug dealer."

Shannon of course no longer really cared about that, but still confusion clouded her face. She could say nothing, so the beautiful young man continued, "And you are still an IRS agent."

"What the hell has that got to do with anything?" asked Shannon. She noticed that this time their verbal sparring was doing nothing to turn her on, unlike their last encounter, and now she was feeling a little chilly in her partial nudity.

"I was hoping that you would make some positive changes in your life," Marcus answered.

Resentment apparent, Shannon answered, "I've been a little pre-occupied with something more important!" She wasn't listening to her own words.

"That is too bad," Marcus said. "I believed in you."

"Oh, don't patronize me like that, buster. I don't need to make any changes in my life. You need to get over this strange idea that you're going to reform 'the evil IRS agent!' You are an over-zealous idealist and you need to just grasp the fact that you're not going to change the world! I'm a good person and I do a good job for my country."

Marcus chuckled again. "It has been a long time since anyone ever called me an idealist."

"You're insane!" Shannon said. What was she doing here? God! What was she doing here in her underwear?!

Marcus turned serious. "You are working on a case right now against a corporation called Bradley Holdings," he said. "The assessment that you have calculated, coupled with all of your bogus fees and fines, and interest, will be enough to bankrupt the corporation."

It all suddenly came very clear to Shannon. "Oh, so you're with Bradley Holdings," she said. "And you're trying to soften me up so you won't get hit so hard. Well, you can just forget that, mister. You're guilty as sin of tax evasion and you're company needs to go down!"

"Go down?!" echoed Marcus. "Should you not mean to say 'pay our tax assessment'?"

"Whatever!" Shannon answered. She moved to the edge of the bed and sat up.

"That sounds awfully destructive," said Marcus innocently.

"Corporations like Bradley Holdings bring it on themselves by not properly paying their taxes," she said venomously. Suzanne Gold had personally brought to ruin more than four dozen private businesses of various sizes. The destruction in her wake had left people unemployed, bankrupt, even homeless.

"But the government does not provide any beneficial services to my corporation," said the vampire, smiling. "We have been over this already, my dear. It would be bad business for us to pay for services that we do not use."

"Your corporation gets its life from the state! I think that's a pretty valuable service!"

"Look again, my dear," said Marcus. "Bradley Holdings is 270 years old. That makes it much older than the state; even the country!"

"It just doesn't matter, Mark. You have to pay taxes. We all have to pay taxes!" She sat on the edge of the bed, her back to him.

"All right," said Marcus. "Let us say that Bradley Holdings did go to the expense of paying taxes. They would just have to raise the price of their goods and services. That would mean that the consumer is actually paying the tax bill; the public masses getting stiffed again, their money becoming less and less effective. Could you imagine how good the economy would be without big government spending and a huge tax liability on corporations?"

Mark had a good point there, but she wasn't going to let him have it. Shannon replied sourly, "I think that it would just make your economy good."

"Well, Shannon, my love, I have some great news for you," said Marcus as he tenderly touched the back of her hair.

She stopped, his touch melting her again. She still wanted him, damn it! How could he be so irresistible? It just didn't matter. If he wanted to fuck her, she would definitely let him, and she would still go after Bradley Holdings with a vengeance.

"What?" she said, trying to change her mood.

"You will not die of AIDS," said the vampire.

III – The IRS Agent and the Drug Dealer

The soothing words were spoken with such integrity, such knowing, that Shannon allowed herself to believe them. Rationally she would have challenged such a statement, but she wanted to believe it, and Mark had just the kind of magic about him that someone could trust for a miracle.

She melted into him; gave herself over completely; felt his mouth on her neck; his hand firmly over her mouth; then suddenly, every sweet sensation was gone. The vampire's victim was rigid, paralyzed, as he slowly sucked the life out of her. There was to be no pleasure for the unremorseful Shannon.

What in God's name is happening?! she thought. This was like something straight out of a nightmare! Shannon wanted to struggle, to fight off this assailant, but she couldn't move. It seemed to her that this bite in her neck was so deep as to somehow impede impulses from her brain to elsewhere. She had never believed in anything so fanciful as vampires, and even now only thought that she was being attacked by a demented Satan worshiper or something of the sort. God! Had she ever been wrong about this guy! The pain of the bite was intense, but quite frankly, nothing compared to the pains of giving birth.

A noise from somewhere was building; a white noise, a static perhaps, that grew louder. It crescendoed as Shannon began to wonder how much louder it could get. The noise shook her to the core, encompassed her, and she suddenly felt very small and alone, even as the noise continued to increase in volume.

Shannon was alone in an expanse of white nothing; a small dot in the middle of an immense blank page, with nothing but the maddening, still growing noise. Infinity stretched out before her in all directions. She was utterly alone, and shrinking; completely isolated, insignificant. She screamed, but couldn't even hear it in her own head for the noise, the mind-shattering noise!!

And all through Shannon's internal madness, Marcus the vampire sucked serenely on her neck in the decaying hotel room. She had tasty blood.

At length, Marcus released his victim, and she tipped weakly until she lay on her side at the edge of the bed. He had been very neat about this feeding – there was not a drop of blood on his face or anywhere else. He had drained her very nearly dry. She would not live much longer.

As Shannon recovered from her temporary paralysis, she began to tremble, sobbing softly. Her confused mind could not grasp the insanity of the situation. The noise was gone, but the memory of it lingered like a deep, subtle rumble from somewhere horrifying – somewhere that beckoned for her to return.

Marcus looked down at her sadly. "Shannon, you break my heart. I could have loved you. And you know the really pitiful thing," he added cynically, "is that there are more people like you in this world right now than I could ever feed on and kill in five thousand years."

Shannon wondered if there was any way out of this for her. She also wondered if she wanted out. Suicide had crossed her mind several times in the last few years, and especially in the last few months, and she realized now that she just wasn't that 'in love' with life. *Life must be a man,* she thought, because it had fucked her over just like every man she had ever known.

Marcus was dressing. "My dear Shannon," he said, smiling darkly. "My dear, dear Shannon. I hope that if anyone else takes on the Bradley Holdings case, that they are as delicious as you have been." The vampire donned his leather trench coat, reached into an inside pocket, and pulled out his extremely sharp hunting knife. This corpse was to be found, and it was time to do some sculpting.

CHAPTER IV

The first week of being back for Mimi had been quite excellent, all things considered. She had gone back to dancing at the Bare Cage. The first night had admittedly been a little difficult. There was a lot of association to cocaine in the environment of the club. She made it through by thinking about Janet's love and support, and, strangely, remembering Marcus's story about Shalimar. Mimi knew that she loved dancing and entertaining men in a sexual way. That passion helped her to stay high on her own.

As it turned out, her shows were the best she'd ever done. Mimi had been 'on' all week. She had always been great – without a doubt the best dancer at the Bare Cage and probably the metro. Now, she absolutely shined, like a super-nova. By end of the first week, she was beginning to feel as if the dingy atmosphere of the Bare Cage no longer fit her.

At the same time, she also found herself with a few hundred extra dollars at the end of the week. It had been her best week ever for tips, and none of it had been spent on a vice. So Mimi decided to take it upon herself to spend a little money on the club in the way of aesthetics.

She organized a cleaning party Saturday morning with as many of the dancers as she could persuade to attend. Surprisingly, it was a roaring success, and the group of about one dozen girls, including Donna the cocktail waitress and Janet, spent the day cleaning, scrubbing, and disinfecting, and just overall removing the 'seed out of the club' as Mimi put it. And she upgraded the dressing room with new furniture and vanity fixtures.

Mimi was aware that she mostly had Marcus to thank for the change in her life. Janet definitely helped, but it had been the old vampire that had totally changed her perspective. Mimi was also aware of her very strong feelings for Marcus. She fantasized about what it might feel like to have the greatly experienced vampire sex her up.

Janet, too, would have been lying if she had tried to deny her feelings for Marcus. After hearing his life story, she loved everything about him. She supposed that that is just what one does when they encounter another person with that much personal power.

The girls had talked about their strong feelings and each admitted to the other that they both loved Marcus as a great friend. They both focused their deep, secret yearnings for the vampire on each other, and their romance grew even more intense.

Janet had also had a great first week back. She had been fired from the hospital, but was immediately hired by Marcus and Gerald to be a live-in nurse for the ever-ailing Gerald and also to do a bit of housekeeping. The gig would not last forever, but Janet thought that it would be the first in a long line of private nursing jobs. She would acquire great references and be a nurse working in the private sector. She loved the idea!

Janet did have a difficult moment when she called Carl and Audrey Reeves to inform them that their son had disappeared. Marcus had commanded that the Reeves not be told of the truth, and suggested that Janet placate them as much as possible. "You will need to show that you are worried about him, without playing it too harshly, or they might attempt something drastic," Marcus had instructed. "Nothing will stop them from eventually going to the authorities, but we want to try to delay that as long as possible."

Janet did as she was told, trying to en-hearten the distraught parents with the news that Chad had recovered much of his health before running away from the cabin. "He's probably just out spending some time alone," Janet had said to them over the phone. "I'm sure that he'll come home very soon." She said the words with just the right edge of worry.

Then, on a much happier note, Janet had informed the Reeves that an anonymous benefactor had come forward to pay all of their medical bills. That news was received with tearful relief. They promised to keep in touch.

Janet had spent the rest of her days this week talking to Gerald, and hearing even more stories about Marcus, some of them four and five times. Like Gerald, Janet found herself fascinated and compelled by vampirism. She pondered about what could be the cause of it. She grilled Gerald about what experimental measures had been undertaken to determine its cause.

"Biologically, he's a perfect male specimen," explained Gerald from his EZ-chair.

Don't I know it! thought Janet as she straightened and dusted around the room.

Gerald continued, "But as to why, I could never figure out. And why the need for fresh blood? You know, we measured the length of

IV – Janet and Gerald Discuss Poop

time that blood could be out of a body before it stopped 'feeding' him; you know, giving him what he needs, whatever that is; and it is less than a minute!"

"How does blood change in one minute?" Janet wondered.

"Well, it can drop by a degree or two in temperature," said Gerald. "Coagulation begins immediately, though it's damn hard to see and even harder to measure in the first minute."

"So that's why Marcus can't just live on the blood from a blood bank?" Janet said it as a statement.

"Exactly," said Gerald. "And then there's the whole mystery behind his photo-sensitivity."

"What did you find there, Jerry?"

"Diddly-squat, mostly," Gerald lamented. "We couldn't figure out the why, but we did measure his tolerance to light."

"How much light can Marcus tolerate?"

"Oh, hell, I don't remember the exact measurements, but you know it has everything to do with proximity. See, he might be in trouble if he got too close to some halogens. Even a flashlight might burn him, if it was held next to his skin. Obviously, the sun is the biggest threat, because once it's above the horizon it can be damn hard to get away from, but Marcus is OK in the pre-dawn and also just after sunset.

"And now you see why the only way we could look at Marcus's blood up close was with an electron microscope. Light microscopy was out! But the specimens always had to be processed so carefully for viewing; I think that the preparation ruined 'em somehow. Did you know that tissue from Marcus can biodegrade even after its frozen? Anyway, we could never come up with a way to view a live blood sample."

"Do you think that the secret to Marcus's vampirism is in his blood?"

"Hell, I don't know. It's how the contagion is spread, we know that. The blood is a good place to start for trying to figure out any human physiological question, and we've never really been able to start there, you know what I mean? Damned frustrating!"

Janet wondered, "Did you ever try any video-enhanced microscopes?"

"Oh yeah. Sure. I've got dozens of films with about one second each of footage showing red blotches getting eaten up by the light. I never even had time to focus the lenses," Gerald grumbled.

"I guess this was all stuff that you tried years ago, before computers?" asked Janet.

"Yeah, back in the day... You know he can re-grow a severed digit in about four hours if he's freshly fed. It just grows back. Amazing to watch! We took some time-lapse photography of that."

"Yeah, I saw him after he had recovered from the bullet wounds up at the cabin. You could not even tell that he'd been shot."

"Did you happen to notice his body temperature before the regeneration?" asked Gerald.

"Yes! I did notice, while we were helping him into his bed in the cellar! He was burning up! I was so worried; I felt like I should treat him for high temperature, but he told me that it was normal."

"Yep! His body temp will rise to levels that are fatal to any normal person. It's a wonder he isn't deaf, blind, or sufferin' from serious brain damage. And sometimes I think he does suffer from those afflictions temporarily."

The wheels in Janet's mind started turning very quickly. "What about his waste?" she asked.

"That's a very good question," said Gerald. "When he does poop, and that's not often, let me tell you, unless he's been eating a lot of regular food... but then, that's the whole thing isn't it?" The old man fought to keep from losing his train of thought and continued. "First, understand that he doesn't have an appetite for solid food like you or me, although he can eat if he wants to. I think that he gets all the nourishment his body requires from blood. Marcus urinates more often than he poops, and even that is usually only once or twice a week. I think his body somehow uses just about everything that he puts into it. And if he doesn't use it for some reason, then he passes it quickly, and it comes out of him looking very similar to how it did when it went in. That's what usually happens if he eats solid food.

"Now, if he's just been sucking blood, then like I said, it doesn't come out of him very often. What does come out him is absolutely devoid of every usable nutrient that a body needs. It usually consists of a material that's mostly carbon and few other elements, metals, always broken down to their molecular base. Nothing living at all! Not a single bacteria or virus to speak of, and you know he's got to be ingesting lots of those kinds of things all the time. Bet your glad you asked, eh?"

Janet actually was glad. Her mind could not stop working on this puzzle, and she was hungry for all of the facts. "Yes, I am. Thank you, Gerald. So what is your general hypothesis?"

"Well, that's a tough one, and I've given the knowns a lot of thought. We've got something that causes Marcus to regenerate from injuries, and to show no signs of aging after centuries. It is some kind

IV – Janet and Gerald Discuss Poop

contagion that can be passed through the blood and other bodily tissues, but not through mucous, saliva or ejaculate. It is not visible to the naked eye. It is highly photo-sensitive. Tissue samples taken from the body are subject to accelerated biodegradation. And finally, it compels our subject to consume fresh human blood."

"Wow!" interjected Janet. "You sure are able to rattle off the facts."

"I should be. I memorized 'em a long time ago. I've been mullin' 'em over since '76!"

"So, what is your prognosis?" she asked.

"I can only think that it is some kind of micro-organism; virus maybe; parasite or maybe one of these prion protein thing-ies discovered by that Prusiner chap back in the eighties. But until we can successfully isolate it, or even just look at it, we'll never know for sure. And that's assuming there is something to isolate or look at."

Hutchinson appeared on the surface to be frustrated and concerned as he carried out his investigation at this latest downtown homicide, but inside he was exhilarated. Another chopped up corpse! His 'Psicko Killer' was obviously feeling confident and cocky.

The pieces of Shannon Goulier lay in a pile on the brick plaza in front of the Edith Green Wendell Wyatt Federal Building. This time there were no clothes on the body parts, and the pieces were cut smaller. Her picture ID tag with the name of her alias Suzanne Gold had been placed deliberately on the pinnacle of the pile.

A large number of cops were trying in vain to keep people from gawking at the gore, while Hutchinson quickly set about his investigation of the crime scene. All the while it was the general consensus among them that the victim must have been some bitch that got what she deserved.

With the KOIN building the south neighbor of the Federal Building, it had not taken any time at all for a news reporter and a camera crew to invade the scene. They had been only minutes behind the cops. The scene had exploded into a grisly circus of gore.

Hutchinson knew that he was wrong for feeling like this, but secretly he hoped that the Psicko Killer would keep on pushing the envelope, seeing what he could get away with, seeing how far he could go. Hutchinson believed that eventually the Psicko would screw up, and the detective would be able to nail him. He could see the headlines now – FEARLESS PORTLAND COP BUSTS PSICKO KILLER. For Hutchinson, it wasn't about keeping the streets safe at all, except for his family. He could have cared less about anyone else in the metro. He just wanted the glory of one great bust. And now he had adopted the Psicko Killer as his nemesis. But he knew he would have to do some discrete digging around in other divisions of the department. The pleasure would be all his.

Additionally, Hutchinson, who felt that he had his own fair share of 'cop's intuition,' couldn't shake the feeling that Jimmy Bechard was the source of the corruption behind this crime. He had a silly fancy that this might be another contract killing! Oh, he'd love to bring the insubordinate wannabe-Mafia-Don down.

Naturally, with this victim sitting out for the entire world to see, it had been a lot harder for the police to prevent the particulars of the homicide from becoming available to the public. The body had first been discovered by a homeless man, who was happy to tell anyone willing to listen about all of the macabre minutiae of his discovery. He even claimed to have seen the big chainsaw welding winged demon that had done the dirty deed. "And he had the head of a goat!" the wino had been heard telling newspaper and television reporters.

Of course, it did not reflect well on the police to have the body (parts) dumped right out in the open and only one block away from police headquarters. Hutchinson readied himself to receive just a bit of heat over that one.

Other reporters were interviewing Police Captain Von Rahal. A reporter asked, "Will this reopen the case against Jamahl Shafer, the man accused of killing Officer Clarence Chapman?"

"Hell no!" answered Rahal. "The evidence against Shafer was iron clad! What we have here is obviously some little nerd that thinks Shafer's work was cute. We've got a copy cat."

And so Portland officially had a serial killer at large. This would put a little pressure on Hutchinson and his fellow peace officers, but it wouldn't be bad. Hell, if anything, it would push the budget through and he'd end up with an increase in pay. He couldn't wait for the next diced body to turn up.

Rahal finished with the reporters abruptly and beckoned for Hutchinson to join him for a little walk. Once the two men were able to converse without being overheard, Rahal said, "Darrel, I've just got word from the 'powers that be' that the FBI will be comin' in on this."

"Oh, come on, Cap'n," whined Hutchinson. "Let's not call those dogs in just yet. Let's try to crack this one on our own first, huh?" And of course, he really meant 'on my own!'

IV – Janet and Gerald Discuss Poop

"It's actually out of my hands, Darrel. The Fibbies want to work up a psychological profile on this guy. They don't want to wait for some diced up body to turn up across the river to make this a federal case."

Hutchinson wanted to say something smart about the FBI's ineffectual profiles, but thought better of it. "I'll work with 'em," he said, hiding his resignation. "Whatever they need." And then thought to himself, *Let 'em knock themselves out coming up with a profile; just keep 'em outa my way!*

CHAPTER V

The night was unseasonably warm, and that made it only slightly sticky for Marcus, as he was never out without his leather trench coat. The odors of filth and liquor along with the sounds of traffic were not suiting the vampire very well either. He stood in the shadows near the downtown corner of Third and Couch Street. It was one of the few remaining places in Portland where one might go if they wanted to see a derelict, and Marcus was looking for a particular derelict – the junky that he had seen at the Public Safety building so many months before.

Marcus had been keeping an eye out for the homeless man ever since he and Janet had had their first conversation at the Bare Cage. He had dedicated several nights to the search before spontaneously trekking out of town with the girls and Chad, but with no positive results.

The old vampire would use the information about the hypo-planting derelict to manipulate Chad and orchestrate an outcome that would serve his ultimate purposes. Marcus was fully prepared to exterminate his unwanted protégé, if necessary. But Marcus did not feel any inclination to seek the other vampire out. He knew that the lovesick Chad would eventually come out of hiding to see Janet; probably shortly after a certain law enforcement officer and a certain judge turned up dead.

Marcus had been back from the cabin for four nights, and had spent all but one of them haunting certain locations of downtown where the homeless folk were known to linger. At least there were less homeless people in the metro than a decade before. His search was not completely like looking for a needle in a haystack – only mostly. However, an immortal can afford to be patient.

The night was unseasonably warm, and that suited Jamie Thompson just fine; he wouldn't have to try to find room at the homeless shelter. Thompson walked unsteadily from a debris-strewn alleyway and turned in the direction of Rose Haven, one of the last remaining soup kitchens and homeless shelters in Portland. It was true that there were less of his kind about the metro these days. Where had

V – Jamie and the Vampire

they all gone? To California – where the days and girls are warmer? To rehab, perhaps? Had the State made room for them at the mental hospital? Had they somehow gotten their lives together and left the streets?

Although his head was bowed, the homeless man was aware of someone walking toward him down the littered sidewalk. Thompson allowed the cowl around his face to sag slightly to reveal a hideous bilateral cleft lip. It was extremely effective for garnering sympathy and handouts from passers-by.

This passerby, a fashionably dressed, muscular young man, would have preferred to ignore the derelict, but he could not pull his eyes away from the shocking birth defect. The mouth gaped open, unable to shut; the two separate upper lips ran up the face from the corners of the mouth to a point under a little hood that might have been a flattened nose. Two crooked front teeth protruded from a glob of gum-tissue that seemed to be stuck there, as if in a futile effort to plug the cavernous hole. A thin scraggly beard framed the monstrous defect. "Dude! Fuck! I'm sorry!" said the young passerby, clearly at a loss for words more articulate. And, handing Jamie Thompson a convenient ten-spot, he passed quickly on his way.

Thompson replaced his cowl; no one would see his grotesque smile of satisfaction. The night was shaping up well for him. He would need only to get a bite to eat at the Rose, then he could be off again, to wherever. The world was his oyster. It was just too bad that he felt like shit!

What he really needed was a fix. Or maybe not. At least not any from his current heroin supply. He made a foggy mental note to throw that bad stuff away the next time he thought about it. He knew he needed to get rid of it, but throwing away heroin, even bad heroin, seemed like such a sacrilege.

How long had he been trippin', anyway? Gin was no longer keeping the shakes at bay. He needed more cash. He needed more of these sympathetic and generous passers-by.

It is said that we are all born naked and equal, with the same opportunity for success available to everyone. Jamie Thompson scoffed bitterly at such sentiment! Life, he felt, had bummed-rushed him at the moment of his conception, and it continued its onslaught upon him at every turn. He felt truly like a victim of circumstance.

His young mother had not wanted a baby, but she had wanted a way that she could manipulate and trap the man who was his father, whoever that was, and so her pregnancy had remained a secret until long after an illegal abortion could be considered a feasible option. She had also been addicted to nicotine, alcohol, crack, and just about anything else that could help her to escape from her own wretched reality. In 1985 Jamie had been born seven weeks premature; small, weak, palsied from crack withdrawals, and with little more than a gaping hole in his face where a mouth and nose should be.

At the behest of one particularly over-zealous social worker, Social Services immediately confiscated the infant, much to the relief of the mother, and probably to the relief of the unknown father, as well. But then the State couldn't find any foster family willing to take the little monster. Jamie Thompson was truly the child that nobody wanted!

In addition, nobody had felt inclined to cough up the money to pay for the surgery to correct Jamie's birth defect. Not the parents, not the State, not God. Guilty eyes looked away from him. On top of all that, Jamie's biological mother died of the mysterious new disease HIV less than a year after he was born. At the time, nobody said anything out loud, but everyone at Social Services secretly suspected that young Jamie might have been born with the dreaded plague.

So, for the next twelve years Jamie had been passed from one reluctant foster home to another. The idea of a normal education in a public school was the height of ludicrousness. Jamie eventually ran away from a particularly unenthusiastic foster home and faded away from the focus of any ardent social worker. Everyone had been relieved by the 'disappearance.'

Jamie had been a little young for a street kid in Portland. Luckily, there are always those older street kids eager to profit from showing a young new-bie the uncomfortable ropes. Unlike most of the other runaways that were only there in an attempt to get away from their over-bearing middle-class parents, (and because they thought it was cool to be a 'street kid'), Jamie had a sadly obvious reason for being on the streets.

The street punks liked Jamie because he was quiet, completely silent rather, and they didn't mind his ugly deformation as long as he kept it covered. They taught him quickly how to benefit from it by using it as a most effective panhandling tool. Young Jamie's 'income' made him very popular with nearly all of the other street kids. And, in no time at all, Jamie had learned also that drugs were the ultimately easy escape from this hard life; they just about made all of the pain worth it!

It is amazing how much abuse the physical body can take and still live! Jamie Thompson was now only twenty-two, and looked much older. Jamie did not care about his health, or lack thereof to be more precise, or his appearance. He couldn't be bothered with taking care of himself. The stench of not bathing clung to him. His long, thin, greasy hair hung down in dark, dishwater gray strands over the collar of a medium-length coat tattered and worn with gapes and wounds displaying lining and stuffing. His head seemed permanently bent to the ground. A cowl covered the lower half of his blotched and puffy face, concealing his underdeveloped nose and cleft mouth. Jamie didn't care about his arms with their red trails that erupted down each vein, though he did try to hide them at times. Showing off track-marks was bad for business. Looking pathetic was actually valuable to the derelict, and he knew only too well that it increased his revenues from panhandling. Getting together gin money was easy enough. But just now, gin would not be enough. The sooner he had enough cash for some smack, the sooner that he could get back to feeling like his regular, fine self. And that was all that Jamie Thompson cared about.

If you should ever spy Jamie around town, you would never see him without his Magic Slate. Because of his tragic defect, and his lack of education, Jamie was essentially a mute. His voice did not resonate in his head and he despised the sound of it. Besides, no one could understand a word that he ever tried to utter through his severely cleft palate, so Jamie carried with him an old, frayed and beaten Magic Slate – the innovative sketchpad owned by every young child of the 70's; the toy that allowed children doodlers to write or draw with a red plastic 'pen,' and instantly erase and start anew by lifting the two thin sheets of plastic away from the soft and malleable, black surface. Jamie's was a dandy 'Land of the Lost' Magic Slate, featuring a picture of the Saturday morning TV show's Cro-Magnon character Cha-Ka, a volcano, a pterodactyl and a few assorted dinosaurs; no sign of the Marshalls. But it was showing its age. The clear plastic sheet had been ripped off a long time ago and the opaque sheet stayed attached by only god knows what. The black surface was deeply gouged and the red 'pen' had long since joined the Marshall family in the land of the lost, leaving Jamie only his fingernail to write with. His scrawlings were childlike, letters often written backwards or capitalized; spelling phonetic or worse; grammar and full sentences never used.

Jamie had lived on the streets of Portland for almost fourteen years now, and he did not care about that either; he had never really known a home. He no longer hung out with the street kids, as he had graduated further and further from their ranks with every new influx of runaways to the streets.

Portland is a pretty good town to be homeless in – relatively mild winters, and lots of sympathetic, generous, liberal altruists. Why, Jamie was practically a Portland personality now; a fixture of the downtown Portland scene! Of course, he was not as outgoing as some of the other homeless folk. He did not play an old guitar on the corner for handouts, or sing, or whittle little thing-ies, or sell pencils, no! Those were not his gig. There were others like himself that played the sympathy card to receive handouts, but there were even more bleeding-heart altruists out there with spare change – plenty to go around.

Jamie just tried now to stay out of sight as much as possible, and stay high. With his gimmick, a junkie like Jamie Thompson could make a fine 'living.' Without the overhead of rent, and with the expense of meals handled by taxpayers and aforementioned altruists, all of his 'income' could go toward improving his quality of life – the only luxury that he cared for – heroin.

So if a low-life drug dealer should approach Jamie with the offer of free smack in exchange for carrying out a little mischief, what should it matter to a guy like Jamie? His conscience wasn't bothered by a little bit of tomfoolery. The dealer had promised that no one would get hurt, and so far nobody had been, really… that bad. The deal had gone rather swimmingly in Jamie's opinion.

But now, after nearly one hundred syringes fixed strategically throughout the downtown area over the course of the past eighteen months, and a fair amount of complimentary heroin graciously provided for Jamie's splendid enjoyment, the long-running arrangement had apparently come to an end. Stan the Man, a relatively successful drug dealer had informed Jamie that his services were no longer needed. As a token of appreciation to Jamie's faithful service over the last fifteen months, Stan the Man had bestowed upon Jamie one last gratis supply of heroin.

The funny thing is, Jamie mused now as he walked groggily down the sidewalk, is that this last batch of brown from Stan the Man, the parting gift, had been terrible! Absolutely horrendous! As was Jamie's general MO, he had enthusiastically tried a bit of the product very quickly after taking delivery of it from Stan the Man, and he had noticed right away that something was 'bad with it.' He had wretched and vomited at least double his normal amount, and then the rush was accompanied by a most disconcerting falling sensation. Jamie was only just now recovering from the bad trip, or so he thought. And he had absolutely no inkling of just how closely death had come to him.

"Hello, my friend."

V – Jamie and the Vampire

The chilling voice had sounded so close to Jamie's ear that his clammy skin crawled and his heart palpitated dangerously fast. After all, his ticker wasn't the strongest to begin with. Jamie wanted to jerk around and see whom it was that had startled the b'jeezus out of him, but his neck muscles were uncooperative. As it was, he only let out a startled noise that sounded like something between a grunt and a squeak, and slowly turned his head. His glazy eyes eventually landed upon a distinguished-looking young man with long brown hair. There was nothing inherently frightening about the young man; still Jamie felt the impulse to shy away from him and get moving, and he acted upon it.

"I'm sorry," said the young man with ice-burg politeness, walking after Jamie. "My name is Marcus. I have seen what you do with your syringes, in the shadows, when no one is looking. Do you plan to do it again?"

"Eep!" Another frightened squeak escaped the sad derelict. He was unaccustomed to anyone accosting him in this manner. Had this dude really seen him plant syringes? Doesn't one homeless junkie look very much like any other? How could the man be certain he had the right junkie? Jamie continued his ambling gait down the sidewalk. Surely this fellow would eventually leave him alone.

Suddenly a bony, firm hand was on Jamie's shoulder, turning him around. The piercing hazel eyes of Marcus inspected the derelict with detachment. Marcus's smooth hand carefully lowered the cowl slightly. It was too grotesque to pass up, even for a five hundred year old vampire.

Marcus looked deep into the dilated pupils of the derelict, noticed the slow, shallow breathing, the slightly jaundiced pallor of the skin. Something here was definitely wrong beyond the normal effects of heroin. "I can't believe I'm doing this," mused Marcus. "Maybe it's true what they say about learning something new everyday." And, holding Jamie's track-marked arm, he sent a wave of adrenaline coursing into the derelict. It was the only thing that the vampire could think of to do to help the dying man, short of taking him to the hospital, and that simply wasn't going to happen.

"You must not die just yet, my dismal friend. Your life has some value, yet; even if only for me."

Jamie felt instantly better, but he was still extremely leery of this suspicious man. He was further relieved when the young man released him and he was able to resume his lurching pace. He just wanted to be left alone!

And sure enough, when Jamie turned slightly again to glance at the young man, he saw to his relief that the dark young man was no longer on his shoulder. Then a nauseating feeling of foreboding rippled through him as he realized that there was no sign of him at all. The disconcerting young man had disappeared!

CHAPTER VI

The clock struck one a.m.

All was dark at the Reeves' home.

But through the house moved a shadow, quite familiar with the layout. The creeping shape bumped nothing, made no sound.

Carl Reeves awoke from his fitful sleep with the paralyzing awareness that he and his wife were not alone in their bedroom. He could see the outline of someone standing at the door just inside the room. Carl gasped in shock even as he thought he recognized the familiar form. In a cracking voice he asked, "Chad? Is that you?"

"Yeah, dad. It's me."

Carl started to rise. "Oh my God! Chad! Thank God you're all right. How are you feeling? Did you have a good time?"

The conversation roused Audrey from her own haunted sleep.

Chad said, "Stop, dad. Stay there. Don't get up. I can't stay, but I wanted to see you, and talk with you." There was a finality in Chad's voice that Carl and Audrey found very alarming.

"What is it?" asked Audrey to her son. "What's the matter, babe?"

"I just wanted to see you," said Chad, his voice breaking with emotion. "I don't know when I'll get the chance to…" His words trailed off.

"Chad!" said Carl. He had his feet out of the bed now and they were habitually feeling the floor for his slippers.

"No!!" And Chad ducked back out the open doorway and into the hall. "I love you," he choked.

"We love you, too, babe," said Audrey, not quite awake enough to fully realize what was going on, but Chad was already moving swiftly out of the house.

The adjustment into vampirism had been easy, Chad fancied. Killing came naturally to the en-darkened youth. He was learning to enjoy feeding, and he was feeling quite clever about his technique. Chad was feeling invincible!

He slept during the day in the basements of any one of several houses around town that he had learned were vacant due to pending bank foreclosures or some other reason. There was some anxiety felt every dawn as he 'bedded' down, not sure if this might be the day that a thorough inspection might be made by some bank official or real estate agent. Of course, if he was found out, he would just be a squatter. They wouldn't be able to throw him out directly, and by nightfall he would be gone.

At night, following the wise instructions that Marcus had inadvertently given him, Chad would walk the night in search of a good victim; someone that wouldn't be missed by family or society was best; and, (something that he had learned the hard way), someone who wouldn't be able to put up too much resistance.

Chad preferred feeding from the wrist. He couldn't wait until he figured out how that charming trick worked so that he wouldn't have to work so hard at controlling his victims. Holding the victim's arm immobile, he would slash the wrist open with a blade and drink the warm living liquid. He would try to leave just enough blood so that it could bleed out after he gashed the other wrist. Hopefully, when the body was found it would be labeled as just another sad suicide. By and large, the whole thing was so easy that Chad wondered what the hell Marcus had been complaining about!

The only thing that really bothered the young vampire was the dreams during day-sleep. The dreams were vivid beyond Chad's ability to distinguish them from waking reality. Chad would be sane and reasonable in the night, and then see the coming dawn and take cover for safety. And then, stowed carefully in a spot that would provide protection from the looming sun, relaxed and falling into the initial throws of sleep, it was as if the shadows would suddenly come to hideous, terrible life. The infinite, endless torment would go on until… nothing. It never ended. Chad would just find himself no longer able to see his tormentors, but he knew that they were still there, lurking in the shadows. He could still feel their pricks and stabs and cuts into him, and he would get out of the shadows as quickly as possible back into the safety of the night.

Chad knew that he wouldn't be able to go on like this forever. Eventually, the authorities would realize that this was just too many suicides and they would start to look closer. When that happened Chad would go to Seattle. He would be able to pull off a lot of suicide jobs up there before anyone noticed!

But first he had to find and pay back all of those responsible for ruining his life. The revenge part would be easy, but finding out exactly whom the responsible parties were proved to be more difficult than he

VI – Chad's Close Call

had thought it would be. Everything was always closed by the time he could get up at night; at least, all of the government offices to which he needed access were closed. And he was quite hesitant to attempt simply walking into the police station after dark.

And that is why he had come back to his home this night. He had wanted so badly to see his parents, but he also knew that there was no way that they could ever find out about what had happened to him. He loved them and missed his family more than he could allow himself to feel. But he had allowed himself only to disturb their slumber to say good-by. Anything more was not practical. Chad was immortal now. He would see his own parents to the grave. His sisters and their children and their children's children would all beat him to the grave. If there was anything that he had learned from Marcus, it was that there is no room for sentiment in the life of a vampire. A bleak glimpse of eternity laid itself out before Chad, and the interminable loneliness of it terrified him at his core. Denial would be the only way to survive it. Or maybe not… he wondered what Janet had told his parents when he had run away from the cabin…

Before waking his parents, Chad had sneaked into his old bedroom. Among some papers, old bills and junk mail, Chad found the old, fateful, difficult to read traffic ticket. 'Bruce Nader' read the name of the police officer issuing the citation. The honorable Perry Wright would be the arraigning justice. So there it was. Everything he needed had been sitting in his old room this whole time.

After the emotional episode with his parents, Chad stole out of the house and ran through the backyard, jumped the fence into the neighbor's yard, and effectively cut through the block. He wouldn't have put it past his father to try to come after him, so he affected a disappearance.

Minutes later he was waiting at the bus stop on McLaughlin Boulevard for the late-night bus to take him back into town. The unobservant young vampire hardly noticed as a black van stopped at a plaza parking lot across the street.

Inside the van, Tim the Vampire Slayer was watching the strange, white-haired man, still nearly a half a mile away, walking methodically toward them.

Desperado said in a low, slow voice, "Man, I've got a feeling about that dude across the street at the bus stop. Look at him. He's a little gothic wannabe. You know, the last time I saw a little gothic wannabe dude like that, he turned out to be a durned bloodsucker."

Tim inspected the black-garbed young man at the bus stop. He had learned to be wary of Desperado's vampire-spotting skills. "We'll see. Our friend is only a few minutes away. If the dude is a vampire, the wizard will spray him."

But it was not to be; not this time at least. Just as the strange man was nearly upon the young man, a bus stopped. Chad boarded the bus and was gone before he even had any idea of his peril. Tim and Desperado watched as the stranger stopped, consulted his crystal device, then turned and walked back in the direction they had come; following the speeding bus, but at walking speed.

"That tears it!" screamed Tim. "We're outa here!"

"Now you're talkin'!" exclaimed Desperado. "Follow that bus!"

Excitedly, Tim spun the rear tires of the van taking off after the bus, but the rush of being in 'hot pursuit' quickly faded as they realized just how slow the bus traveled. It stopped frequently along its route, and all they could do was try to watch for the young man to disembark. They followed the slow moving transport all the way downtown. Presently, the bus entered the short span of the Sixth Avenue bus mall where normal vehicles were not permitted. Tim was about disregard the traffic rule and follow the bus when he saw a police cruiser up the street and prudently decided to turn, and that was where they lost their quarry.

"Dammit! Now what?" said Tim.

"I dunno," grumbled Desperado. "You're driving."

CHAPTER VII

"What is Bradley Holdings?" asked Detective Darrel Hutchinson, hoping that this nerdy little IRS bean-counter that had taken over the case files of one Suzanne Gold wouldn't take the question as rhetorical.

Gary Fox looked up from the documents he was reading and answered succinctly, "It's a conglomerate of sorts; pretty large; lots of fingers, lots of pies; deals mostly with its numerous subsidiaries which in turn deal mostly in real estate, but they're into a lot of other things as well. Very diverse," he added with admiration. The IRS agent was in his late twenties and dorky beyond the point of typical. The front of his brown hair was carefully combed over but the back was greasy, disheveled, and sporting an obscene cowlick. His tie was immaculate, while his suit looked as if he had slept in it.

Hutchinson could smell the scent of sour milk on the IRS agent's breath, but he was just glad that someone at the IRS had agreed to work with him. He had heard that the FBI, with its usual blunt lack of finesse, had been unable to coerce any cooperation out of the IRS on gathering a few details about Shannon Goulier; laughable.

"Is its stock traded publicly?" asked Hutchinson.

"It has the organization, the look and feel of a publicly traded corporation, but no, its not. Totally private."

Hutchinson sat across from the IRS agent at a desk stacked high with papers and files. Gary Fox's plain, windowless office was claustrophobic and cluttered.

"And I am correct in understanding that Bechard Properties has a deal pending with this Bradley Holdings?" asked the detective.

Fox answered, "One of Bradley Holdings' subsidiaries, yeah."

"Which one?"

"An outfit called the Ava Group."

Hutchinson's pulse raced at the mention of the corporation. "Do you have the details of that?"

Gary Fox looked at the detective quizzically. "Why would we have the details of a pending real estate deal? The only reason we even know about the deal at all is due to a Notice of Interest recorded at the county building."

Hutchinson knew of the Notice from his own search of the public records, but the document hadn't told him anything more about the private contract that it referred to. "So how much money are we talking about here?"

"Well, the Notice of Interest doesn't actually contain any numbers, but the property in question would probably be assessed in the millions," said Fox confidentially. "Several tens of millions."

"Could the IRS complicate or prevent such a big deal from going through?" asked the detective.

"Oh, you bet," answered Fox with a bit of gusto. "We could pretty much stop a deal like that dead in its tracks if we wanted to."

"How could you do that?" Hutchinson asked and blanched as his hand touched something slimy under the armrest of the chair in which he sat.

"Oh, one little Notice of Lien against the name of the sellers filed at the county building would probably be enough to give the buyers cold feet over the deal," said the nerd.

"But you would need a judgment or an assessment or something like that before you could do it, right?" asked Hutchinson, looking nonchalantly for a tissue.

"Naw." Fox shook his head, silently laughing and pointing an imaginary finger of ridicule at Hutchinson. Obviously this detective, like so many other patriotic Americans, had no idea of the lowdown, unlawful lengths that Uncle Sam's collection agency could go to achieve its ends.

"Okay. So what is the significance of this Bradley Holdings corporation?" No tissues anywhere!

"Well, it's like I was telling you about Bechard Properties. Neither corporation has ever paid a lick of taxes."

"Because of loopholes in the law?" Hutchinson guessed. Not a single absorbent surface to be found!!

"No," answered Fox. "They've just never paid."

"How can that be?" Hutchinson asked incredulously as he wiped the offended finger on the back of his pant-leg.

"I'm not sure exactly," wheezed Fox. "In the Bechard Properties case the office could never get through an audit. Arthur Sherman, Suzanne's direct boss, has been in charge of the case for years and hasn't really done much with it for as long as I've been working here. Suzanne would have inherited the case when Sherman retired. Now, I'll probably end up with it."

"And Bradley Holdings?"

VII – Profiling a Killer

Fox continued, "Bradley Holdings is a very similar story. Suzanne had not been able to pin them down to an audit. According to office records, no agent ever has, and the case had been in the office for over twenty years! There is a rumor going around the office that the case is cursed."

Hutchinson was getting tired of the silly bullshit. "Cursed?" he said, skepticism giving the word a cutting edge. "How?"

"Apparently, some kind of harm has befallen every agent in the office who ends up with this case," said Fox spookily.

"What exactly?" asked Hutchinson with only slight interest.

"Well, I don't know all of the details but the first agent that received the case in 1980, Paul King, was killed during a mugging. Eric Sweeney inherited the case from King and was the victim of a hit-and-run. The third agent disappeared. They've never found him. The guy to have it right before Suzanne went crazy. Remember the shooting they had at that gay porn theater in southeast?"

Hutchinson nodded, "Oh yeah. The dude took out four fags before someone finally wrestled the gun away from him."

"Yeah," continued Fox. "That was our guy, Mitchell Johnson. And then poor Suzanne. You see? Now the Bradley Holdings file belongs to me and I'm afraid to touch it!"

"Who owns Bradley Holdings?" Hutchinson asked.

"Our records don't have that information."

"Who runs the corporation?" asked the detective.

Fox answered sheepishly, "We don't have that information accurately, either."

"Well, what the hell was Ms. Goulier doing on the case, anyway?" barked Hutchinson.

"Who?" asked Fox.

"Suzanne! Whatever," growled the detective. His patience was dipping on empty. Apparently Fox was more familiar with her alias than her real name.

"Oh! Right," said the geeky IRS agent. "Well, according to her file, not much. Just knocking on a few doors, kicking over a few trash cans. The file doesn't show her finding much of anything that we could use. Nothing but big bad company no-no's that so far we haven't found any way to exploit."

"Like?"

"Like get this – Bradley Holdings doesn't seem to have one single employee. Same with all its subsidiaries! No employees; just independent contractors. Can you imagine that? Over 20,000 people nationwide, all getting paid cash under the table! Most are probably illegal aliens to boot! The IRS has open files on every known Bradley IC, but so far I have heard of little success in nailing anybody for anything. The company moves its people around if the IRS starts hounding them. It's almost like a Mafia organization, except that I don't see any signs of criminal activity, other than the tax evasion, and we can't pin 'em down for that."

Clearly, the beleaguered IRS agent was tapped of any more information that was going to be useful to the detective. "Thanks for your time, Mr. Fox," said Hutchinson, and he stood to leave Gary Fox's cramped IRS office. "I appreciate your help. Just one more question. Is it a possibility that Bechard Properties might be a subsidiary of this Bradley Holdings?"

"Nothing in our records indicates anything like that," said Fox. "But stranger things have happened."

Hutchinson turned these new little tidbits of information over in his mind as he descended in the elevator and exited the Federal building. His theory was a little weak, but he had seen worse. As far as the detective was concerned Jimmy Bechard now had the means and motive for the Shannon Goulier murder. Bechard had more money than God and could afford to hire a pro to do the job, and he was protecting his interest in Bradley Holdings by preventing the IRS from stopping the real estate deal or worse. Perhaps Shannon Goulier had been planning to make life hard for Bechard Properties directly. So he had her killed. With a little more digging, Hutchinson felt sure that he could figure out how poor little Preston had been connected to the deal. Had similar circumstances in 1985 led to the demise of Harvey Madison?

It was all circumstantial, but Hutchinson's hunch told him that he was close. The necessary evidence for a proper arrest and conviction couldn't be far away.

A guy like Bechard gets his power from having certain government officials in his pocket. If Bechard could be stripped of his political connections...

Within minutes, Hutchinson was back in his own office. Just in time, too, because it was time for the dreaded conference call that he had committed to shortly after the IRS lady had been found cut into stow-able pieces. It would be easier for Hutchinson to endure the call between Captain Rahal, Chief Lemmon, Special Agent Bill Rhodes, and himself if he remained isolated in his own office; not together in a room with his superiors. Why did Rahal and Lemmon have to be privy

VII – Profiling a Killer

to everything that the FBI agent had to say, anyway? He picked up his desk-phone and waited for the connections to be made.

Presently, everyone came on the line, and the four men exchanged polite, but tense pleasantries. Agent Rhodes started by verifying the facts of the two homicides – forensic evidence, victim information, medical examiner's reports, and many other details, some seemingly immaterial. Hutchinson's pointless partner Gene Miller had carried out the tedious task of collecting copies of the crime scene photos, various reports and other materials, and mailing the whole mess to Bill Rhodes at Quantico so he could review everything. Hutchinson was surprised at how quickly Rhodes had gotten back with them, but he still felt like this was pretty much a waste of time. Of course, as far as he was concerned he could have been taking the day off.

"Now," said Rhodes to the other three on the phone line, "I don't want anyone to mention anything about any of your current suspects. My profile has to be based solely on the facts of the crimes; no bias."

We heard you the first time, thought Hutchinson. Rhodes had already spelled these guidelines out in detail in a letter of instruction to the department.

Rhodes continued, "Speaking first of the Preston homicide, the crime scene has both organized and disorganized elements to it. The mutilation itself suggests a high level of aggression and mania. The location being so public hints that this specific crime wasn't particularly premeditated or planned, however it would seem that the killer or killers, I will refer to them as the unsub, may have been 'equipped,' you might say, with the tools and the means to kill whenever the feeling struck them just right.

"Notice the amount of blood throughout the elevator compartment. You don't get a mess like this by just killing and mutilating a body. Judging by some of the smear marks, I would say that the unsub actually made most of the mess on the walls intentionally. Even though this looks more like a crime of opportunity, or more likely necessity in the mind of the unsub, you can see that he still takes the time and the risk of being discovered to basically write a message to the authorities. It might be that the unsub considers himself an artist and this is his signature, but I would be more inclined to think that he is just being arrogant and saying, 'Look what I can get away with and you can't stop me.'

"There is a fair amount of dirt on the floor of the elevator. According to the janitorial staff of the Bancorp building, the car had been vacuumed out at approximately eight o'clock, roughly one hour before the discovery of the body. Therefore, it is possible that the dirt was tracked in by the unsub. Analysis of the dirt showed that it came from somewhere close to a high traffic thoroughfare. It also contained compounds consistent with being near or under a large body of water, specifically the Willamette River. So our unsub may have recently been down by the river. Judging by the amount of dirt, it's possible that whoever tracked it in there didn't realize or care that the dirt was on him.

"Now, about the victim. He's your basic quiet nobody, and he wasn't lighting any fires in the DA's office. He was a smoker, and was known to occasionally enjoy a cigar, which apparently he was doing at the time of his death. One of the witnesses, a Travis Noonan, stated that he had given the cigar to Preston before dinner, which is what Preston was doing there in the first place, having dinner with Noonan and one James Bechard. I have no information on the exact nature of the dinner."

Hutchinson cut in sharply, "Bechard claims that it was just a friendly dinner among acquaintances, but I got the idea that there was more –"

"Yes, thank you," interrupted Rhodes. "To continue! Now, the condition of the body is troubling to me. The autopsy found no sign of defense wounds. Our victim was caught completely by surprise and subdued or rendered unconscious before he even had a chance to react. The medical examiner's report suggests that the severings were done with a serrated-edged blade. For our unsub to be able to do this much damage in the supposed time window suggests a lot of strength, power and speed. Again, even though this is a crime of opportunity, our unsub has come prepared, I would say even experienced; he knows exactly what to do; he does it, and he even allows himself just enough time to leave behind his signature. Although, the fact that the severed limbs still bore their respective clothes does suggest that the unsub was aware of the short time and wasn't gonna be bothered with removing them.

"The other element of the crime that suggests a high level of organization and sophistication in the unsub is the dismantling of the building's surveillance system. After analyzing the blueprints of the building I have come up with a reconstruction of the events.

"But first, let me give you my analysis of the second mutilation case. I'm going with the assumption that both homicides were carried out by the same guy. 'Cause if they weren't then the only thing that I can suggest is that you guys check for something in the water out there!

VII – Profiling a Killer

Uh, heh heh heh!" Rhodes laughed a compressed laugh and then stopped abruptly. "Uh, that was a little joke, fellas."

Hutchinson, Rahal, and Lemmon remained stoic on their ends of the line.

"You guys still there?" asked Rhodes after a moment.

"Ahem," Captain Rahal cleared his throat. "Please continue with your report."

"Um, right," said the FBI agent. "So, the second body, Goulier, was found mutilated in a similar manner right in plain view. The body being left out in the middle of a highly visible public place is again an indication of that arrogance on the part of the unsub. The placement of the victim's name-tag directly on the pile of limbs speaks to a high level of aggression, not to the victim as a person, but to something else, probably her profession. I think that the unsub was lashing out with anger that he feels toward the IRS itself. The location of the body supports this. However, this one could not have, in all likelihood, occurred at the location of where the body was found. That would have been just too risky."

Hell! Impossible! thought Hutchinson. *Tell us something we don't know!*

"Again, no apparent defense wounds on the victim's body. No signs of vaginal entry, and frankly, nothing on either victim to suggest that the homicides were of any kind of sexual nature, unless you count the fact that the female victim was naked. This doesn't seem sexual to me, though; instead it suggests that the unsub was somewhere with the victim in private, and able to take his time. He may have been wanting to humiliate her by having her found mutilated and naked. Extensive victim-ology showed that Goulier was a divorced, single mother. Sources suggested that she may have been… kinda promiscuous. Our unsub may have seduced her, then did the job on her after she got naked.

"I see here that she had been recently diagnosed with AIDS. Police reports say that a few of Goulier's past sexual partners that are now infected as well showed signs of bitterness during routine questioning. Now, I don't want to tell you guys not to pursue all leads, but I gotta tell you, given the level of sophistication and the apparent high level of psychotic behavior, I really don't think that this was committed by some guy that got pissed just because she gave him AIDS. If that was the case I think we would have found her cut and/or stabbed in the face or the genitalia, and left in her home, not cut into pieces and left out in the open.

"It almost seems like too much for one man to pull off, and that is why I have given consideration to the possibility that we could be dealing with a team of two or more. That idea supports the theory that the jobs were hits, planned out in every detail. However, when you take into consideration the level of certain disorganized elements along with the shear psychotic mania of the murders, I think you'll realize how unlikely that possibility is. On the other hand, it could have been a team that engineered the crime scenes specifically in an effort to mislead the FBI. But because there is no evidence to support that, I'm going with the theory that it was one guy, who is a very talented killer.

"So, again assuming that the same unsub pulled off both jobs, I think we're looking for someone with extreme anti-social tendencies, primarily anti-government. He is going to have a high level of technical expertise. He'll be charming if not handsome, in spite of the fact that he may go long periods of days without bathing or taking care of himself. He is absolutely a homicidal maniac. I think he has killed before, so you may be looking for someone that is ex-military – fought in either Vietnam or the Gulf. He'll be strong, but not necessarily in good shape. I imagine that he'll have pretty severe financial problems, probably something to do with the IRS."

"This is kinda how I would reconstruct the sequence of events surrounding each of the murders. First Preston's – our unsub is depressed, and emotionally disturbed. He's walking around town, down by the river, probably just thinking about how badly he would like to kill some poor slob that he blames for his miserable life. He's probably thinking something like, 'If one more yuppie bastard gets in my face and tries to tell me something I'm gonna rip him to pieces, and I'll love it!'

"So, he ends up walking around the Bancorp building; it's nice, and warm, quiet so he can think. He's just killing time.

"Now here's Preston. He's just finished dinner and in a pretty good mood right now. Something that he's doing, maybe even smoking the cigar especially if he is on the elevator, tips off our unsub and the guy attacks Preston before the poor guy even knows to be scared.

"The unsub cuts our victim into Preston-ettes, then exits the elevator through the ceiling hatch. Now, the unsub still doesn't have anywhere to go until the elevator gets back to its parked position on the first floor. Once there, however, he can cross along the tops of all of the other elevators in the shaft and, if he is a good jumper, climb out of the shaft into the main security office on the second floor of the building. Now he re-initializes the digital recorder, effectively erasing any

VII – Profiling a Killer

footage that might show him doing any of this, and sneaks out of the building unseen."

Hutchinson protested, "But there was a security guard in the office the whole time. How could the perp do all that right under –"

"Maybe the security guard wasn't accurate in his report," Rhodes interrupted. "Maybe he was out having a smoke. Maybe he was in the bathroom jerking off. Or maybe this guard is your killer; these reports you've sent me don't reflect nearly the amount of lookin' up his ass that I would be doing if this was my investigation."

Alone in his office Hutchinson reddened. He was glad that Rahal and Lemmon weren't there to actually see it even though they had just witnessed the trouncing by phone. He hadn't included information about his interrogation of Jensen in the reports to the FBI. Hutchinson had also been meaning to investigate deeper into the Bancorp security guards, especially Dan Jensen; he just hadn't made any real headway yet. Time management wasn't his forte, although you had to admit that anger management certainly was!

"Now, as for Goulier, whether this was also a crime of opportunity or something with a little more planning is hard to say. But if I was to reconstruct it I would say that our unsub found himself in a private place with the victim. He may have arranged it somehow, or he may have just gotten lucky. If he did arrange it, then we need to go over every case file that Goulier was working on, because one of them might be our unsub. Anyway, he's thinking here's his chance to get this bitch for screwin' up his life, or more likely, here's a chance to get *back at the IRS* for screwin' up his life. This may have all gone down at Goulier's house, since her daughter was away with the father at the time. Goulier probably has no idea what's going through his mind; she thinks the guy is charming and is ready to get it on with him. Instead, he subdues her and pulls out his famous knife with the serrated blade. She never even has a chance to put up a struggle. He cuts her up, loads up the pieces, drives downtown to the federal building, and dumps them when no one is looking. We might be able to figure out more when you can find the container or the vehicle that was used."

It seemed to Hutchinson that Rhodes said this last bit rather smugly. *If we could find the container or the car we could find the damn perp!* thought Hutchinson. Then he said with mock heartiness, "Well, is that it?"

"Yeah, pretty much; for now," Rhodes answered.

"Thanks for your time," said Captain Rahal, and Chief Lemmon issued a similar sentiment.

Hutchinson was already hanging up. "Smug bastard!" He grabbed his overcoat and bolted out of the office before Rahal or Lemmon could corner him. He wanted to touch base with Travis Noonan.

As he walked the few blocks from the police station to the courthouse, he prudently gave due consideration to the thoughts and opinions that had been presented by Rhodes. Hutchinson knew that he should probably stick to the conventional wisdom of the 'expert,' but he simply didn't want to. His hunches had never let him down. Besides, it was still pure speculation on Rhodes's part anyway! The FBI was only speaking from experience, but what did Rhodes really know? There were still so many other possibilities. To Hutchinson the murders still looked professional. They smacked of purpose, not random crimes of opportunity. And Hutchinson now felt sure that they were dealing with a team instead of just one single guy.

When Hutchinson arrived at the judge's chambers, Noonan took him right in. "I'm so glad you stopped by," said the big man. "I hear you have your hands full. That sure was a shame about that poor IRS agent."

"'S' happens, your honor," said Hutchinson, head hung.

"Same MO as poor Preston; same guy?"

"We're pretty sure."

"Do you have a psychological profile on the guy?" asked Noonan.

"Yeah. More than one actually, and they all disagree; but they're all weak. Opinions come pretty damn cheap when you're looking at an apparent serial killer. The only thing we've been able to agree on is that the unsub has a beef against public servants, which may mean he's some kind of anti-government zealot." He had used the FBI agent's word…

"The perpetrator, or the person who hired him, right?" amended Noonan.

"Right," agreed Hutchinson. He was glad to hear that Noonan seemed to share his opinions of the nature of the crimes.

"Keep digging, detective. You're the only one at that department with a lick of sense. I know that if anyone can get to the bottom of this, you can. And don't let Jimmy Bechard intimidate you. I'm behind you all the way. Got it?"

The detective breathed a huge sigh of relief as he exited the office. He had Noonan on his side! That would go a long way in dealing with Rahal and Lemmon and other department politics. What's more, his hunch, his totally reliable gut feeling, was leading him down a path that ended at Bechard. It would be a treacherous path to follow; Bechard

VII – Profiling a Killer

was powerfully connected. But Hutchinson had Travis Noonan on his side; Travis Noonan, who had been leading the parade for more police support and a larger budget for the department. Noonan wouldn't let Bechard walk over the detective. He would be safe under Noonan.

CHAPTER VIII

The damn light didn't look as if it was going to turn green anytime soon, and Officer Bruce Nader was anxious to get home; actually to his girlfriend's house. He had recently moved in, or closer to the truth, had let the lease run out on his own apartment. Why pay rent on a place when you're not even there half the time? He was tired of waiting for the traffic signal to turn, so Officer Nader hit the switch that controlled the chase lights of his police cruiser and 'bwooped' the siren three times as he cut through the intersection at Thirty-ninth and Division. He had been waiting for a whole two seconds.

Officer Bruce Nader was a hard-working cop who loved his job. He felt lucky to have stumbled into the career because after his stint in the army he had felt like his life had no direction. Nader had been a cop now for about two years, and he had the gig nailed. He'd be making detective soon, so long as he kept hitting his quotas, and he had no problem hitting his quotas. Nader actually enjoyed completing all of the necessary paperwork after issuing a citation, and his work was prompt and thorough. He could issue as many as two dozen on a good day; all good citations – the kind of tickets that don't usually get dismissed at the arraignment. Yes, he was sticking it to all those slobs out there who thought that the traffic laws applied to everyone else but them!

Nader was appalled at the number of moms in minivans he would stop for speeding through school zones, elderly folks for rolling through stop signs, and brand new teenaged drivers for just being reckless behind the wheel. He took a lot of pride in thinking of all the automobile accidents he prevented, and other crimes that he surely thwarted. How satisfying his job was!

He was also quite amused at the games people played behind the wheel. It was hilarious to see how everyone would slow down whenever they caught sight of his cruiser. But he always got the biggest laugh from clocking people after they had passed by him – without fail everyone sped back up to whatever speed they had been driving before.

Nader stopped his cruiser in front of his girlfriend's house. He was certain that Rachel's neighbors loved him because having a cop car

VIII – Officer Nader and the Vampire

parked on the street was an extremely effective neighborhood crime deterrent.

A child's bicycle sat upside-down on the front walk. It belonged to Adam, Rachel's eight year-old son. Nader managed to just tolerate the child because, like it or not, Adam was part of the Rachel package. It seemed to Nader that women over twenty-two years old without children were getting more and more scarce. And a guy like Bruce had to take what he could get!

He stepped past the bicycle and continued up the walk, to the front door of the quaint neighborhood house that having been built in 1978 was just older than he was. Rachel wasn't the picture of neatness, but then, neither was he. She certainly spent more time picking up the house than he did maintaining it. The structure was showing its age. Hell, weren't the landlords responsible for taking care of any of this shit?

Nader opened the flimsy screen door, wondering what was still holding it to its hinges, and turned the knob on the front door. It wasn't locked and that lightened his mood a little. For one thing, the lock was stubborn; he would eventually need to stick a little graphite in the damn thing. And it always seemed to Nader that if the door was unlocked that Rachel was anticipating his arrival; he felt like a welcome guest. You see, deep down, Bruce Nader felt like an intruder everywhere he went, especially when he was behind the shield.

But that was one of the things that he loved about being a cop – it gave him the right, along with his co-intruders, to go anywhere they deemed necessary for the sake of the public good. Society needed his rough insertion. His uniform provided him a sort of costume, anonymity; the badge provided him with the indemnification to take the necessary measures. Without them he was just the unwanted and unwelcome Bruce Nader. But with them it did not matter if he was unwanted or unwelcome; his intrusion was somehow requisite.

"Hey baby!" he called as he entered. It was oddly quiet. Bruce stepped through the dingily furnished front room and into the kitchen, expecting to see his girlfriend, but she wasn't there. "Rach?"

Bruce stood quietly and listened. Had he just heard a faint sniffle from the bedroom? What the hell was she balling about now? He walked softly down the hall. The door to the master bedroom was open and in the dim light Bruce could see Rachel lying on the bed, her face wet and red. She was definitely upset! He prayed that it wasn't something stupid that he had done… or not done.

"What's the matter, baby?" he said in his most tender voice as he entered the room; then he saw what was upsetting his girlfriend.

Sitting comfortably on the laundry hamper in the corner was a young skinhead holding tightly to Adam and touching the end of a gun barrel to the child's head. "Don't move," said the punk coolly.

Officer Nader's police academy training, token at best, was momentarily lost to him. Not that it would have helped him much anyway. He was paralyzed into a terrible state of acute indecision. It took him a full three seconds to even tally his options. By the time he had done that much the young man was breaking into a wide grin.

The man said, "I've dreamed of this moment, Officer Nader." He seemed oddly more relieved than malicious, as if peace might finally be washing over him.

Bruce would liked to have come back with some snappy answer. Something like 'Well, here's your wake-up call, asshole!' would have been perfect, but he simply did not dare. He would need to remain perfectly polite and compliant until he ascertained whether or not this punk actually had the balls to pull the trigger. However, testing a gunman's resolve is extremely tricky, for obvious reasons. Bruce couldn't let anything happen to little Adam, no matter how many times he had wished that the little shit would disappear.

Bruce realized that the room was dark because the curtain had been drawn tight. Rachel lay on the bed unrestrained, but afraid to move for a very good reason. Clearly, this intruder wanted leverage against Bruce, and right now he had it! An intense rage began to boil in Bruce's blood. How dare this asshole invade his house and terrorize his girlfriend and her son!! Let the men fight like men! Leave the women and children out of it! Bruce would crush the little pansy coward if he ever got the chance! God! He felt so helpless! He couldn't do anything with the boy so compromised.

Bruce couldn't stand the idea of this asshole getting the best of him. He was supposed to be the hero after all! He longed to do something heroic, something that would save the day. A fleeting fantasy of an immensely grateful Rachel throwing her tender little body against him played in his mind; Rachel feeling his bulging muscles as he holds the dripping heart of his enemy tight in his large hand.

The smooth voice of the young man brought Bruce back to the frustrating, infuriating moment. "Well! Now that you're here, let's get on with the fun."

Bruce did his best to smile through his rage. He had been taught at the academy to remain genial and stress-free when confronted by a

VIII – Officer Nader and the Vampire

gunman; anything to help keep the gunman at ease. The last thing you need is a stressed-out man with a gun. "Can we talk this thing over?" Bruce asked as accommodatingly as he could.

"We're going to," said the young man. "But first you're going to perform a very slow striptease. Throw your weapons on that pile of clothes over there."

Bruce entertained the fantasy of going off and capping everybody in the room. He could start by putting a bullet into Rachel. That would wake that stupid little son of a bitch up – so much for the goddam leverage! If the dude actually had the presence of mind to cap the kid then Bruce could fill the little punk with lead. And if the little asshole actually shot at Bruce, the bullets would bounce off his Kevlar and Bruce would *still* fill the dude up with lead. And if a stray bullet caught the kid, too bad; life would go on. *'Cause little punks need to learn that they can't just come into your house with a gun and expect you to take it up the ass!*

But Bruce just did as he was told, tossing his gun and night-stick across the room to a pile of laundry that had made it only as far as the doorway from the master bathroom on its journey to the hamper. Hopefully, the gun would be close enough for Rachel to jump for if a fight broke out.

"Keep going," said the kid with the gun. "I want to see your underwear."

His frustration mounting, Bruce slowly removed his precious uniform. Maybe if he took his time something would give. He started methodically on his Kevlar vest, stalling as much as he dared, and it seemed like an eternity until it was finally off. He placed it nonchalantly on the foot of the bed, hoping again that Rachel might be able to reach for it if bullets started flying.

The young man didn't seem at all bothered by the slow pace, but he didn't let the Kevlar vest get by him. "No, no, Officer Nader," he said, contempt and scorn permeating the name and title. "Off to the side!" Again, Bruce complied.

At length, Bruce stood before the gunman in his briefs. "Now," said the young man. "Handcuff her."

Again, Bruce tried to get by with leaving the cuffs loose enough for Rachel to slip her little wrists out of them, but the gunman wouldn't have it. "No, no, Officer Nader," he said even more contemptuously. "Behind her back. Interlock the cuffs. Tighter!"

"I'm sorry, baby," said Bruce. He could hardly maintain his own composure over her terror-filled sobs.

"Use your belt on her ankles," said the punk, still cool as ice-cubes as he held the whimpering boy. Bruce obeyed.

The young man continued, "I want you to know that you are going to die. Put any hope of surviving this out of your head. There is nothing to be discussed or bargained for, except for possibly the lives of this woman and child, but you will have to convince me that they are worthy of living. I am simply going to kill you, and you will have the exquisite pleasure of seeing death coming from a long way off. Before death comes to you, however, you will lose all hope; you will feel damned!"

Bruce wanted to say something – anything! But his heroicness would not allow him to put the boy at risk. This guy was sick, without a doubt. But the situation was far from hopeless. Every passing second was a chance for something to break; a chance for the tables to turn. Finally, with astounding contriteness, Bruce asked, "Who are you?"

The young man looked full at the cop. "I was Chad Reeves before I died. Now, I am simply Death."

Bruce racked his brain trying to recall anything about a Chad Reeves as he finished securing Rachel's feet. He came up fully blank.

"I see you're trying to remember where you know me from," said Death, and he leveled the gun at Bruce.

Rachel lay on her stomach, still on the bed, and she could just see what was going on by twisting her head. She let out a breath of relief as the immediate threat against her son was abated. Bruce was also somewhat relieved, but now also saw his own peril looming closer. The words of the young man echoed in his ears.

Death now directed the boy to face him as he held the gun steady on Bruce. "Adam," said Death without a trace of condescension. "Do you have a lot of friends at school?"

The boy was frightened beyond his ability to respond at first.

"Its okay, Adam," said Death in a sweetly soothing tone. "Do you have friends around the neighborhood?"

Timidly, the boy nodded.

Death nodded, too. "Do any of the bigger kids pick on you?"

The boy continued nodding.

"Do you pick on any of the other kids that are littler than you?"

Adam stopped nodding abruptly.

"Do you?" Death persisted gently.

The boy shook his head slowly, still not uttering even a peep.

"Don't lie to me," said Death softly, but firmly. "Do you bully any of the smaller kids?" Chad had followed the child's after-dinner

VIII – Officer Nader and the Vampire

activities the previous night and knew that he in fact did. Relatively harmless bullying, perhaps, but even now the terrified boy had in his pocket a red-colored felt pen that he had forcefully taken from a smaller child that lived two doors down.

Still, the child denied it.

"You can't lie to Death, Adam. I already know. What do you have in your pocket?"

Guilt morphed onto the face of the boy.

"Its okay, Adam. Pull it out."

Slowly, fearfully, the boy did as he was told and produced the red-inked magic marker – a simple, little item that is a commodity if only for a brief flash in the span of many childhoods.

"Good," said Death. "Does that belong to you?"

The child was frozen.

"Does it?"

At last Adam shook his head slowly.

"No, it doesn't, does it? Did you take it from the smaller child?"

Still, the child hesitated.

"You can't lie to me," said Death.

Adam finally nodded his head, looking contrite.

"Do you bully the smaller children?"

Looking even more penitent, Adam nodded a little faster.

Death nodded as well. "Yes. You do. Is that a good thing? Is that right?"

Adam shook his head, almost quickly.

"No, its not," said Death. "There. You see? It's good to tell the truth. Now tell me, Adam, what do you want to be when you grow up?"

Bruce was starting to put this together in his head. He was aware that the boy fully idealized him, and he was afraid that if the boy answered it might enrage this insane gunman. "Adam," he said apprehensively, and then Death cut him off.

"Quiet," he said coolly, not changing his tone. "It's not your turn to talk. I'm talking to Adam. Adam, its okay. You can tell me. What do you want to be when you grow up?"

Hesitantly, the boy said in a small cracking voice, "A policeman."

The eyes of Death turned even colder, if that was possible. "Adam, the police are very bad men, don't ever forget –"

Bruce blurted, "You're the one with a gun!"

Chad sprang from his seated position on the laundry hamper and had the barrel of the gun against Bruce's head in a split second, with the hammer pulled back. "SHUT UP!! Shut up! You don't talk unless I tell you to talk!"

That was the moment when the last of Bruce's heroism crumbled away, and stifled sobs began to bubble out of his red, hot face. Rachel emitted a short shriek.

Death continued, "Tell him you're a bad man, Officer Nader."

Bruce could only choke on a trembling sob.

Death pressed the barrel harder into Bruce's head. "Tell him, Nader. Tell Adam that you are a bad man!"

"I am a bad man." It was a hardly understandable mumble.

"What's that?" said Death. "I didn't hear you."

"I am a bad man," Bruce repeated slower.

"Do you bully people, Officer Nader?" asked Death.

"Yes! Yes, I bully people."

"Is that right? Is it good?"

"No, it's not. It's bad."

"A policeman is a bad man; isn't that right Officer Nader?"

"Yes! Yes it is. I am a very bad man." He bawled out the words.

"Very good, Officer Nader," said Death in a very condescending tone. "You may have just saved young Adam's life. You see, Adam, because Officer Nader is a bad man, he is going to die. If he was not a bad man, he would live. Do you understand?"

The eyes of the boy no longer registered fear. He appeared stoic. For him this would be the beginning of a life filled with repressed emotion, severe psychosis, and therapy. He nodded.

Death nodded too. "Okay, Adam. Can you write in the dark?" The arbitrary nature of the question further frightened the boy's mother, but not Adam. Death continued, "I want you to practice writing on the wall in the closet with the door shut. You can write or draw anything you want. Use the magic marker. You may want to write the name 'Chad Reeves' and you can also write about what's happening here today and what we've talked about."

"It's okay, baby," said Rachel finally mustering some bravery. "Don't be scared. Just do what the man says."

Slowly, the boy opened the sliding door of the closet and stepped in. He felt strangely comforted by his mother's scent on the clothes. He slid the door shut. Faint light leaked past the edges of the door, and slowly his eyes adjusted to the darkness. He held the felt pen tightly in his hot grip, and pulled the cap off.

Bruce had stopped puzzling over the question of who Chad Reeves was. Now he was trying to figure out why the crazy punk had put the

VIII – Officer Nader and the Vampire

kid in the closet with a magic marker. It frightened him even more for what might happen.

And hope did indeed abandon Bruce Nader.

CHAPTER IX

Marcus sat comfortably on the couch between Sarah and Tina. Lying peacefully asleep on the floor was Jagger the Pit-bull. It looked nothing at all like a conventional family, and yet there was certainly something very homey and family-esque about the three of them sitting there. The scene could have been a Norman Rockwell painting on the cover of the Saturday Evening Post.

The girls were enthusiastically catching Marcus up on their lives. Tina was working hard at the supermarket and had already received a small raise. It wasn't much, but it did make her feel like a valued employee, and Marcus knew that she would go far in anything she tried. He encouraged her without sounding patronizing, condescending, or pious. The little girl looked even more healthy and vibrant – alive!

Sarah had also entered the labor market for the first time in her life. She had managed to land herself a position in telemarketing. She pretty much hated it, but at least it was something. Sarah just wasn't quite ready to relinquish her claim to government benefits at the death of her husband. Marcus blanched at hearing that, nevertheless he believed that Sarah would continue to work hard to establish her independence.

On the positive side, however, Sarah was already looking five years younger and fifteen pounds lighter. Just getting up from the bed and out of the house had done wonders. Tina had also been putting slight pressure on her to quit smoking, and Sarah was now in the process of cutting down.

Tina was still obviously quite enamored with Marcus. She was increasingly exerting less effort to hide it from her mother. But honestly, what red-blooded girl wouldn't be totally into him? With that long beautiful hair, those brilliantly light brown eyes, and that perfect body, he was absolutely gorgeous – marvie! What's more, Tina also knew his incredible secret; that made him all the more desirable.

Sarah was, of course, also quite taken with Marcus, and, except for the obvious reasons, couldn't figure out why – specifically, why it was that she should feel like a giddy schoolgirl whenever he was around!

At length, Tina asked kittenishly, "Marcus, would you like to go for a walk?"

IX – Marcus Asks a Favor of Tina

The vampire's dark gaze fell to Tina's left hand where a large, suspicious-looking bandage spotted with relatively fresh blood was adhered to her palm. Where had he seen that before? "That would be nice, darling," he said, and he excused himself to Sarah as they rose to go.

Outside it was an enchanting night, notwithstanding that only a handful of stars could pierce the glare of the metro lights. Endless rows of virtually identical three bedroom, two bath homes manufactured from a cookie cutter by some slick developer over twenty years ago stretched over the gently rolling terrain. Being a fair distance from any major roads, the neighborhood was mostly quiet, with the constant roar of traffic reduced to a mere ambience. Marcus and Tina talked very softly as voices would carry easily down these suburban streets.

"I was hoping we would get some time alone," said Tina. "Since you refuse to spend the night." The little girl would be lucky to pass for fifteen any more. Six weeks of not dancing, smoking, drinking, and doing whatever drugs happened to be around had transformed her nearly completely back to the young girl that she was supposed to be at seventeen. Her visible tattoos seemed severely out of place, and most of the body piercings had grown over and healed. Marcus now had high hopes that she might grow into a greatly empowered and productive individual.

"I need to talk about something in particular," said Marcus. "I gather that you are pretty familiar with the downtown scene?"

In the past, such a question would have opened the door for Tina to boast about how hip and down she was with the coolest of the cool. Being socially connected with one or more of the charisma-endowed street urchins could be considered bragging rights for any low-self-esteem teenaged loser that turned to downtown as both a source and an outlet for their angst. But Tina somehow felt 'over it' now. She did not understand the growth and change that she was going through, but she liked it. She answered simply, "Yes."

"Do you know a particular homeless chap with a severe hair-lip?"

"That could only be Jamie," she said.

"What do you know about him?" asked Marcus.

"He's been on the street forever and he's addicted to heroin. Jamie is one of the sadder cases downtown. We've hung out. He bought H from me a few times."

"Does he have AIDS?"

"Um, I think so," Tina replied. "I think he was born with it."

"Does he have any friends, partners, lovers?"

"Not that I know of," said Tina. "He can't talk and he's not real sociable."

"How does he buy his drugs?" asked Marcus.

"I'm sure he gets the money from begging. He probably makes a hundred dollars a day. Maybe even more. He has a thing-ie that he uses to write on when he needs to communicate. What is your interest in a guy like Jamie?" asked Tina.

"I've been following the chap for four nights, and I haven't seen him interacting with anyone," Marcus said with mild frustration.

"Why have you been following Jamie?"

"I saw him plant a syringe, Tina. I believe he might be the one who has been planting infected syringes around town."

Tina's face registered shock, but she did not doubt the vampire's word.

"But," Marcus continued, "Someone else either knows or is in on it, because the news reports disclosed there has been an anonymous call to the police with a warning every time a syringe has been planted. Jamie could not have made such a call."

"Wow," was all that Tina could say, and it came out in a stunned breath.

"I know I have just laid a lot of shit on you, and I am sorry, but I believe you are mature enough to handle it. It is not any bigger than the secret that you already keep for me. Anyway, Jamie must be doing all of his heroin purchases during the day, because I have not seen him talking to a single soul. I was really hoping that you could shed some light on the subject. Who made those phone calls? Who might Jamie's accomplice be?"

Tina could not hide the pleasure she felt at having the vampire again come to her for assistance. She glanced at the bloody bandage on her hand. *It's working!* she thought. Then she said, "What would you like me to do?" in a sensual tone that more than hinted she would be willing to do anything for the vampire.

"Perhaps you could take a day and watch him for me." Marcus was aware of Tina's servility, and the significance of her doe-eyed, adoring gaze hadn't escaped him either. Maybe he should not be doing this; she would undoubtedly feel very much invested.

"Oh, yes!" she said, excitedly. "I will do that for you!"

Well, it is done, thought Marcus. He said, "Fine. When is your day off?"

"I can go the day after tomorrow."

IX – Marcus Asks a Favor of Tina

"Good. The sooner the better. Follow him discretely from a distance and find out whom he talks to on an average day."

The two of them walked along for a minute, silently. Tina was entertaining fantasies in her head of Marcus lavishing love and every kind of gratuitous affection upon her. She was certain that she was already seeing the positive results of the magic spell she had cast.

Marcus's thoughts, as usual, were a bit darker. There could be no doubt that the girl had a lot of emotional healing yet to do from the damages done to her in early adolescence. To her credit, she had already made outstanding progress. She did not fit the victim profile. That is why she had chosen at such a young age to run away from the abuses of her step-father and the co-dependence of her mother. She had already felt all of the pain that she was going to allow herself to feel over that situation. Her strength was in her ability to forgive – both others and herself. Her maturity was quite beyond her seventeen years; there was no denying that. Marcus had definitely taken a liking to Tina, but not in a romantic way. Maybe in few years, a decade more likely. It would be delightful, he thought, to watch as she grew and developed. In the mean time, the girl would have to be set straight.

"Tina," Marcus began.

"Yes, love?" she answered quickly; she had been startled from her daydream and hadn't quite emerged back to reality yet.

"Tina, my sweet, you are dear to my heart, but you must put any romantic notions that you may have for me out of your head."

Disappointment and frustration washed over the girl. At first she thought that she should try to deny it, to play it cool, but she knew she was talking to a clairvoyant. He obviously could tell that she was into him; she would not be able to lie to him. She said, "But it's not fair."

Marcus said nothing for the moment and she continued. "You get to use all kinds of magic on me. You get to live forever. You already have my heart and I get nothing. Marcus, I don't want to grow old and die… alone."

"You mean, like your mother is doing?"

"Yes," she answered quietly.

The vampire mused at this girl. Even as young as she was, she still had a sense of her own mortality. It may have been partially the result of having been suicidal in the past; partially the result of watching her mother age beyond her years in too short a span. "Tina," he said tenderly, "It will be hard for me to say this without sounding self-righteous, but I'm going to try. For what it's worth, neither one of us has any guarantee to immortality. But I would never wish this life of mine upon you, my love. Living by ending the existences of others is the ultimate immorality. Would that I could quit it."

"But you wouldn't have to kill, Marcus. We could create a secret clan of donors; people that would all keep your secret." Apparently, the little girl had been giving this some thought.

"Yes, and people that would incessantly badger me to make them into a vampire," Marcus added. "That has been tried in the past with extremely limited success."

The disappointment and frustration redoubled on the girl. "But I love you, Marcus. It's not fair that you can make me love you and I can't make you love me."

"Tina!" Marcus said in a mock scolding. "I do not make you love me. And if you do indeed love me, you could hate me just as easily."

"But you're a vampire. You charmed me. If only I had your magic, I could charm you; I could make you fall in love with me."

"Tina, my sweet, you have been reading too many vampire stories. What did you think, that you could cast a spell of fixing upon me?" Tina looked sheepish on top of her disillusionment. "Let me guess," said the vampire. "You had a little ceremony with candles and statues of saints. You probably used my shirt that I imprudently left behind when I last visited. Is that why your hand is bandaged?"

"Something like that," said Tina. The ritual she had performed was beginning to seem rather silly.

"Ah, my sweet, sweet Tina. You are as adorable as you are romantic. But listen to me carefully. I do not want to try to tell you that there is not magic in the universe. But I do wish to impart with you this one wisdom – there is no such thing as calling upon unseen forces to carry out your wishes. In all my life I have never seen any kind of evidence that would support the notion of magic in its most popular sense. There are a lot of truths in this universe that we do not yet comprehend. These unknown truths, for the moment, may seem as magic to us. The real magic lies in the pursuit of truth and knowledge."

"But you're magic," Tina protested. "You are immortal and you have amazing powers."

"I regenerate," Marcus corrected gently. "And I do have some amazing skills, but I am not magic. I do not know what it is that allows me to do what I do, but I can assure you that it is nothing supernatural."

"But how can you know that for sure, Marcus?"

"Remember Ockam's Razor," said the vampire.

"What can I do, Marcus, to make you love me?"

IX – Marcus Asks a Favor of Tina

"Tina, my love, there is nothing anyone can do to make another person fall in love with them, or do anything else. You have control over one person! And right now in your life, I would say that you are exercising excellent control over yourself. You are working hard; you are improving your life and your mind. You are bettering yourself and you are growing. You are doing the things that lead to happiness and a good life. These things do take time, however. Even though we do not know what will be after this mortal coil finally comes to an end, I believe that you will be more empowered by living as if you already knew that you were going to be around fifty million years from now. It helps to keep you focused on what is truly important, and will prevent you from wasting your time on the immaterial.

"You will have forever to develop and grow into a splendid being; a being that will attract and have many friends and loved ones over the course of eternity. You will not have the power to make people love you; no one does really. But that is not really what you would want, is it? What you do have is the power to make yourself a lovable person, and believe me, you are already skilled in the use of such power.

"Tina dearest, do not be frustrated if you do not receive certain desired feedback from certain individuals. Hoping for or expecting more from people around you opens the door to disappointment. You can save yourself heartache by simply accepting from people what they are willing to give to you."

The dark couple had stepped into the shadows of several trees growing at the edge of a public park area. The vampire now stopped and faced the small girl, tipping her head up with a gentle hand on the tip of her dainty chin. Single streams trickled down from each of her dark eyes, but there was no longer any sign of frustration in her face. She had been profoundly affected by Marcus's words, and now her young, angular face reflected determination, power, with only shadows of fleeing doubts.

"And Tina," Marcus continued. "I do love you."

He kissed her lightly on the forehead.

"Now," he continued, "How do you think your mother would react to learning of my secret?"

CHAPTER X

This was a hell of way to start off the day. Hell! To start off the week! Detective Darrel Hutchinson entered the residence of Rachel Keller. Uniformed street cops were everywhere! Word travels fast when a fellow officer gets taken out. It's almost as if it is compulsory for everyone on the force, whether they know the guy or not, to show up at the scene and make a show of how well-bonded the members of the police force are. Hutchinson had been forced to park his unmarked Crown Victoria over two blocks away for all of the patrol cars in the street.

At the sight of all the uniforms, Hutchinson groaned. The crime-scene was bound to be tainted by all of the activity and foot traffic. He stepped down the hallway and looked into the bedroom over the hardly recognizable pieces of Bruce Nader; difficult to recognize perhaps because the severed body parts were mixed together in a gory pile with the body parts of someone else – a female, probably Rachel Keller, though Hutchinson had never met her and would have to check it. The real difficulty lay in trying to get over the expansive pile without stepping in gore, as it obstructed the doorway to the room.

Several of the uniformed police officers had already attempted the jump with negligible success and were looking around the room. Careless bloody tracks spanned from the pile in all directions over the carpeted floor. Hutchinson exploded, "What the hell are you doing!?! You fuckin' clowns are contaminating the crime-scene!!"

The first impulse of most of the cops, (which they successfully suppressed), was to respond belligerently. But, one by one, they adopted a hang-dog posture and moved in a congested attempt to exit the room.

"Goddammit!!" yelled Hutchinson in frustration, as he surveyed the obvious disturbances to the evidence. He breathed deeply trying to calm himself as the cops exited the room one at a time, then he asked, "Who was first on the scene?"

"I was, sir," said the last cop inside the room. "I was radioed and asked to check on Bruce after he didn't show up at the station this morning." Guilt was tattooed on the officer's face and Hutchinson was

X – Detective Work

certain that this was one of the imprudent cops that had called everyone with the grotesquely fascinating news.

"I don't want anyone else in or out of this room," barked Hutchinson. "Until I've had a chance to retrieve all the forensic evidence."

Hutchinson tiptoed gingerly through the area trying vainly to step between the strewn limbs. Once past the macabre obstacle course he examined the scene. Seconds later a dry heave doubled him over. Detachment abandoned the battle-scarred detective. Hutchinson was horrified. His illusion of safety was fast dissolving. He could imagine finding his own family like this and the mental picture struck a chill through his core.

"You okay, lieutenant?" asked the remaining cop.

"He's graduated to the next level," Hutchinson muttered dramatically, even as he wondered how much worse than this any deranged person could get.

The detective regained his composure just enough to examine and analyze the scene. He noticed that Nader's uniform and vest were piled near the bathroom doorway. A blood-encrusted pair of handcuffs had been dropped near the main pile. There was no sign of Nader's gun. Laundry seemed to be just about everywhere, some of it stained with blood. How would the FBI profiler try to reconstruct this mess?

Hutchinson had wanted the Psicko Killer to strike again, but not like this. This double job was especially grisly. Of course, something deep inside the detective was actually glad that it had been a cop. Now he would be justified in employing extreme measures to apprehend this killer. It wouldn't matter if no one cared for or even knew Nader; every cop on the force would take his murder as a personal attack. Collectively, cops always enjoyed playing the victim because then they could all come back snarling and biting like a cornered wild animal. It is fun to dispense righteous retribution.

At length, Hutchinson had bagged everything that he could see to bag. He had taken the crime-scene photos himself. He had, in fact, taken it upon himself to do just about everything that was normally carried out by one of the lower-ranking officers. It pissed him off because it was obvious that the killer had arranged the pile in the doorway on purpose just to make it difficult; and it pissed him off even more that his comrades had fallen for the booby-trap.

Even in the midst of his pissed-ivity, Hutchinson discovered one major difference between this murder and the previous jobs – this scene was comparatively loaded with forensic evidence. There was a fourth set of fingerprints this time; on the handcuffs, the bedroom doorknob, the bathroom sink. This job had plainly been sloppier. The detective was actually a little encouraged, hoping that the additional evidence wasn't simply the trace of clumsy policemen.

At last, Hutchinson turned his attention to the closet. He slid the door open and used his flashlight to illuminate the space, rather than employ the light switch just outside the door. The light beam fell on the detached eyes of a young boy, and Hutchinson's heart leapt in a start. He recovered quickly, and said softly, "Hey. What's your name?"

There was no answer from the boy.

"Are you okay, little guy?" Hutchinson asked.

The uniformed officer stood behind Hutchinson, trying to wear a reassuring smile. The boy shrunk back into sweet-smelling clothes.

"It's okay. I'm a policeman. You can come out. My name is Darrel." But the boy was not put at ease.

"Stand back," Hutchinson said to the other cop. Then it suddenly struck Hutchinson like a brick. *You idiot! You can't let the kid see his mom all mutilated like this!* He said, "Uh, on second thought, if you would rather stay in the closet, that will be okay, too. Okay? Are you alright?"

"You are a bad man," said the boy without emotion.

"No, no. I'm not the bad man. I'm one of the good guys. I'm a policeman. See?" Hutchinson displayed his badge. "My name is Detective Darrel.

"Police are bad men," said the boy.

"No, I'm a good man, and I can prove it. Would you like some candy?"

"NO!" yelled the boy, and he shrouded himself in his mother's clothes.

"Okay," said Hutchinson, at a loss. He shut the closet door and beckoned to the other officer. "Go make a call to the child psychologist."

While the coroner picked up the body pieces, Hutchinson carefully slid the closet door open and flicked on the light. "Hey buddy, can I come in?"

"No!"

"Please? I just want to see how you're doing."

"No!"

But Hutchinson was slowly invading the space as he talked. Then he saw the red marks on the wall. "Hey, this is cool. Did you draw this?" Hutchinson noticed that the child's hands were covered in red ink. The scribbled pictures and words on the wall were terribly difficult to make out. "Can you tell me what this is?"

"No! You're a bad man!"

Hutchinson knew that he was bungling at trying to establish rapport with this child. "Okay, I'm gonna go now. Do you want me to leave the light on for you?"

"No!"

Fine! thought Hutchinson. *Is that all you can say, you little shit?!*

The child psychologist, a nice young lady named Pamela Winn, had no more success with Adam than Hutchinson had. The police finally removed the child kicking and screaming from the closet. A sedative was at last administered to make the child manageable.

Before leaving to return to his office, Hutchinson spent a few minutes sitting on the closet floor, trying to make heads or tails of the red marks on the wall. Everything had been scribbled over. The only discernable writing he could actually make out was the words 'bad man', and the writing preceding those words might have been 'police'. There appeared to be something of a drawing, but it, too, had been defaced with frantic scribbles. The picture consisted of two stick-figures, one holding a disproportionately large gun on the other. Maybe the shrink would be able to dig some information out of the kid. Hutchinson was certainly baffled.

The kid appeared to hate cops. Had a cop done this to his mother and her boyfriend? Or maybe it was someone wearing a uniform…

Upon arriving back at police headquarters, he quickly prepared his compares and then ran a check for the unknown set of fingerprints on every database available to him. An hour later the results were in – no matches.

Stymied again! At least the prints didn't belong to any of the cops. Hutchinson was just about to look for his favorite brick wall when the SWAT theme chimed. "Yeah," he said flatly after punching the button on his cell.

"Hutchinson? This is Mike Stone," said the apprehensive voice. "Uh, you still investigating that Nader murder scene out in southeast?"

"I just finished up. Why?"

"Well, uh, I was hoping that we could compare notes on a couple of my cases that show some similarities to a few of yours."

"What the hell, Mike? Have you got missing persons cases that connect to the supposed serial killer?"

"You could say that. But right now I'm working on another murder case – Judge Wright and his family! And I've also got another –"

"Excuse me?" interrupted Hutchinson, then he immediately tried to soften his tone. "I mean, when did you start working homicide?"

"Since yesterday morning," said Stone. "One of my missing persons turned up dead. Rather than turn the case over to someone on homicide, Rahal just decided to transfer me and stay on it. I mean, you guys have kinda had your hands full."

"Well, congratulations," Hutchinson said lamely. His mind churned. First the FBI, and now Stone was crowding him. Were they chasing the same guy? That was the first thing that Hutchinson would have to verify. Apparently Stone thought that they were.

It was true that the homicide division had been quite busy lately. Dead bodies with slashed wrists had been turning up with disconcerting regularity; mostly homeless people, some drug dealers, gang-bangers, and prostitutes. It would have been easy to just say 'Hey, they couldn't live with themselves anymore – good riddance!' But it was becoming obvious that they were the victims of a very clever repeat killer. Hutchinson was just grateful that the case had been assigned to someone else in the unit, so he could be free to put all his energies, lame as they were, toward tracking down the Psicko Killer. But why couldn't the Cap'n have put Stone on the suicide case and left Hutchinson to his own devices on the Psicko Killer?

On the other hand, what if it was all the same guy? The words of Travis Noonan echoed in the detective's ears. Just how many sickos could one metro area accommodate? Could these mock suicides also be the work of the Psicko Killer?

This would be the beginning of the information exchange game with Detective Stone. Hutchinson didn't like playing it, but he was very good at it and sometimes it was the only way to get the edge over the other competitors in the dog-eat-dog glory race that was homicide, or any other division at the police department. Sure they were supposed to be on the same team, but under the surface everybody knew that that was baloney. Still, pretenses had to be carefully maintained.

"Yeah, thanks," said Stone in response to Hutchinson's felicitations, with equal insincerity. "So, uh, anyway, you know the judge, don't you?"

"I know who he is," said Hutchinson.

"He was cut into pieces along with his wife and daughter," Stone said with a measure of reverence.

Again Hutchinson's mind reeled. It was official – Stone was working cases that by right belonged to Hutchinson. Son of a bitch! But, there was no use crying over Rahal's spilt milk. Hutchinson would

X – Detective Work

just have let Stone do his thing, and then weasel information out of him slyly. His next trick would be to get as much data about the Judge Wright murder as possible. This would be done by offering some information; hopefully making some little tidbit sound far more important than it really was and getting Stone to open up. "That sounds like the serial killer alright," affirmed Hutchinson.

"Yeah, but I was under the impression that the perp on your jobs left no trail," Stone said.

"That's true," said Hutchinson with syrup. He smiled devilishly; apparently Stone had found traces of the Psicko Killer at his latest murder scene as well. "I believe Cap'n Rahal has a written report of the FBI's psychological profile if you want it. It would contain the FBI's analysis of what little forensic evidence we did turn up on the Preston and Goulier murders."

"Yeah, Rahal already gave it to me," said Stone.

Jesus! thought Hutchinson. *Cap'n must be pullin' for Stone!* He was feeling left out and dejected. He asked nonchalantly "So, what did you find on Wright?"

Stone could hardly hide his superciliousness. "Well, I think I've got the killer's fingerprints for one thing."

"Wow!" Hutchinson tried gamely to sound surprised and impressed. He was pretty sure that he had pulled it off. His gut feeling was telling him that Stone's mysterious prints would match his own mysterious prints, but they still wouldn't lead to anyone that they had on file. "That could bust this thing open."

"I hope so, Darrel. We need to catch this guy. It's pretty nasty up here."

"Yeah, I can imagine. Do you need me to come up and lend a hand?"

"Oh, naw. We're pretty much finished up here, but thanks."

"Sure. Just let me know if you need anything," said Hutchinson. He felt confident that Stone would tell all at some point. "Say, you said something about a missing persons case that turned homicide; who was it?"

"Do you remember that guy named Bob Wilson? Disappeared from the Public Safety building a few months ago? He was suspected of stickin' those AIDS infected needles all over town; you remember?"

"Oh yeah," said Hutchinson. "He turned up chopped? Where?"

"Are you sitting down? Get this – his body was found cut up like the others, and stuffed into an exhaust ventilation shaft on the roof at the county jail. Judging by the decay I would say he'd been up there since the disappearance."

Of course he's been dead since the disappearance, thought Hutchinson. He was taking for granted that little time had elapsed between Wilson's disappearance and his death.

Stone then went on to tell Hutchinson the unbelievable story of how the decaying pieces of humanity might never have been found except that a smooth inmate had somehow managed to slip from his cell the previous Saturday night, and had made a break for it through the hazard-lined ventilation shaft. His escape attempt was thwarted when he came across the ghastly remains of the former probation officer and had the nastiest fright of his life.

This new engaging bit of data turned itself over in Hutchinson's mind like a rotisserie chicken. So, Wilson turns up diced like the rest! It would appear there was a connection between the Psicko killings and the hypodermic needles after all. Noonan had called it!

Hutchinson was at a loss for words. He managed, "How do you suppose the body got up…?"

Stone shook his head even though Hutchinson wasn't there to see it. "No effin idea."

CHAPTER XI

This was Travis Noonan's big moment.

It had turned into a bright and beautiful autumn day. An enormous crowd had gathered downtown at the red-bricked Pioneer Courthouse Square for the event. The band Flash in the Pan had been retained to play a short set, then, with the masses properly hyped up, the MC announced Travis Noonan and then handed him a wireless handheld microphone.

Noonan stood on the large construction of risers that were put together to form a stage. Behind him was all of the music equipment, abandoned for the moment, as the stage had been fully relinquished to the politician. He had decided that this rally speech should be a little more casual, so there was no podium for him to stand behind. This wasn't going to be a lecture after all; he was going to stir the people up with righteous anger, pride, hope, and enthusiasm.

Allowing the intoxicating applause to ring on for a moment longer, Noonan looked out over the diverse crowd that was assembled before him. One of his aids had estimated approximately four thousand people. Of course, not all of these people here today supported Noonan. As with any large assembly, certain special interest groups would take advantage of the crowds to demonstrate. Activists for everything from animal rights to anti-globalization were on hand to gain sympathy for their cause. Leeches as far as Noonan was concerned. He had put this extravaganza on himself.

Getting the necessary permits had been a breeze for the city councilman, and one of Bechard's more apt secretaries had been loaned to Noonan to coordinate the entire event. She had booked the band and the production company. She had chased down the vendor's who had been so willing and quick to commercialize the event. Money from the participating vendor's had more than paid for everything.

Still, he was glad that the activist groups were there. Those certain, more controversial groups that did not garner a lot of support from the general public would be wonderful targets for the occasional comical and political potshot.

There was even a small group of people showing their support for another politician running against Noonan. The competition was a semi-solid citizen named Von Raines. At that moment Raines' campaign manager, a very able and handsome man named Kevin Greene, was fretting over the show of support that Noonan was receiving from the massive crowd. Greene turned to one of his assistants and complained, "Damn! This crowd is suckin' Noonan off right now. Couldn't we find anything to smear him with?"

"We're still lookin' into that," answered the stalwart assistant. "But so far he's squeaky clean."

Presently, the solemn politician raised his hands in a modest gesture and the applause died. "My fellow Portlandians," began Noonan. "I had originally hoped to come before you today with great tidings, but alas, my heart is heavy this day. I have just learned that one of this city's finest peace officers, Bruce Nader, and my colleague on the bench, Judge Perry Wright and his family, have all been the victims of the most heinous and terrible murders. I would like to call for a moment of silence to remember and pray for these lost friends."

With that Noonan bowed his head in an attitude of prayer, but he wasn't praying. He was listening to the hum, the murmur, the gentle roar of the crowd as it subdued and went very nearly silent, solemn; reverent. Then he stayed alert to the vibe of the assembly. In order to work this crowd Noonan would have to be in sync with the collective mindset of the crowd, and he was definitely working this crowd. He waited, head bowed, for about a minute, until finally the gentle rumble of the crowd began again to rise ever so slightly. The light-rail train was pulling up to the square, and even though it was generally very quiet, against the backdrop of the silent crowd it seemed quite irreverent, so Noonan, not missing a beat, prudently began again.

"Thank you! The losses of these men and their families are a great blow to our community. The police are certain that the murders were committed right in the victims' homes by the Psicko Killer, and I find that to be very disturbing. I can remember a time not so long ago when we could feel perfectly safe inside the walls of our homes and walking in the neighborhoods of our fair city at any hour of the day or night.

"As a judge I have seen the worst of the criminal element of this city pass through my courtroom. In the interest of keeping our streets safe I have been very tough on my sentencing of those found guilty. As a city councilman I have always pushed for increased police protection for Portland. It is the fine, hardworking officers of the law who deliver to me in my courtroom that vile element that would take away your freedom and safety if they could. It is these fine, hardworking officers who everyday, put their lives on the line for you; to keep you safe and

XI – Noonan's Big Moment

free. And it is these wonderful, brave officers who will bring to justice the Psicko Killer, and anyone else who threatens your safety and freedom."

The crowd erupted into applause. Noonan waited for the crowd to quiet only slightly before continuing. He spoke as if he alone led this mass of people.

"I'm told that the authorities are investigating the possibility that the Psicko Killer might also be the one who has been depositing hypodermic needles in public areas around downtown. The police are working hard to bring this despicable person to justice, but they need your help. They need more money from the city. I hope that you will stand behind me as I push for Portland city to budget more money to the police department."

Again the crowd roared. Noonan had them. His magnanimous eyes scanned the crowd seeming to make eye contact with everyone as he talked.

"I don't have to tell you that it's a little scary living here right now. However, we deserve to be able to walk down the streets of our beautiful city, and not have to worry about getting stuck by an AIDS infected needle. We have to send a clear message to the criminal element in this town! We're not going to take it anymore!!"

The crowd went wild with cheers and applause. Noonan's eyes smiled down upon the people as he waited for the hubbub to die down so he could continue.

"While we're at it, we must put more money into our schools, so that our children can be educated and trained for the bright, wonderful future. They must be taught morals, and citizenship. The hypodermic needle scare has been a frightening wake up call for all of us. We must teach our children what must be done to stop the spread of this evil disease!"

As he spoke his gaze meandered around a particular activist group demonstrating for the legalization of drugs, and finally came to rest on one person that was standing a short way from the group. Noonan focused on the person across the distance and stiffened. The person was a disgusting life-chewed homeless man. His face was half covered by a filthy cowl.

Noonan's next line escaped him, and as the applause began to subside, an intense sweat broke from his brow. He stammered, "We, uh, uhm, we have to, uh, give our support…"

Blessedly, applause rippled gently through the crowd and gradually grew into a tumult as Noonan lowered the mic and raised one fist triumphantly in a gesture that meant only god knows what. The crowd obediently mimicked his gesture and cheered. Noonan smiled broadly with the response. He said quickly, "Thanks for your support. Make me your governor." His campaign slogan was momentarily forgotten so grasping at straws he added, "I love you all!" It was well received.

He stepped hastily off the stage handing the mic to the MC and hissed to anyone within earshot, "Get the band back up there, quick!" The big man was soaked with sweat.

No one out in the crowd, least of all Jamie Thompson, really noticed that the politician had lost his composure and cut his speech dramatically short. Jamie wasn't even paying attention to what was going on. He was just standing near that particular group because one of his suppliers happened to be demonstrating and Jamie was, as usual, desperate to make a purchase.

And standing a short distance away was Tina, faithfully keeping an eye on Jamie. Because it had been several weeks since she had been downtown, she was now surrounded by a small group of street kids and other downtown personalities; friends with whom she had associated when the street had been her life. They were curious and inquisitive about how she was doing; and how much money she had.

So far, her surveillance had revealed little. She decided that if this went much longer without result, she would approach Jamie. There was at least a little rapport established between them.

Noonan had stepped away from the backstage area to a payphone, and made a call where he said nothing, but punched a few buttons on the phone. By the time he had made his way back to the backstage area, his cell phone was ringing.

"We need to talk," was all he said after he pressed the button. He had to raise his voice to be heard over the din of the band, but he was also trying to be careful to not be overheard. "You know where. Ten o'clock." He terminated the phone call.

Tina at last walked up to Jamie. He smelled horribly offensive, but she hugged him sweetly as she said, "Hi, Jamie. How ya' been?"

Jamie shrugged and made a 'so-so' gesture. This is where it got really difficult to carry on a conversation with Jamie. His condition kind of put a nix on the notion of small-talk.

Tina put her arm around the pathetic derelict again. "It's good to see you, Jamie," she said sincerely. "I worry about you."

Jamie's eyes seemed to smile for a moment; apparently he was touched. He produced his tattered Magic Slate and with the ragged tip of a brown fingernail scrawled, *"H?"*

XI – Noonan's Big Moment

"No, Jamie, I'm sorry. I'm clean. When are you gonna get clean?"

The derelict shook his head vehemently, lifted the one remaining grey sheet on his Magic Slate to clear his previous note, and then wrote, *"FiND GoD?"*

"No, I moved home."

"Step DAD?" Jamie was aware of her background.

"He died in a car crash. Drunk," said Tina, showing no grief.

"GLAD?"

Tina wouldn't bother upholding pretenses with Jamie. "Yeah."

Jamie scribbled *"i AM HAppy 4 U"*.

"Thank you, Jamie," and she gave him another half hug.

Jamie was feeling comfortable with the streetwise little girl. She had always been nice to him. Now, as he waited for his heroin contact to finish demonstrating, he decided that he could use a little sympathy from the sweet girl. He wrote, *"i ALMoSt DieD"*.

Concern flashed over Tina's face. "You almost died?! How?"

Lifting the sheet to again clear the pad, Jamie scrawled, *"BAD H"*.

"You took some bad heroin? Jamie, that's terrible. I wish you would quit."

As Tina spoke, the junkie cleared his sheet and wrote more. *"StAN tHe MAN GAve"*.

"Stan the Man gave?" asked Tina, and Jamie responded by underlining the word 'gave'.

"I don't understand, Jamie," she said.

In tiny capital letters, Jamie added, *"BAD H"* to the end of the message.

"He gave you the bad heroin?" Tina asked incredulously, and the derelict nodded. She had no idea why Stan the Man might feel inclined to give Jamie heroin, let alone bad heroin, and her first inclination was to locate Stan the Man and confront him. However, she had to admit that the idea scared her, so she decided that she would simply report this back to Marcus. The vampire would know what to do, if action was even necessary. She said, "Please be careful Jamie. I worry about you." And, standing on tiptoes, she left a kiss on Jamie's grisly cheek, just above the filthy cowl that covered his regrettable birth defect.

CHAPTER XII

The black van was parked at the same location up the street from the house where Tim and Desperado had most certainly seen a vampire about a month before. They had been watching the house for three days now, but this time there had been no sign of him.

"We should have stormed the place when we had the chance," grumbled Tim.

"We still can," said Desperado. "That place could be crawlin' with bloodsuckers."

"Maybe," said Tim, "But all we've seen comin' and goin' is those women. We're just gonna have to be patient." But he was seriously tired of being patient.

"Where has Marcus been the past few days?" Janet asked. "I have a huge, huge idea."

Night was falling upon the city. Gerald sat on the front porch swing watching the city lights gradually becoming more and more present and luminous against the darkening background. He frowned for a moment thinking it over, then said, "He's out, I imagine; stalking somebody, planning an execution; else he's keeping his distance from his friends because he's fasting again. I think he's been gone for three or four nights, so if he hasn't fed then he'd be starting to lose his sense right about now."

"Why does he do that?" asked Janet with concern lining her voice.

"Well, Marcus simply can't abide the idea of having to kill somebody, so he'll often put off feeding until he's mad with hunger. Or he may just be working out the details of a kill. Believe me, its much better when it's planned. Spur-a-the moment killings are usually risky," Gerald stated as if he knew first hand all about it.

Janet said, "Well, I think we should go out and find him. I have a great idea about how we might be able to look at Marcus's blood under a microscope."

"Don't be silly!" Gerald's tone was patronizing. What made this girl think that she could solve the problem that he and Marcus had failed on? She was just a nurse, for Pete's sake; Gerald was a doctor,

XII – An Eventful Night

and Marcus was a doctor several times over. "You need to leave Marcus alone just now. He'll come home soon enough. Whatever it is you want to show him, it will keep."

"I can't wait," said the girl as she stepped off of the porch and strode purposefully to where her Mustang sat parked in the street in front of the house. "Besides, why should he have to worry about feeding when he's got donors? He won't need to kill if I can find him."

"Don't be a damned fool!" called out Gerald. "If Marcus has gone grey, he'll be very, very dangerous!"

But Janet paid no heed to the warning as she got into her car, started it and drove away. The black van parked up the street did not catch her attention in the slightest.

"That girl's talking estrogen nonsense," muttered Gerald, but he wasn't overly worried about her. The city was large; Marcus could be anywhere. She would never even find the vampire.

Downtown on a weeknight isn't crawling with nightlife like a Friday or a Saturday. Still, there was plenty of young people cruising up Broadway. They were in bright, noisy, shiny cars that were still being paid for by loving parents who had more important concerns than that of where their child might be on a school night.

Manuel Stanley, the man with the exotic sideburns, stood on the corner of Broadway and Alder street watching the slow moving cars go by. Once upon a time he would have been supplying these awkward little teenagers with all the diversion they could afford, but now he had to let that lucrative opportunity pass him by. Through carelessness he had been caught, more than once. The only thing that had saved him from an extended stay in the hoosegow was a special business arrangement. The opportunity had not been as profitable as selling drugs, but then, when faced with the option of jail, Manuel had seen the merits of agreeing to the arrangement.

It was really okay, though. He had gotten into dealing in the first place only to pay for his own drug habit, and under the terms of the arrangement, he still got all of the junk he needed, plus cash bonuses. All he had to do was follow instructions and keep his nose clean, and so far the instructions had been relatively elementary. And he had still been able to sell a little smack here and there, on the side. None of that tonight, however. Tonight, he could only stand and watch the revenues flow past him in a river of booming, bouncing, under-lit cars.

One such car, a black pimp-mobile with gold trim and darkly tinted windows, boomed slowly along, prowling up to the curb, stopping where the tall, thin, dark-haired man stood. Manuel Stanley, aka Stan the Man, opened the passenger door of the car and ducked quickly into the vehicle.

"Jesus, man!" said Stan the Man. "This is so tacky."

"It's the best way for us to meet without anyone seeing us talking, or overhearing our conversation," said the driver.

"Whatever! What do you need?"

"Jamie Thompson is still alive."

Stanley's jaw dropped open. "No way! No one could live through the dose of shit I gave him."

"Well, he did. He must have a stronger constitution than we thought."

"I'll take care of it," said Stanley. He had no compunctions about murder.

"Wait a minute. I want this done a certain way. This thing has gotten way out of control. The body count is far higher than I ever wanted. With all these serial killings and pan-handler suicides, the police and the media are buzzing. It's too much, and we need to pinch it off."

"Jesus!" said Stanley. "I had no idea you were behind all of that shit, too."

"I'm not," said the driver of the pimp-mobile. "But something good can still come from all of this chaos if I just work it right."

"Cool! What's your plan?"

"The police know who is responsible for the all of the killings; one man, but he's too slippery for them. The killer hasn't left any evidence that they can use to get a conviction. They need an eye witness! So we're going to give them one. We're going to do our civic duty and bring this killer to justice!"

It was 1:35 a.m. Janet had been combing the city streets for hours looking for Marcus. No luck. Mimi would be getting off at the Bare Cage in a few minutes, so Janet decided to head in that direction. She simply had to find Marcus; that was all there was to it. Patience abandoned her in the face of something this compelling.

Within minutes she was turning her Mustang into the parking lot of the strip joint. Janet was just exiting her car when she heard footsteps approaching her. She whirled, her heart racing, and saw a dark form moving quickly toward her. It might have been Marcus except that the figure didn't have his movement. She gasped a short precursor to what

XII – An Eventful Night

was surely to be a scream, but then the dim light of the streetlamp caught the face of the dark form as it slowed. It was Chad.

"Oh my god, Chad!"

Chad was silent as he closed the remaining distance to Janet. He was dressed in black jeans and a black leather jacket. His fuzzy scalp was covered by a black leather skull cap.

Janet's speeding heart had not yet relaxed. "Chad?"

"I'm sorry if I startled you, Janet. I needed to see you. I need to talk to you."

"Chad, are you okay?" It took only an instant for Janet to fall right back into caregiver mode. "We've been so worried about you. How are you feeling? Where have you been?"

Chad did not answer her questions. She would find out how he was feeling soon enough. And a retelling to Janet of his adventures as a vampire would probably not be prudent. In point of fact, Chad had been feeling very fine; quite excellent since exacting his revenge. But he was also ready to admit that in his waking hours he had been feeling a little down; 'empty' was a good word. Chad had tried female companionship as a possible cure or at least a diversion from the empty, lonely feeling, but when it hadn't helped, he had ended up feeding on the prostitute and faking her suicide. His mind kept coming back to the same thought, the same realization – that he wanted Janet. And that was what had brought him to this place. He had come here knowing that Janet would eventually show up to watch her girlfriend dance.

Now that he was an all-powerful vampire, he was sure that he could have Janet. What mortal could resist the charms of a vampire? But first, Chad needed to verify his safety. As much as he felt omnipotent, the young vampire also had a healthy fear of his vampire 'father.' He asked bluntly, "Does Marcus want to kill me?"

"He did," Janet answered truthfully. "But he may have calmed down by now," she added, as if the whole thing had been years ago and Marcus had been hopping mad. Marcus was right! He had told her that Chad would seek her out. And Marcus had instructed her to tell Chad about what he had learned about who had planted the hypodermic needle. But first she wanted to give Chad the good news. "But Chad! I have the most exciting news! I may be able to find out what causes vampirism!"

Chad did not even try to feign interest. He now had an idea of where he stood with Marcus – primary objective achieved. Now he had only to convince Janet of the splendid benefits of vampirism. He would use his astounding vampire powers and charm her.

Except, that now, suddenly there was another need that Chad felt – that now familiar, overwhelming hunger for blood. To Chad, it was as if all else could be put on PAUSE while this one need was adequately satisfied. His voice lowered ominously as he said, "Janet, you can save a life tonight if you will just give me some of your blood."

Janet's face reflected a mix of horror and disappointment, and more; mostly confusion at feeling so much at once. Chad seemed not the least bit interested in her ideas! Moreover, he was now imploring her to let him feed off of her. Janet had been hoping that maybe Chad would be willing to accompany her to the lab, saving her from having to locate Marcus, but now she wanted away from this killer that used to be the sweet and lovable Chad. The worst of it, however, was that she knew without a doubt that Chad, true to his word, would go out and kill this very night if his hunger was not assuaged.

Wordlessly, sadly, Janet bared her neck. She would at least prevent one death this night. Chad bit with his newly formed fangs and drank, hardly remembering to be careful to not suck too long. The bite made Janet go rigid with pain, as Chad had not yet mastered even the basics of secreting pain blockers. Marcus's bites had been deeply pleasureful, sensual, even erotic; a very fair trade for the blood that she had given him. Chad's bite, however, was merely the feeling of her life being sucked away; no pleasure, no passion; just all-consuming pain in a fathomless void that seemed to be the sum of all her fears to power of infinity.

Chad was rhythmically sucking like a nursing infant lulled to sleep by its mother's warm breast milk. Finally, in a wrenching of all her will, she whispered a solitary, "Chad." It was all she could do and it was just enough to bring him out of his trance.

Shame washed over the young vampire as he pulled away from his victim. Now that he was satiated, Chad could not remember what it had felt like to be hungry. The bloodlust was once again appeased. Why had he been so compelled to feed on Janet? The hurt, confused look on her face told Chad all that he needed to know about how she was feeling about him just this second. His own face fell, head bowed deeply in disgrace, then he turned and ran as fast as his could move, disappearing back into the shadows to which he had become so accustomed.

Janet's head bowed as well but for a different reason. She had managed to stop him before the blood-loss got too bad; she would be okay, she just needed a minute to rest. Janet did not know how to feel about Chad. She had always tried to give him the benefit of the doubt,

XII – An Eventful Night

but it seemed now to her that she had simply been her usual naïve self. Confusion hung over her like a thunderhead as she slumped back into her car. Marcus would know what to do – but, then again, she wasn't sure if she should tell him about the visit either.

It always started with an annoying, grating tingle in his molars, accompanied with a heightening of already heightened senses, primarily the olfactory senses. He could literally smell the blood; the life in the people near him. The teeth wanted to gnash and gnaw. It was an overwhelming appetite stimulator.

The vampire could deal with these relatively minor discomforts. However, over the course of a night they would grow to a point somewhere beyond mere nuisance. The day-sleep after such a night would be especially horrifying, and provide no rest and little regeneration, if any was needed.

The next night would be shear hell. Every part of the vampire's body would be sending signal after painful, pulsing signal to the brain that it was starving, actually dying; breaking itself down just for the energy to keep going. Shakes, cramps, and random points of intense, stabbing pain would gradually increase through the ever-slowing night. This pain, the vampire knew, was as easy to abate as drinking blood; take a victim and the torture ends, it's as simple as that. If the vampire could withstand that temptation, then by the end of the night his rationality would be slipping.

For a final day, the body of the vampire would go into a hibernative shut down, in which the vampire would experience the most unspeakably horrifying nightmares of all; dreams in which he had no consciousness. The vampire would not regain consciousness again until the body had fed. In the evening the body would rise under the control of something else, something primitive, something base. The vampire would be gone; only a wild and very dangerous animal would remain. It would feed upon the first victim of convenience.

Of course, this timeline wasn't static. It was subject to shortening or lengthening by certain variables. And Marcus had become extremely well-practiced in his ability to go without feeding and still keep the grey madness at bay. The pain was endurable. It was his nightmares that he hated the most; the nightmares that became living reality for him as his body took over and did what it had to do to survive.

Just now, Marcus was still mostly himself as he shuffled along Pacific Street. The driving pain was already enough to stop him every few feet, but that was only because his body knew that he wasn't moving toward any potential victims. Even though Marcus knew that feeding was inevitable, and he already had a few hapless victims in mind, he was currently playing the game of staying as far from people as he could; keeping a fair distance between himself and the fine scent of that fresh blood, and his body was hating him for it.

Nearby, camped out underneath the Grand Avenue overpass over the Banfield freeway, was a handful of unfortunate homeless sorts. The disappearance of one of them would go completely unnoticed. But Marcus would put off the feeding for as long as he could, dreading it as much as he dreaded the nightmares of grey madness.

The vampire was looking like a homeless man himself. Personal appearance was always pretty low on the priority list whenever he fasted beyond his hunger. He was covered in loose dirt from the day's sleep. Choosing to spend the day partially buried rather than at home in a comfortable, secure cellar might have been considered an indication of his loss of rationality, but it really didn't matter to Marcus. Sure, there was less risk of being uncovered and destroyed at his house, but he would still have the terrifying dreams no matter where he bedded down for the day. He was, even after all these centuries, still just a creature of habit.

Marcus was vaguely aware that he was walking past a construction sight. However this fact was only logged somewhere deep in his memory for later use. There was something about the property that nagged at the back of his brain. Normally, he could recall everything perfectly, instantly, but not on the edge of grey madness like he was. It would come to him…

He lurched down the street, walking in a broad, meandering circle of blocks around his pathetic and unsuspecting quarry. There were only a few people out and about in his wide circuit, and he avoided them. He generally tried to stick to the shadows; another habit. The shadows provided all the security he ever wanted. But the life of a shadow is so fragile. Shadows can be easily cut through, pierced, driven away, and disintegrated by light.

Marcus was aware of the rustling of a cool wind. Movement caught the corner of his eye. His head snapped to see what it was, but there was only shadow; a slightly less inviting shadow.

A prickly chill inched down Marcus's spine. He was being watched – he just knew it! His nose told him that there was nobody near him, but he also knew from experience that the nose does not always tell the whole story. He turned back to continue his loping along, now just skirting the edges of the shadows.

XII – An Eventful Night

Looking into another shadow he saw it again; the black swirl of movement. For a short second he could distinctly see dozens of pairs of eyes glaring at him from the shadow. Then they were gone and Marcus was just about to convince himself that he was seeing things when the unmistakable smell of rotting corpses crawled up his nose. Now here was a nasty scent that warranted moving away from. But it seemed to surround the vampire; his nose could not lead him away from it.

The air grew thick and putrid. Marcus's lungs no longer wanted to work. With all the pain and starvation, and now the deathly air, it seemed to Marcus that his ability to survive had finally reached its limit. He had already given up long ago, and so it would be here that he would finally lay down his body and await oblivion. It had never worked before, but it would work this time.

The shadows swirled again then and suddenly the hordes of faceless tormentors were there for him again. Marcus was unable to move away from them. The shadowy creatures moved around him in a jerky, macabre dance; their malice and hate emanated from their faceless forms. Several of them stepped forward and lay their bony hands upon Marcus, lifting him up with sharp, icy fingers.

A voice boomed, "Marcus Lanchetta! You are damned to feed on death! Death will keep you alive! You must feed!"

"No," cried Marcus weakly. "I want to die. I do not want to cause death."

"Death is inevitable for mortals! You are Marcus the Vampire! You are damned to live from death! Such is your sentence!"

"Lies!" cried Marcus. "Death must somehow be avoidable, for I live! Do not make me cause death in order to serve my sentence!"

From out of nowhere the shadow figures produced a rotting corpse. It had been dead for only a few months and Marcus recognized it as his late love Maria. Even looking at the decayed, brown face Marcus could still envision the fresh, young Maria. Why did this have to happen? It seemed so senseless, so wasteful. Where was the warm, loving, productive individual that had animated this body?

"Eat of this body!" boomed the voice from nowhere.

"I will not!!" cried Marcus.

"Feed!!"

"No!!"

"Just do it, Marcus. Damn it!" The voice was different; it was no longer coming from nowhere.

Marcus looked tenderly over the shrunken corpse of Maria. Grief overwhelmed him, but it did not overwhelm the pain and discomfort of the grey madness. Trembling nearly to the point of seizure, he fought to keep himself from satisfying the terrible hunger.

"Feed!!" One of his shadowy tormentors jumped on his back and began pushing his head forward and down. Still, Marcus used the last of his strength to resist.

"Be sensible, and drink," said a voice. It was a soft voice, a woman's voice. It was Mimi's voice calling from the darkness.

"Miriam?" Marcus called, groping blindly. Monstrous, swirling shadow creatures were still all that he could see before him against the shadowy waste-scape.

"Marcus, I'm right here. Drink my blood!"

He still could not see her, and it even seemed difficult for Marcus to interpret the sensations his hands were feeling as an outside force seemed to animate them momentarily. He decided that he would trust Mimi.

An unseen vein pulsed with blood very near his mouth; he could smell and hear it even though shadows filled his vision. He had but only to move slightly to bring his lips into contact with the vessel, where he bit and sucked tightly. The life of the blood flowed into him like a spreading stain. Rationality and peace returned…

"Ow!! Damn, Marcus! This hurts like a bitch! How about some fuckin' endorphins, buddy?!" The pain-filled voice belonged to Mimi, and Marcus found himself standing near the edge of the empty street, clutching tightly to the en-weakened amazon, and sucking mightily on her neck.

Janet was pushing against Marcus's forehead in an attempt to make him stop. She said, "That's enough, Ghandi!"

Marcus did stop. And he sent a wave of endorphins and other pleasure chemicals coursing through Mimi, causing the voluptuous girl to swoon. "What are you girls doing here?" Marcus said finally, after catching his breath.

"I've been looking for you all over town," said Janet. "It's a miracle we found you. I have an idea for a way to examine your blood and I'm anxious to try it!"

"You must be anxious to have put yourself at this kind of risk," said the vampire. He was amused that the young nurse had taken such an interest in solving the riddle of his vampirism, but he could not in all practicality see how she could succeed where a great mind like Gerald had failed. Still, at this point, there was no harm in humoring her. But he made a mental note to sometime soon reiterate to Janet and Mimi

XII – An Eventful Night

just how dangerous it was to approach him while he was 'fasting.' It didn't seem right to chastise her at this particular moment.

The trio got into Janet's idling Mustang and the nurse began to explain her ideas as she drove. "Marcus, are you up on the latest in computer enhanced microscopy?" She immediately had his interest, though the vampire had to admit that with all of the advances being made in every field of technology, it would be quite a feat for someone to 'stay up' on anything. Marcus had been relatively slack in his studies. He had been too depressed, and time had run away from him.

For the vampire there was no time of day or time of night; there was only sunset and sunrise, sandwiching a few futile, perishable activities, and regeneration nightmares. He'd seen it all before. The centuries of the habitual behavior of survival were becoming a blur, even though every specific memory was in his head somewhere; perfectly, easily accessible, like running a video in his mind's eye. As if in the blink of an eye the decades now flew past him. Why, it seemed like only yesterday that he was working long nights in the lab with a younger Gerald, trying every conceivable method for a way to get a look at what was going on inside the vampire's body.

Janet asked another question. "Did you and Gerald ever try using infrared differential interference contrast to look at your blood under a microscope?"

"Hah! Gerald helped develop that technology," said Marcus. "It was the only method of microscopy that did not disintegrate the specimen; however, we were still unable to see anything out of the ordinary."

"And what is the biggest problem with light microscopy, especially a method like IR-DIC?" Janet quizzed.

"Lack of contrast, of course," said the vampire. The girl knew her stuff alright, but was she really onto something? "Now, tell me more about this computer enhanced microscope technology."

"Well, a huge innovation in microscopy came with the development of the digital camera. Digital cameras use a chip called a charge-coupled device. Are you familiar?"

"Only vaguely," said Marcus.

"Well, simply put, the CCD is essentially a photo-sensitive computer chip. CCD's have been developed in the past few years that are actually more sensitive to minutely varying light-waves than the human eye. They can 'see' things that we can't, and because they're digital, the computer can be used to increase contrast, making it possible for us to see microscopic things that were previously invisible to us."

Marcus felt his pulse quicken. Could this be true? Could he really at long last examine his blood for some abnormality? Realism slowed him back down. He would approach this skeptically, if for no other reason than to not get his hopes up.

Jamie Thompson woke from a funky fuzz, aware that someone was coming down the debris-strewn alley in his direction. His filmy eyes focused as best they could, and the form of Stan the Man resolved itself. Fear seeped sluggishly into Jamie's slow heart and froze his already immobilized body.

Stan the Man had not as yet noticed the junkie lying in the dark among the garbage. The derelict was effectively camouflaged by refuse. Stan the Man walked right past him, continuing to the end of the darkened alley, and it seemed to Jamie that the man had a truly murderous look about him.

At last Jamie could stand it no longer. In a frantic, awkward movement he climbed to his feet. Stan the Man yelled behind him as he scrambled out of the alley. "Jamie! Wait!"

There was not another soul to be seen anywhere along the quiet street. Jamie ran for all he was worth, which wasn't much. From behind he heard the quick footfalls of Stan the Man. Just ahead of Jamie was the vehicle access door into an old warehouse that he knew to be abandoned. The vertical door had been jammed slightly askew in its runners, creating a one foot gap between the bottom of the door and the cement. Jamie threw himself down and scurried through the narrow gap just as Stan the Man caught up with him. Stanley made a grab for Jamie through the gap, but the derelict had just managed to scramble out of reach of the long arm. Cursing quietly at having missed his quarry Stan the Man trotted a little further down the worn sidewalk. He wasn't about to mess up his suit; he would have to find another way in.

Jamie's worst fear was being realized. Even in his foggy mind he could figure a reason for why Stan the Man would be trying to kill him. Jamie knew that he had come to a fool's end. Moving with surprising stealth, Jamie climbed an old metal staircase up to a railed second level that overlooked the large interior of the warehouse. A door from the balcony led into an old, debris-cluttered corner office where light from a street lamp shone directly in through a window overlooking the street below. From a broken window on the facing wall, Jamie could look right down into the darkened alley where he had been blissfully

XII – An Eventful Night

tripping only a minute ago. In the stark light Jamie's gnarled fingernail gouged a final message into his Magic Slate. The battered doodle toy was then dropped out of the broken window, followed by the dingy cowl and the ragged, sleeveless coat. Jamie could hear Stan the Man still down below, trying without success to creep silently.

It was time. Expertly, efficiently, habitually, Jamie engaged the activity that was his one talent. He could have been a doctor, he mused, with his skill of handling a needle; knowing right where to find the vein; knowing just the right amount of drug to use for a quick fix, or a good high…

Or an OD.

With luck, the Goddess would take him before Stan the Man could find him.

The campus of Portland State University can seem quite gothic at night. It is a grand old campus cut through the middle by a long, public park one block wide, and spanning for twelve blocks. Marcus, Janet, and Mimi stayed to the many excellent shadows cast at all points throughout their covert sneaking walk to the biology building. With both the talents of Marcus and Mimi at their disposal, getting by security and gaining access to the lab was trouble-free. Having attended PSU, Janet was quite familiar with the interior of the building. It was her show as she brought the infrared DIC equipment and integrated computer system online. The trio then doused each of their penlights making the glow from the computer monitor the only illumination in the lab. It lit up Janet's face as she performed the necessary computer operations. Worried about bumping something in the dim light, Mimi stayed out of the way and tried not to move.

Without a word Janet pricked her own finger, prepared a blood sample on a glass slide and placed it on the stage of the microscope. She flicked switches on the microscope activating the light source and adjusted the focus knob. The three of them watched the grainy image on the computer screen as it resolved into a field of mostly black with numerous white circles. Other lines and specs of white floated among the bubble-like shapes.

"OK. Those round things we're looking at are my red blood cells. This is at a magnification of one hundred times."

"Yes," Marcus said. "And that other strange outline must be one of your white blood cells. Also, I can make out what looks to be crystals, possibly uric acid, but that would be difficult to determine without color. Some of your RBC's appear slightly traumatized indicating stress or perhaps the presence of a parasite. And it appears that you have a mild erythrocyte aggregation."

"Never mind all that," said Janet. "We're here to analyze your blood, not mine. The computer is recording this image so that we can have something to compare your blood to."

"If this works," Marcus amended.

"Right," said Janet only slightly peeved and in a deft movement she had pricked Marcus's finger and squeezed.

Marcus sighed. "It usually requires a gash," he said, as the poor girl was unsuccessful in acquiring a drop. He pulled out his knife and cut a tiny slash in his finger. "Once you have the specimen on the slide, you'll have about sixty seconds before it completely breaks down."

Janet captured a drop of blood on a slide and quickly replaced the slide containing her blood with Marcus's specimen, gratified to see that it seemed unaffected by the infrared light. Working quickly, she refocused the microscope and for the first time ever, Marcus beheld his own blood under magnification!

It looked very much like Janet's had, for the most part, except that there were no signs whatsoever of toxins or even the slightest malfunction in the cells. But there was something very different - obviously different about Marcus's blood. The abnormality lay in the little lobster-shaped objects that darted about at relatively high speeds in the field of black.

"Oh my god! What is that?" asked Janet.

Marcus was equally stunned. "I have never seen anything like it before. Is there any way you can adjust the phasing to bring out the image?"

"I can try, but we're already looking at an image courtesy of the CCD. If it weren't for tremendous contrast enhancement by the computer, we wouldn't be seeing this at all."

The trio watched as the strange little shapes swam around. The little 'lobsters' were maybe a tenth the size of the red blood cells, but easily ten times as numerous. They seemed to be attacking the red blood cells and destroying them. After nearly a minute, the red blood cells were virtually gone and the tiny foreigners began themselves to break up and disintegrate!

Marcus was quiet as Janet transferred the two videos from the computer hard drive to a compact disk. They would be able to analyze the footage later on Marcus's computer. Marcus could hardly wait to show Gerald!

XII – An Eventful Night

As the trio crept out of the biology lab and safely away, the vampire felt truly lighthearted and optimistic for the first time since he could remember. This night had seen the occurrence of a breakthrough! Nothing would ever be the same again. What other mysteries waited to be uncovered with the new and exciting technological advances of the twentieth century? *Whoops! The twenty-first century!*

The night was drawing to a close. They drove directly to Marcus's house and quietly entered the fine home, unaware of the black van that was parked up the street in which Tim the Vampire Slayer dozed.

Once inside the home, Marcus knew that something was wrong! There was a foul odiferous presence, unmistakably fecal. "Gerald!" Marcus called with no effort to hide the worry in his voice. The lifeless form of Gerald lay back in his recliner in the front room. Marcus knew before he checked the old man's pulse that Gerald was dead. The old man looked as if he might only be sleeping, but his body was not the warm temperature of life, but rather a sickly cool.

Marcus estimated that Gerald had been dead for only an hour or so, and he felt the beginnings of guilt and regret creeping into his heart for not being there when it happened. But now was not the time for emotion. Not a minute could be wasted in calling the emergency unit at the Oregon Cryonics Institute. The sooner that Gerald's body could be put into cryo-stasis the more likely that he would have a successful thaw and restoration at some point in the future, or so it was postulated. There would be time to grieve after Gerald was safely preserved. Marcus was on the phone with the Institute dispatch in a heartbeat, and in another pair of heartbeats a special ambulance was on route.

"Please take care of this," he implored to Janet. "You know what to do. I must get to safety. You have full authority."

Janet, for as emotional as she could be, was almost always strong and cool in a crisis. "I'll take care of it, Marcus. Don't worry."

He flashed a smile of genuine appreciation and love at the girls, then left the room. Marcus needed to be alone. He had lost another dear friend to death. Like so many before Gerald, Marcus had seen the end coming. The end must eventually come even if a body appears to be in perfect health, and to the old vampire the end always came with alarming suddenness. Time flies… It was doubly sad that Gerald never even got a chance to look at Marcus's blood.

"I don't understand why Marcus is bothering with this cryo-freezing thing," said Mimi. "He always makes so much sense in everything he does. He has a way of cutting through the bullcrap and getting to the truth. How could he buy into this nonsense? As if they're going to be able to someday thaw Gerald out and bring him back to life. I don't mean to sound negative, but it seems like a waste of money."

"It might be a waste of money," said Janet. "And I'm pretty sure that Marcus doesn't expect it to work. The thing is, he doesn't know for sure. It just might be that in a hundred years they will develop the technology to somehow preserve Gerald's conscious, his memories, or whatever it is that makes him Gerald Harper, and then somehow transfer it to a clone created from his own DNA. OR maybe they will develop some other technology, maybe nano-technology, that will be able to restore Gerald. It might work to freeze Gerald, and it might not, but just puttin' him into the ground will definitely *not* work."

"But you're the religious one," said Mimi. "Don't you find this idea of freezing a corpse like an abomination? What about Gerald's soul?"

Janet sighed. "I don't know, baby. I've had to re-evaluate my belief system since I met Marcus. The god I was taught to believe in would never have created something like Marcus. I mean, he really *is* a vampire! To me that means that if there is magic in the universe, then anything goes, ya know what I mean? So much for order in the universe!

"But if he is the product of some kind of science, as I am inclined to believe, then the universe must be truly ordered as science always maintains, and right now we simply don't have any physical evidence to support the god hypothesis or the existence of the immortal soul, or even the traditional vampire.

"When I was younger I used to want very badly to have a perfect knowledge of God. I know that the bible said it is sinful, but I used to pray for a sign. I thought that if I could have just one little miracle, one little sign that God was really there and that he loved me, then I could live a perfect life. But what sign did we finally get, baby? A sign that there really is no god; that the concept was invented by certain men in an attempt to rule and oppress the masses."

"That's what I love about you, Janet," said Miriam. "You know how to make me think."

Tim was awakened suddenly from his early morning doze by a commotion from down the street. Partially dried spit ran from the corner of his mouth to the edge of his stubble-spotted jaw. He blinked several times, trying to wet his tired eyes, then focused through his grungy spectacles on the goings-on in front of the house he and Desperado were staking out.

XII – An Eventful Night

It looked like an ambulance, but the words Oregon Cryonics Institute were printed on the vehicle. Three men and one woman were hurrying back and forth from the vehicle to the house with equipment cases. Presently, the activity stopped as the four spent a period of time behind the closed front door of the house.

"Damn!" said Tim. "We've missed it again! I just know they've gotta be doin' some kinky shit in there."

"Watch yer language!" growled Desperado.

The sky had lightened considerably when the team finally exited the house wheeling out some kind of special gurney with a cumbersome, human-sized tank upon it. The equipment cases were then loaded back into the ambulance, and finally the vehicle sped off.

"Now what?" asked Desperado.

"We still haven't seen any vampires coming or going," said Tim.

"Well, I say we storm the place," said the rogue enthusiastically.

"No!" said Tim decisively. "We gotta wait a little longer."

CHAPTER XIII

It didn't look good for Dan Jensen. Here he was again, sitting in an interrogation room at the police station, waiting nervously but without anticipation for Detective Darrel Hutchinson to any minute come back in and harangue him about what he had been doing and when.

Dan's track record as a security guard was sucking. This was the second dead body, (cut into pieces, no less!), that had been found on his watch. Dan had been the night watchman at one of Jimmy Bechard's construction sights near Lloyd Center. He knew that something bad might have happened when he woke up lying on the ground, missing a few hours out of the night. All he could remember was patrolling the area on foot, then an aerosol can floating in front of his face, a fine, sweet, pungent mist, then coming to himself at last feeling like an elephant had tap-danced on his sinuses. Obviously, he had been chloroformed, or exposed to some other such knockout gas, but he had been hesitant to report the incident. He had felt that after the incident at the US Bancorp Tower his new employment with Bechard might be hanging by a string.

Dan had checked the entire area over carefully with his flashlight after coming to, and had seen nothing out of the ordinary. All of the expensive equipment that he had been commissioned to protect was perfectly undisturbed. So he had decided to keep his unscheduled downtime to himself.

But then, shortly after dawn, just as construction workers were arriving and he was preparing to go home, one of the workers had seen blood on the inside of the large dumpster, and the hideous chopped up body was discovered only a little deeper inside of it. It was the body of a homeless man. A generous supply of heroin had been found with the body along with several hypodermic needles. Later, cops had found blood in Jensen's car. Dan cringed at the thought of what this would do to his employability as a security guard, or anything else for that matter.

Hutchinson entered the small room with the movement of a man that believed he was deity. The temptation for the detective to flaunt a smug smirk was strong, but he fought it. He said, "Mr. Jensen, its

XIII – The Framing of Jensen

lookin' kinda bad for you. But I assume you are maintaining your innocence."

"I am innocent. I haven't done nothin'."

"I believe you," said Hutchinson, smiling. "I really do. This whole thing could be cleared up if you will just consent to standing in a lineup."

Dan was definitely wary of this change of demeanor in the cop, but he knew that he was truly innocent. The only thing that he was guilty of was being a victim of circumstance. He agreed to the lineup.

Hutchinson could not officiate at the lineup. He could not even be in the room while the witness was making the identification, lest he should subtly or subconsciously tip off the witness to whom he suspected for the crime. But Hutchinson had already extensively interviewed the witness, one Manuel Stanley, and the witness had described Jensen almost perfectly. Stanley claimed to have been a sort of business associate of the victim's, one Jamie Thompson, (and Hutchinson could easily guess just what sort of business they might be transacting), and he happened to see a man fitting Dan Jensen's description putting the unconscious form of Thompson into the passenger seat of a small car with the tell-tale markings of a security vehicle sometime after midnight the previous night. At the time, Stanley hadn't been sure if it wasn't a public officer picking up the passed out derelict, and so he had said nothing until this morning, when he had learned of Jamie's death. Hutchinson had already verified that the blood found in Jensen's car was in fact the blood of the victim, Jamie Thompson. Having a credible eye-witness just secured the conviction.

Inside the small, dark room, Stan the Man and two cops stood looking through a window into another brighter room where two more cops herded and instructed the lineup of unsavory looking characters. Stanley knew most of those guys from the street. Presently, number five was instructed to step forward. Number five was a tallish, balding, tired-looking man wearing the uniform of a security guard and aging by the minute. "That's him," said Manuel Stanley. "Definitely."

Dan Jensen was escorted back to the interrogation room. Hutchinson let him sweat a little more by making him wait another five minutes by himself. The detective's manner had returned to aggressive when he finally re-entered the room. "I'm sorry, Mr. Jensen. Your alibi for last night is so thin it doesn't even qualify as an alibi, and we've got an eyewitness that says you were downtown last night at around 2:10 loading Jamie Thompson into your company car. That, along with where we finally found Thompson's body, uh, parts, is all we need to charge you with murder one and hold you over for an appearance before a grand jury. And, quite frankly, we've pretty much got you for the Preston job as well. You get one phone call; I hope you've got a good lawyer."

Dan turned ghostly white. "I don't have a lawyer."

"Why don't you call your boss?" Hutchinson cracked. "I hear he's got a real shark of a lawyer! But I have a better idea. Why don't you sing on your boss, instead? We know you ain't got no motive for the murders; not personally anyway. My hunch told me a long time ago that the killings were contract jobs. If you can confirm that hunch, I'm sure I could make things go a lot smoother for you. Quite frankly, I'd be damn disappointed to find out that you are really just a sick bastard and not a pro after all." The detective watched the confused face of Dan Jensen as he spoke. *This guy sure keeps up a good act,* thought the detective. But he was nearly positive that he had pretty much solved the case.

Dan was confused, and frightened beyond anything he had ever felt before in his life. He couldn't figure out what kind of game this cop was playing with him, but he surmised that now would be a good time to remain totally silent; at least until a better idea struck him. As for whom to call, Jimmy Bechard seemed like as good a candidate as any. As it turned out, he didn't actually need to make the call.

The sudden clattering of the door startled both men, mostly the beleaguered and fatigued Dan Jensen. Entering the room as if on cue and whirling almost like a Tasmanian devil was a skinny man, shorter than the detective. The brown-haired man wore an immaculate double-breasted suit and carried a leather attaché. Moving quickly, he fairly slammed the briefcase down on the metal table across from Dan. The fractured click of the dual spring-loaded latches released and flicking open resounded ominously through the live little room and seemed to send out the signal that it was time to get down to business.

All of this happened before Hutchinson had even finished saying, "What the hell?!" His first impulse was to be belligerent and demand that the intruder exit. After a split-second decision he chose to go with that initial urge, even though his hunch was telling him that this little guy was a lawyer – probably Bechard's lawyer! But before he could bring his temperature up to a sufficient boil for a good, indignant eruption, the little man had a card in the detective's face.

XIII – The Framing of Jensen

"Philip Lambert, Attorney," he said, shortly, with clipped words. "I'm acting as legal representation for Mr. Jensen. Why are you holding this man?"

The aggressive demeanor of the little man instantly put Hutchinson on the defensive, however the detective realized it almost immediately and he silently vowed that he would not let himself get on the losing end of a verbal joust. "Dan Jensen is suspected of murder."

"Is my client under arrest?" asked the attorney in his staccato speech.

"Not yet, but he will be. I was about to –"

"What have you got on him?" Lambert demanded in a voice that suggested that any charges made against the man must be false.

Hutchinson considered not telling him, just out of principle. But the detective knew that there was nothing the attorney could do at this point, so why not put it in his face? "The dismembered body of Jamie Thompson was found on a site where Jensen was supposed to be keeping watch."

"So?"

"We've got the victim's blood in Jensen's car."

"So?!"

"And we got an eyewitness!" said Hutchinson, thoroughly enjoying the impending victory that playing this ace was sure to bring. Surely this would slow this lawyer down.

"What exactly did your eyewitness supposedly see? Did he actually see my client commit the crime?"

Hutchinson suddenly found himself floundering. He had fully expected the lawyer to snap his briefcase shut and excuse himself. "Well, not exactly," he stammered. "But he saw Dan Jensen putting the victim –"

Lambert interrupted again. "Pretty weak, detective! No grand jury will ever indict. You have no case!"

But Hutchinson firmly believed that he had found the killer and he would not be so easily put off. He wished like crazy that he could think of something witty and sarcastic, but "The hell I don't!!" was the best he could manage for the moment. He rallied quickly and continued. "And I don't care what you say, Mister Big-shot Lawyer! His ass is mine! I don't even need a reason to hold him. There are a thousand little shit things that I could book him on. Or you! How would you like to spend the night in jail?"

"I am well aware of the many superfluous statutory laws on the books that you can exploit at any time to serve your ends," said

Lambert. "But there are a thousand and one ways to get out of any one of them. So, detective, I'm going to suggest that you let my client go free right now for lack of evidence."

"You're high!" blurted Hutchinson. "I'm booking him right now for murder one!"

"Or, you could do that, too," said Lambert, sounding like some kind of nerdy game show host. "But I think you should be aware of the consequences of such an action. We'll sue for damages."

"Are you threatening me?" God! It sounded so trite to the detective as he said it.

The attorney was not defensive or denying. "I'm simply pointing out the logistics of cause and effect."

"I can't be sued!" said Hutchinson. "I have immunity. I'm a public official."

"You're half right," said Lambert. "As a public official you are fairly well indemnified, as in the old saying 'you can't fight city hall.' But as an individual, you are as responsible for your actions as any other citizen. And this is where you, as a law enforcement officer run into a hard place. You cannot enforce statutory law on any citizen without violating their civil rights. It's logistically impossible. And it doesn't even matter if the person is guilty as sin. The second you take them into custody, you've violated their civil rights. You have caused a damage, and any moderately decent attorney could get a judgment against you personally. I do it all the time."

Hutchinson was pretty sure that that last part, at least, was true. He had heard the rumors. "So you're suggesting that I just let you walk outa here with the Psicko Killer?"

"My client is not guilty of killing anyone, and if you let him leave right now we might see fit to excuse you for wasting his valuable time this morning."

Doubt formed like a cloud over the detective. He bit his lip pensively, deciding. "Wait right here," he commanded, unable to hide a note of resignation.

Hutchinson walked down the hall and through the door that led to a stairwell. He could have taken the elevator, but he opted instead to plod slowly up the stairs and think about his situation. He had heard the 'I'll sue you' threat from a million lawyers before in his twelve years working as a cop. You learn early on as a cop not to give any regard to such pathetic mewlings from lawyers and indignant arrestees and their ilk. But coming from Lambert the threat seemed to carry substance. Lambert spoke as one who has total confidence in his ability to execute

XIII – The Framing of Jensen

such a threat, as if he was an old hat at such activities. And the detective had a lot to lose.

Inside Captain Rahal's office, Hutchinson related the situation to his superior, summing up with his reluctance to make the arrest. Rahal's response surprised the detective. "Well, Darrel, I gotta be honest with ya'. I'd be nervous to make the arrest myself with that hellhound Lambert around. You're just gonna have to dig up some more evidence on Jensen."

Hutchinson was shaking his head all the way back down to interrogation room. It was still shaking, bowed, as he re-entered the room saying, "Alright, you're free to go."

But the room was already empty.

Because many of the sidewalks of downtown Portland are brick, it can be difficult to ride a skateboard in some places. Tina, however, was an expert. This morning she fairly zipped down the gentle decline of the Sixth Avenue bus mall. Once north of Burnside Street, the going was even easier, since the city beautification efforts had stopped at that street, making it a border that seemed to separate the happy and safe southwest from the wretched, ugly and evil Old Town.

As per Marcus's latest instructions she was looking for Jamie, prepared to entice him with smack to get him off of the streets and to the safety of Marcus's house. There was cause to believe that someone might wish to prematurely end the life of the junky, and the vampire wanted one more chat with Jamie before fate caught up with the pitiful derelict.

Tina knew many of the habitual haunts where street people like Jamie went to be out of the way and get high. Now she skated around, looking, asking discretely, learning nothing. Finally, she caught a glimpse of his familiar coat down an alley as she was zipping down the sidewalk on her skateboard. She stopped abruptly and walked casually back to the alleyway.

It was his coat, alright, and his cowl, and his Magic Slate! But there was no sign of Jamie! The Magic Slate was blank, but when Tina lifted the single grey sheet, Jamie's last message was read easily, gouged deeply into the malleable black pad. Tina feared the worst as she looked at the message – *"StAN tHe MAN"*

Marcus might want to examine this stuff, she thought. But she wasn't really hip to the idea of carrying the smelly items on her skateboard. She deposited the worn coat and the grimy cowl behind a trash can and underneath an empty cardboard box. She would take the incriminating Magic Slate with her to show the vampire.

CHAPTER XIV

When Marcus had arisen the next evening, he was nearly overwhelmed with news, on top of being very much in grieving over Gerald. The mood around the house was very solemn. It wasn't so much Marcus mourning Gerald's death as it was simply Marcus missing his old friend. As always, Marcus had to acknowledge that his grief was a completely selfish emotion. He grieved for himself now having to live without his friend.

Tina had been waiting all day to tell Marcus about what she had found. "I suppose we must acknowledge the possibility that harm has befallen Jamie Thompson," he said wryly, after she told him. The vampire made plans to go on a little hunting expedition.

But first, Janet needed to discuss the biology of vampires. She had been analyzing the video files of the IR-DIC microscope footage. For the millionth time Marcus wished that Gerald could have been there to offer his opinion on the incredible footage.

Marcus postulated that the tiny lobsters were some kind of microbial bio-organism. It looked as if the little creatures might be capable of affecting any bodily function; probably for the positive, it seemed. "Assuming that my body is full of these unknown microbials, they could be the cause of my condition."

Janet was of a slightly different opinion. She spoke as the video footage continued to run in a loop on the computer around which they stood, in a lavish office at the house. "That much is apparently correct, but I would hesitate to label them as a microorganism. They don't seem 'natural' to me, or, I should say, they would appear, to me, to be fabricated. Look at how they disintegrate after they break the blood down. It's as if they're covering their tracks."

"My dear, what you're suggesting would also imply some other rather improbable ideas," said Marcus, musing. "Assuming that they are also the reason for my craving for fresh human blood, what do you suppose is in the blood that they need?" But Janet had no quick answer.

"Look at how perfect the blood in your specimen is," said Janet. "Absolutely no sign of free radical damage, no parasites, no undigested proteins. It's perfect! Can I take one more blood sample for more testing?"

"Certainly, dear. Are we going to have to break into any more labs?"

"No, I got what I need from the medical supply store earlier today. Gerald told me about one time when you guys were able to prevent some of the blood break down by extreme centrifugal agitation. I'd like to duplicate that experiment and then run some tests on whatever is left behind."

"As you wish," said Marcus, and he noticed at that moment that indeed there was a small centrifuge sitting on a table in the corner of the office.

Janet cut the lights off, leaving only the computer monitor to illuminate the room, then she stepped up to Marcus in the glowing light with an empty hypodermic needle.

"Allow me, dear," said the vampire, tapping the vein in his arm. He took the syringe and extracted twenty cubic centimeters of his own blood, pulling the plunger skillfully with one hand. Janet then took the loaded syringe from him and quickly squirted its contents into a test tube. After securing the vessel in its place in the carousel, she activated the device, which began spinning the test tube and the blood at blurring speed.

"How long should I leave it running?" she asked.

"Oh, three minutes should suffice," said Marcus. "What you will have left will be mostly blood, but I can tell you right now that you will not find a trace of those little micro-lobsters. It will no longer be photo-sensitive, however, so you will be able to view it normally in any light microscope."

"That's exactly what I figured, but I've got other plans for it," said Janet, and she glanced at Marcus as if to ask permission. Marcus was pretty sure that the blood would be safe. Whatever contagion that the blood contained was somehow neutralized at the point that the blood lost its photo-sensitive nature and stopped breaking down. Maybe Janet could find something by examining the neutralized blood that he and Gerald had missed.

"With that, I shall leave you to your own devices," said the vampire. "I have business to attend to."

Tina sat in a fine armchair out in the front room. As Marcus stepped out the office turned laboratory, she asked, "Are you going to go find Stan the Man?"

XIV – Marcus Meets Tim the Vampire Slayer

"Yes," said Marcus. "And I shall need your help. I don't know who he his, what he looks like, or where he might be most easily located."

Tina beamed; she loved being needed by the vampire.

Not even 200 feet up from the house, Tim in the van watched with anxious vindication and anticipation as the vampire and a young female victim exited the house by the front door. Dusk had nearly completed its transition into full-blown night, so Tim was using his super cool infrared night-vision goggles.

"That's him," he cried, almost not believing his eyes. "That's the vampire!" He had been watching the house for so long he felt blind! "And that's the girl that we saw riding up this morning on a skateboard."

"She's gonna be vampire-bait unless we do something!" said Desperado. "Let's move!" And the two of them threw off goggles, grabbed guns and bolted out of the van.

Tim was not thrilled about the idea of confronting a vampire after dark. It was so much better to get them in the daytime where they slept. That way if he got into trouble, he could retreat to a place where the vampire could not follow. At night, there was nowhere to run. But he had to save the girl! He would have to make short work of this vampire so he readied his shotgun as he ran.

Marcus and Tina cut across the small yard to the driveway where the Cadillac SUV sat parked. As he was letting Tina into the passenger-side of the vehicle, he heard the growing sound of light, quick footsteps. Glancing across the roof of the vehicle and up the street toward the sound he saw the man bringing the sawed-off shotgun to bear. Marcus quickly closed the door, securing Tina inside, then dashed around the front of the vehicle. He could only guess as to the reason why this man would be chasing him carrying a gun.

The man with the gun was charging around the rear of the vehicle. "Die, bloodsucker!" yelled Desperado.

"Wait!" Marcus ducked just as an explosion ripped through the hillside neighborhood. It was extremely loud and seemed to echo across the area like rolling thunder. The angry swarm of buckshot pellets blasted just over the vampire's head, tearing a 'permanent cavity' into the dense shrubbery that separated Marcus's yard from his neighbor's.

"Jesus Christ!" yelled Marcus as the sound began to fade. "Do you want every single cop in this town up here?" He stood up just enough to see where his attacker was and caught the acrid, metallic smell of a body at war with itself; the scent that was often times an indication of mental imbalance. Marcus also saw where several errant pellets of buckshot had laid lines across the hood of the previously pristine automobile. Tina had ducked down at the first sound of the gun.

Tim resumed running around the automobile, having recovered after the tremendous kickback of the firearm. However, Marcus moved with him, successfully keeping the vehicle between them. Tim finally stopped near the front of the vehicle as Marcus was at the rear. The nerdy slayer fainted to the left, then to the right, then again to the left, but whichever way he moved to go, Marcus moved the other way.

Marcus took note of the sawed-off shotgun and felt grateful for the length of the SUV. A gun like that would have incredibly explosive blasting power at close range. He hoped that the gunman was not trigger-happy; one more report like that last one and the cops would be investigating. The situation would be resolved much easier without that complication. As it was, Marcus could only hope to have everything under control before the neighbors started peeking out their windows; fat chance of that!

The big question that ran through Marcus's mind at the moment was did this guy really *know* that he was a vampire? And if so, then how? The gunman would have to be subdued and questioned. Marcus would have to disarm the gunman, first mentally, then physically. To do that he would need to respond to the situation in the way that a person could normally be expected; with realistic denial. He cried, "What do you want?" trying to sound decently scared and willing to negotiate.

Tim turned toward Desperado who happened to be several feet off to his right just at the moment and exclaimed, "Get him! Cut him off!" Then he jumped again around to the left trying to close some distance between himself and the vampire.

"I'm trying, but he's too fast!" Desperado growled back.

Marcus witnessed the one-sided exchange with amusement and curiosity as he continued to keep the large vehicle between himself and the gunman. He could see no one standing where the gunman had been looking. "Please! Let's talk this over," he said.

"Nothin' to talk over, bud," said Desperado.

Movement on the front porch momentarily grabbed the attention of everyone chasing around the SUV. Janet and Mimi both screamed when they saw the gunman.

"Stay back, ladies," Desperado was heard to say. "This dude's a vampire!"

XIV – Marcus Meets Tim the Vampire Slayer

Marcus was very aware of the change that had come over the gunman as he spoke, especially the sharp increase in his pheromone secretion, a subtle change in body odor above the pungent smells of sweat and urine. Was that guy exhibiting symptoms of Schizophrenia or Multiple Personality Disorder? The vampire continued his plausible denial. "Are you crazy?! I am not a vampire. There are no such things as vampires!"

Tim came back out. "You can't fool me. I can tell vampires because they killed my sister, and you're a vampire!"

A drop in pheromones; a change in odor! Marcus saw his opportunity and took it. "I'm very sorry about your sister. Were you close?"

"Of course we were close!" Tim yelled angrily.

"Dude! This guy is trying to mess with yer head," said Desperado, again standing a little way off to Tim's right. "He's got to be a vampire."

But Tim was starting to second guess himself, especially now that Desperado had spoken with such a surety. The rogue biker and comic book hero was handy to have around in a fight, and great for conversation, but his abilities in spotting vampires were weak at best. Most of the time, those whom Desperado labeled as vampires turned out not to be vampires at all. Tim looked at his partner and yelled, "Desperado, wait!"

"Yes! Please, Desperado!" said Marcus, trying to focus on the place where he had seen the gunman looking. "Wait! Let's talk about this."

Desperado spoke audibly, "Don't look at *me*; he's the one running this show. I'm just the side-kick. I take orders from *him*."

On the porch, Janet and Mimi huddled inside the doorway. Under her breath, Janet whispered, "Schizophrenia!"

Tim kept the sawed-off shotgun leveled in the direction of Marcus and continued moving around the SUV, albeit a little slower now. Marcus matched the gunman's movements, keeping the vehicle between them, preventing him from using the weapon. It seemed to be a momentary stalemate.

Tim said, "If you're not a vampire, you're gonna have to prove it to me."

"How?" asked Marcus, doing a good job at sounding frightened and helpless.

The vampire slayer knew that such a proposition was indeed difficult. He had learned from his years of travels and hunting vampires that many of the points of vampire folklore were completely wrong. Holy artifacts did not always work against vampires. Garlic did not repel them either, but it could help you against their charms. Vampires could also cast reflections in mirrors, or at least create the illusion of it. They didn't always have their fangs out. They really could pass for a normal person, and a normal person could pass for a vampire, though god only knows why they'd want to. Even sunlight wasn't a completely reliable way to tell a vampire, because Tim had seen a few times when vampires had walked right out into the sun after that strange, white-haired dude had flashed them, or weakened them, or whatever it was that he did to them with his little crystal device. But for now, the light test would have to do.

Tim holstered his weapon and said, "Desperado! Keep him covered. If he vamps out, let him have it!"

Marcus put his hands up and tried to focus on the place where he believed Desperado to be according to the imagination of the little madman. Tim walked warily around to the front of the SUV and gestured for Marcus to join him.

"Have your girlfriend turn the headlights on," said the slayer. "If you can put your hand over the headlight without it getting burnt, then I'll believe that you're not a vampire."

"Oh shit!" whispered Mimi.

As Marcus stepped around the passenger side Tim exclaimed, "Wait! Have your girlfriend turn the headlights on first! The high beams!!"

Marcus nodded to Tina and she activated the switch, bathing Tim in the stark, bright halogen light. The slayer stood close to the driver side headlight, knowing that he would be relatively safe from a vampire in that amount of light.

"Does he really have to point that gun at me?" Marcus asked, gesturing in the general direction of Desperado.

"Until you step around here, he does!" commanded Tim.

Marcus the Vampire held his hands high as if in respect of the imaginary gun that was surely trained on him. Held above the intense beam of light the bare hands would be safe. Marcus had only to hope that the leather of his trench-coat, his starched slacks, and his black turtleneck shirt would provide enough protection from the intense halogen beam that was bright enough and close enough in proximity to actually burn him. He stepped into the light, nonchalantly trying to keep his distance.

XIV – Marcus Meets Tim the Vampire Slayer

Inside the cab of the SUV, Tina watched the tentative steps of the vampire. She had no way of knowing whether the light from the headlights would be harmful to Marcus or not, but being an all around clever girl, she prudently kept a hand on the switch, which she deactivated the second she saw Marcus make his move against the crazy gunman.

Tim was momentarily blinded as his eyes made the adjustment back to the darkness. He felt only a nudge, then a sort of enlightened feeling, and he realized only a half a second later that both his shotgun and his pistol were no longer on his person.

Marcus had both guns as he now charged to the place where he hoped that Desperado was standing in the alternate non-reality of this mad little would-be vampire slayer's psychotic mind. He was hoping that his imagination might be at least temporarily in synchronization with that of the gunman. Apparently, this gunman hallucinated a partner that occasionally took over as an alter. Perhaps by establishing a sort of familiarity with the imaginary Desperado, the alter would be brought out. Occasionally in cases of schizophrenia, the alter can be actually be more empowered and reasonable than the principal. Marcus felt confident that this was the case in this instance. For his purposes, he would need to talk to the more reasonable delusion. To bring off this hair-brained scheme, Marcus would let the imaginary man kick his ass.

He ran at Desperado ready to make use of the shotgun, but Desperado spun out a high side kick that sent the weapon flying across the length of the yard, (away from the slayer). Another very quick blow from Desperado's left hand knocked away the pistol as well. Marcus tried a silly right-handed roundhouse punch, but Desperado blocked it with ease and sent his own right fist into Marcus's solar plexus. As Marcus doubled over, Desperado knee-ed him in the face, throwing his head back. To Mimi and Janet on the porch, and Tina in the SUV, it looked as if Marcus was engaged in a beautifully choreographed pantomimed fight – which he was!

Marcus rallied weakly, trying this time to land a quick left jab followed by a right upper-cut. But Desperado seemed almost to anticipate his attack and his muscular forearms deflected the blows. Desperado then grabbed Marcus's collar and held him as he delivered three more powerful blows to his gut, followed by a wide right cross that spun Marcus fully around in a three-sixty before sprawling him flat on his back on the lawn. Tim watched the whole thing with wide-mouthed amazement.

Desperado was clapping the imaginary dust off of his hands. "See?" he said to Tim. "I told you he was a vampire."

Tim drew his sword, the only ready weapon that he had at his disposal; he would locate his guns later, just now he had a vampire to slay. Standing over the fallen form, holding his sword high in preparation for the killing blow, Tim said in his best slayer voice, "Die, blood-sucking vampire scum!"

On the porch, Mimi gasped and moved out of the doorway as if to try to do something to prevent the inevitable, but Janet stuck out an arm to stop her. "It's OK," she whispered. "Marcus knows what he's doing."

As the slayer began to bring the sword down upon Marcus, the vampire's leg shot up, catching the slayer squarely in the crotch. The blow seemed to fold the slayer in half, and as he toppled over sideways like a felled pine tree, paralyzed with pain, Marcus's left foot kicked the hilt of the sword from the slayer's grasp, sending the sword spinning straight up into the air. Moving with amazing speed and grace, Marcus bounced to his feet and caught the sword in its descent. In another flash he had the en-pained slayer back on his feet and held immobile with the sword at his throat.

Desperado probably said something like "Whoa, man. Let's be cool here!" But only Tim heard it.

"Desperado!" Marcus called. "Stay calm. I am not going to kill your partner. I just want to talk to you!" And with that Marcus shoved the still throbbing slayer away from him with a slight spin. After the poor little guy had regained his balance Marcus asked, "Desperado?"

"Yeah," came the voice of the gunman, but the pitch and quality was again that of the alter. Again came the boost in pheromones, and the increase in personal power.

"You're right," said Marcus. "I am a vampire. But I am a good vampire. I do not kill people." Marcus knew that that was a lie, but for now it sounded good.

"Whatever!" said Desperado. "We're just doin' our part to protect the American way of life."

"Great!" said Marcus. "Let us just talk this thing over, and after we are done, if you still want to slay me then I will not try to prevent you."

"OK. So what do you want to talk about?"

"How did you find out that I am vampire? How did you locate me?"

XIV – Marcus Meets Tim the Vampire Slayer

"Hah!" Desperado grunted. "You blood-suckers stand out like neon signs. I can spot you a mile away." Desperado knew that that was lie, but, like Marcus's from a moment before, it sounded good.

"How long have you been doing this? How did you get your start?"

"Well, I've been a crime-fighter ever since I was a kid. I am the result of government experimentation to create a super-soldier. I was side-kick to Captain USA for years. You've heard of him? Anyway, I hooked up with little Timmy a few years back when his sister was kidnapped by a bunch of blood-suckin' vampires. I helped him try to rescue his sister, but we were too late – she died. That was when we ran into the funky Einstein-looking wizard dude. And we've been hunting vampires and slaying them all over the country ever since."

"Whoa! Back up! What about the funky wizard?" asked Marcus.

"Oh, he's just some strange dude with white hair that goes straight up instead of down. He has a vampire tracker, and another doohickey that he uses to make vampires weak so their easier to kill."

It would have been difficult to notice, but Marcus turned pale. He was certain that the white-haired 'dude' that Desperado spoke of was the one Slayer, the very same that John had so vehemently warned him of all those centuries before.

"Please, Desperado. Tell me more about the wizard."

"Well," he hesitated, "There's not much to tell. I don't really know him. I've never just sat down and chatted him up, if you know what I mean. He just walks around and when he finds a vampire, he zaps him or sprays him with some little crystal doodad and that's it. And we're right behind him to mop up."

"Walks around?" Marcus repeated, and Desperado then told of how he and Tim had followed the white-haired man across the country from Detroit.

"So the wizard is currently in Portland right now?" asked Marcus.

"Yeah, we saw him hot on the trail of another vampire the other night."

Marcus knew that Desperado could only be speaking of Chad. If the Slayer got to Chad, then it would seem that the situation did indeed solve itself. However, a glance over at Janet told Marcus that she was now nearly beside herself with worry.

As they conversed, everyone migrated back into the house, so that they were all sitting around the front room when Marcus finally asked, "So, Tim, do you still wish to slay me?"

The Desperado alter was gone, and Tim was suddenly back. He frowned a little shamefully. "No, I guess not."

"Believe me," said Marcus. "I appreciate what you are doing more than you know. A part of me wishes that you had been successful in slaying me. But I have to admit that dying right now is not a good time for me. Lately, I have learned things, and met certain special people that have caused to me rethink my life. For the first time in decades, centuries, perhaps for the first time ever, I am feeling a distinct passion for life. It seems to me that it would be a shame to die just now. Maybe the Slayer will get me, I do not know. But for the first time in my life, I hope not."

CHAPTER XV

As Halloween parties go, this one was rating quite high. The music pulsed and lights were low around the old state room at the Bismarck Hotel. Alcohol flowed as if from a fountain. An extensive assortment of goblins, ghouls, demons, monsters and characters danced, writhed, meandered, staggered, and crawled around the area. Half-naked, fully-stoned girls were everywhere. Every male in attendance would have in the course of the night at least one opportunity to be serviced; it would just be a matter of how much it would cost him. Stan the Man, costumed only in his standard lime green silk double-breasted suit, wasn't sure who was actually throwing the party. But if he happened to locate the host, he would be sure to give them his finest compliments.

The Bismarck, like the San Teresa, was a hotel from a different era, but its story for some reason was less known and less colorful. The Bismarck was a little younger, and it had never been as luxurious as the San Teresa. So now, as a cheap hotel, it lacked much of the charm held by its older sister, even though they both averaged the same number of used condoms and needles on the floor, and the same amount of graffiti on the walls. The Bismarck was just one among a dwindling collection of hotels around the downtown area where you could still rent a room by the hour, or by the week. The city wrecking ball was already on its way, but until it arrived there would be nightly parties held in the state room by the local downtown night life. Wild parties! And Halloween night boasted one of the wildest parties of the year!

The state room was at the top of the five story building. It had housed political dignitaries of the 50's and rock music celebrities of the 60's. Along with a spacious main room and dining room, the suite had three once-lavish bedrooms and three bathrooms matching in age and wear. A rickety balcony overlooked Morrison Street, and through a fire-escape one could also gain access to the roof of the Bismarck, where a large humming neon sign proudly displayed the hotel's name in flickering red and blue lights.

This was just what the doctor ordered for poor Stan. He had been deeply bothered all day after carrying out his grisly assignment from the night before. Stan the Man had killed a few times already; he didn't like having to do it but it was no longer any big deal to him. If it was called for, he could carry it off. But Jamie Thompson had been different. Stanley had never before been required to dismember a dead man. He was only vaguely aware of the reason for it. Stan the Man would have preferred to have recruited help for the macabre task but his boss had forbidden it. Oh, the stresses of a career criminal! He needed this party bad!

Stan the Man marveled at how busy the party was as he walked around socializing. A DJ, who in return for his services had probably been promised sex, fame, and all the drugs he could do in one night, mixed stolen MP3 files from the internet on a computer connected to a large stereo system. People, tripping on everything from pot to X, danced and grinded wherever there was a spot. Three girls were engaged in making out on the couch in the main room, and there was still room for two guys to be sitting on either side of the pile up; and it wasn't that big of a couch. Writhing bodies were everywhere – the main room, the bedrooms, the bathrooms, the balcony, the fire-escape stairs and the roof. Discarded bits of costume were strewn about the place.

All this, and the strip clubs hadn't even let out. This party would go on all night long. Once the first batch of party goers had passed out, they would be replaced with an influx of more people arriving after the clubs had closed. Strippers from the Bare Cage and other nearby strip-joints would be along shortly after two.

Tina and the Vampire ascended the stairs that led to the state room. The walls vibrated with bass. The little ex-goth girl felt stoked beyond anything she had ever felt before. She was about to enter a party of the most beautiful of the beautiful people and she would be on the arm of the most marvie and amazing hunk that ever graced a party at the Bismarck. She felt only a little awkward that neither of them was wearing a costume.

The little girl's disillusionment was complete as she pushed open one of the double doors that led into the state room and laid her sober eyes upon the scene. It hadn't been that long since her last party, but this was not the way that she remembered it. Having been a little high, and usually a lot drunk at her previous parties, it had always seemed to her that everyone there was so beautiful, interesting, witty, sexy, bright and shiny! But now they just seemed silly, stupid, shallow, childish in a bad way, not sexy at all, dull and ugly. She was instantly over the whole thing.

XV – Death with Dignity

"That is Stan the Man," she said, pointing across the room to the slick-dressed Hispanic man with exotic sideburns growing across his cheekbones.

Just around the corner from the Bismarck and across the street, at the parking lot of the Bare Cage, Janet stood next to her car. Naturally, as was her habit of late, she was there to meet Mimi at the end of her shift. But Janet was also hoping for an appearance from Chad again. She was not disappointed.

Chad, as was *his* habit of late, had been watching the Bare Cage from the safety of the shadows, waiting for Janet to show up. Now that she was there, he fairly flew to her. He had again made the mistake of not feeding before he came to her, but he vowed to be stronger this time.

"Janet," he said with a soft voice.

Janet looked up, her eyes bright. "Oh, Chad. I have wonderful news!"

"What is it?"

"I have analyzed some of Marcus's blood, and I think I have an idea about what it is that makes you crave blood."

"That's amazing," said Chad, consciously trying to do a better job of sounding interested than he had the night before.

"Yeah, it's been a weird night," said Janet, unloading all that was on her mind. "Marcus was attacked by a vampire slayer!"

"Wow!" said Chad. "Is he alright?" Not that he really cared. His own situation would be greatly simplified if Marcus conveniently died.

"Oh, he's fine. He's at a party right now over at the Bismarck Hotel. He's talking to someone who knows something about who was planting all those hypodermic needles around town."

Chad's face darkened. "I gotta go," he said and like a breeze he abruptly left Janet's side, with the girl calling after him. Within a minute his newly sensitized ears were picking up the pumping of the music from the state room. Silently, he stole up the fire-escape and into the fifth floor door that led to state room.

Inside the state room Chad saw a scene that fascinated his young wannabe-worldly eyes – costumes dancing, naked bodies heaving and arching, the air thick with cigarette smoke and something else. The entire room pulsed to the heartbeat-like thump of the kick drum and bass. The smells of sweaty humanity, beer, and assorted smoldering herbs served to remind the young vampire that he yet to feed this night.

Chad scanned the room looking for Marcus, hoping to catch sight of the old vampire before the powerful predator caught sight of him. A very drunk, young preppy wearing a ridiculous Saddam Hussein mask on the top of his head staggered toward Chad and slurred, "What are you supposed to be – a vampire?" He lurched away laughing.

Chad exited the state room, back out onto the fire escape, then climbed past a few enraptured couples taking up space on the narrow steel stairway, to the roof where he immediately saw the vampire that he was looking for. He ducked into the shadows, hoping that Marcus would not smell his presence. In addition to the large neon sign and all its rigging, the roof was also dotted with several large ventilation fans. In the dark, back-lit only by the neon, they seemed like giant mushrooms growing in a stark gothic wonderland. Just behind the sign on the far end of the roof was the maintenance access door that led back down to a stairwell on the other side of the building. The edge of the roof was bordered only by a concrete lip about one foot high. There were plenty of places to hide. For the moment, Chad could see no one else on the roof; only Marcus, some little teenaged girl with him, and a tall thin, dark-headed man, all near the rear of the building. He could just hear their voices over the pumping of the music below him.

Marcus was holding the dark man's head almost tenderly with both hands and saying, "Believe me, Mister Stanley. You could live to pay for your sins. But you will die right now if you do not tell me what I wish to know. Why did you kill Jamie Thompson?"

Stan the Man's cool had abandoned him. His face was damp with tears. It seemed that he had no strength, no energy; that if he should try to strike out at this pale young man, he would move with nightmare sluggishness. Stan had always survived by staying one step ahead of fate. There had always been someone that he could cut a deal with who could stave off fate's collection agent for just one more caper. But not this time, it seemed. Fate had finally called its note on Stan the Man due and payable, and was now collecting; all of it; with interest!

"Noonan kept me out of jail," said Stan the Man while sobbing. "Jamie was a contract. Travis Noonan paid me to kill him and set up some guy named Bechard for a fall by fingering one of his employees. Noonan had me supply Jamie with heroin in return for sticking the needles around town."

Marcus interjected, "You would call the cops with the anonymous tips."

"Yeah. At first we expected Jamie to die of AIDS, so everything would be nice and clean. Noonan would have his crisis and nobody

XV – Death with Dignity

would ever find out the truth. But Jamie didn't die and Noonan became afraid that he would expose everything."

His story was slightly less than coherent, but it worked. "That is enough," said Marcus. "I see now exactly what is going on. You will not die right now. However, you will be soon forced to make restitution with one who feels that his life was destroyed by your actions. Taking into consideration what he will do to you, you may wish to beg me to do my worst right now. You may have bought with this confession some time. I hope that you use it wisely."

Marcus turned to leave, pausing only for Tina to join his side. They left Stan the Man curled up against the short wall that bordered the edge of the roof. Just before stepping onto the fire escape ladder, Marcus paused. "You can come out, Chad. I will not harm you."

When no one appeared Marcus added, "I can smell you distinctly. It is alright; I only wish to talk with you." A hesitant shadow poked out from behind one of the large ventilation fans, stepped forward, and resolved itself into Chad. Marcus continued, "You are looking quite fit. It would seem that you are getting your revenge on those that you hold responsible for ruining your life."

"Yeah," said Chad. "You said yourself that they deserve it."

"Has it been everything that you imagined it would be?"

Chad did not even try to hide his enthusiasm. "It's fucking great!!" And Tina's own face betrayed her envy. "I was able to give it to that fuckin' cop and judge that got me into that AIDS mess in the first place." Chad opened his coat to show the older vampire his trophy – a police-issue Glock taken from the late Bruce Nader. Chad wanted very badly to impress the older vampire, much like a student might wish to gain favor in the eye of his teacher. The young vampire continued, "And I've been disguising my kills as suicide victims."

"I know. Very clever. It will work for a little while," said Marcus. "I take it that you heard everything that Stan the Man just told us."

"Yeah! That's unbelievable stuff!"

"What do you plan to do now that you know?" asked Marcus.

"Heh!" Chad scoffed. "I'm going pay 'em fuckin' back! For me and for everyone else that got their lives destroyed by this!"

"I would admonish you to not do anything rash, my young friend," said Marcus. "There are other dangers nearby right now. Dangers to you that are greater than myself. I would urge you to go far away for a time. Come back in a few months, when it is safe. Then see if the idea of further revenge still strikes you."

Chad was not about to argue with the vampire, but he was also not about to alter his plans either. He could not quickly think of anything to say to placate Marcus, and the old vampire also could not disguise his mild disappointment. Marcus smiled coolly and said, "You will do whatever you want. It is up to you to either forget your injuries, or to exact revenge. This situation will now resolve itself without any further involvement on my part." He had given Chad just enough of the truth to indemnify himself with the girls. Tina would tell Janet and Mimi that Marcus had warned Chad. No one would be wise to the fact that Marcus was manipulating Chad into destroying himself.

Chad lingered conspicuously as Marcus and his small female companion climbed down the fire escape and exited the roof. As Tina and Marcus left the Bismarck, she asked, "How did you make Stan the Man talk so easily?"

"Its amazing what the right concentration of dopamine and estrogen can do to a man," he answered. "These are the little tricks that Chad does not yet know."

"So what are you going to do about him?"

Marcus knew that if Tina ever came across Chad in the right circumstances she would try everything in her power to persuade the young vampire to turn her. Her question was undoubtedly a fishing expedition for information on Chad's standing with the old vampire. Marcus decided that he should nip this one in the bud. "I will kill him."

"Why didn't you kill him just now?"

"That is not something I wish for you to see. Come now. It is past your bedtime."

The girl sighed. She wanted the vampire to take her to bed, but she knew it wasn't going to happen.

Back on the roof, Stan the Man huddled alone near the roof's edge. He didn't know exactly why, but he could barely move. Perhaps it had something to do with getting the shit scared out of him. And that hit of X he had washed down with some Captain Morgan's couldn't be helping right now, either. The euphoric buzz was long gone, having been interrupted by the obtrusive and scary-as-hell young man with his mind warping interrogations and his horrific revelations. The only thing to be done right now was to wait until the sensation passed.

"Hey, are you OK, man?" asked a young male voice.

Stan the Man turned his head and saw the shape of another young man silhouetted against the light of the large neon sign. "I'll be fine," he croaked.

XV – Death with Dignity

"Damn," said the young man, bending a little closer to the victim. "I didn't want it to be like this."

Stanley could see now the white fangs in the mouth of this young man. Fear seized his already paralyzed body. "Who – What are you?"

"I am Death. You killed me."

"Fuck!" cried Stan the Man. "Don't you think I've had enough for one night?!"

Chad, Death, the vampire, was hungry. He moved over his victim with the slowness of a romantic lover. Stan the Man felt powerless to move or even cry out. With his teeth, the vampire applied slowly increasing pressure on Stanley's neck until finally the fangs pierced the elastic flesh, sliding in as if there had been a slot reserved for them.

A pair of girls, wasted off their asses, hardly able to negotiate the steps of the fire escape, climbed onto the roof giggling and staggering. When they saw the young man with his mouth locked to Stan the Man's neck one of the girls said, "I always knew Stan the Man went that way." And the ditzy girls didn't even give the pair of men a second glance.

While the capricious girls writhed and fondled each other in their X-induced euphoric passion, Death cut off pieces of Stan the Man using a knife that he had conveniently found in the ex-drug dealer's pocket, the very same knife that Stan the Man had used to carve Jamie Thompson, and casually tossed the pieces over the edge of the roof and into the back alley below. First a right arm, then a left arm, then a foot. The pieces struck the pavement with nauseating thuds and splats. Finally, the head flew over the edge, followed by the de-limbed torso, forever disguising the true cause of death.

After performing the grisly chore, a chore that Chad enjoyed perhaps a little too much, the young vampire walked nonchalantly back down to the state room. Laying about everywhere were tangled bodies; people too high or too involved in the pumping bass of the music to notice the vampire. As he proceeded to the bathroom he casually smeared dabs of blood from his hands on the naked, unaware bodies.

Chad washed the blood off of his hands and leather jacket in the bathroom sink while a guy and girl, high out of their minds, did it on the toilet, paying him absolutely no heed whatsoever. Running through his mind the entire time was what he was going to do to Travis Noonan, the splendid judge and politician extraordinaire. At last his vengeance would be complete! It would be a thing of beauty.

The only problem was that it wouldn't last near long enough. Chad wanted the guilty politician to suffer long and terrible. His warped, dark mind schemed and fantasized about the possibilities. He also knew that he would have to disappear afterward if he expected to survive. No problem there; he was fully burnt out on this burg. But he still wanted to take Janet with him. He wanted her to share his triumph and suffering. And he wanted her to be his forever.

Freshly fed, cleaned, and vindicated, Chad left the party and walked back over to the Bare Cage. A few of the dancers were already exiting the club, so he knew that it would not be long before Janet and Mimi would also be along. While he waited out of sight, in a shadow near the Mustang, he thought about what he would say to her. *"Hello, Janet. Come be a vampire with me!"* It had a bad ring to it. *"Janet, I love you! I want to be with you forever."* At least it was honest. Too bad it just sounded hokey.

Presently, the entrance of the club did produce the girls. They walked across the small parking lot, looking as sweet on each other as they ever had. A dark thought crossed Chad's mind, and he realized that he would have an easier time of charming Janet if Mimi was out of the picture. *Who was the man here, anyhow?!* He reasoned. Who now had the supernatural strength of a vampire?! He could take what he wanted!

Except that he didn't want her like that. He wanted her to want him.

He would have to make her want him. There was no other way; no other alternative! And besides – who in their right mind would ever turn down immortality when it was offered to them?

"Janet," he said as he stepped out of the shadows, startling Mimi.
"Chad?"

The young vampire looked deep into Janet's eyes and spoke quickly. "Janet, I love you. When I was sick I used to dream about being with you. I dreamed of it because the way things were I would never have imagined any way for it to actually happen, and that dream, as sweetly painful as it was because of its impossibility, was the only thing that could numb the physical pain that I was feeling. Janet, I still have that dream, only now things are different! I'm not dying, and I'll never have to worry about that again. I have the power to make all of your dreams come true! And I will, Janet. I'll make you so happy; I'll give you everything you ever wanted. I will make all of your dreams come true!"

The question of becoming a vampire had been in back of Janet's mind ever since Marcus's unbelievable revelation on the way to the cabin. The girls had mused together about the idea, notwithstanding the

XV – Death with Dignity

fact that Marcus spoke adamantly for never turning anyone. They had tossed the possibilities about the same way one might ponder over what they would wish for if they should happen to come across a genie living in a magic lamp. Surely, the immortality aspect of vampirism was the most attractive feature. Pitted against that fine advantage were several cons, the biggest one being the need to drink fresh human blood. In their discussion, Mimi had kind of suggested that she might be able make such a trade for eternal life. Janet, as much she liked the idea of never having to die, could not get past the fact that she would be compelled to kill for such a gift.

But she hadn't been seriously faced with the decision. She and Mimi had only mused on the idea because they had assumed (correctly) that Marcus would never willingly go against his wishes. Now, here she was, with the dark gift being offered to her in exchange for her heart.

Janet realized that she was not overly tempted by the proposition. She cared deeply for Chad, maybe even loved him, but certainly without passion. She did not wish to be beholden to him. However, she had to admit deep in her heart, if it had been Marcus making the offer, she would have had to think about it a little longer.

But how was she going to be able to stand there and tell Chad, a vampire, (and one disconcertingly scary, Janet noted) that her answer was 'no?' Janet had never been very good at rejecting the advances of an unwanted suitor. But then, her life had put her in that situation only once or twice. Janet just hated the idea of breaking someone's heart; she didn't want to hurt Chad. She hadn't quite grasped the concept that she had no control over nor responsibility for other people's feelings.

Her mind racing, searching for the right words, she looked at Mimi and found strength. The answer was held in the dancer's beautiful, steady face. Janet was free to do as she wanted, and Mimi, as her intimate friend, was ready to support her decision, and deal with the effects of the cause set in motion by that decision.

"Chad, I love you as a friend, and I care deeply for you, but I don't want to be a vampire. I'm very happy with my life as it is." Janet would have loved to express some of the feelings of her deep love for Mimi, but she supposed that it might be prudent not to bring that to the center of Chad's focus just now.

As it was, the announcement was enough to blindside the young vampire. He had fully been expecting for Janet to take him up on his offer. Dark clouds seemed to form around him now. Hope was very quick to abandon him. Foul darkness bubbled up from Chad's core threatening to consume him completely.

But, from some hidden reserve in his heart, he summoned the very last of his good will, and pasted on his face a bitterly impassioned smile. He had to convince her!

In a movement not absent of grace, he stepped close to Janet. His arm reached around the small of her back, and pulled her body tight to his. Still looking deep into her eyes he said, "This *is* life, Janet; what I have! Only I hold the promise of forever. Me! And I will share it with you! I love you!!"

Chad was caught up in the exhilaration of the passionate feelings. Time seemed to hang for moment as he held Janet's soft, warm, voluptuous body against his. His free hand tenderly caressed the back of her neck under the volumes of silky hair. Her smell filled his head and made him feel lighter than air. Looking into her deep, soulful eyes, he believed that he could see her internal conflict. What could possibly be clouding her judgment so as to make her bock at such a generous gift? Chad wished that this moment could be his eternity.

But his eternity was interrupted with the force of Janet's arms pushing him away. Chad had no sooner finished speaking his words than Janet managed to get her arms up and against him and push with all of her might. Mimi stood ready to defend her lover if Chad showed signs of becoming physically abusive. She would liked to have gotten the attention of the bouncer, but she wasn't about to leave Janet's side.

The darkness that had previously gathered around Chad abruptly returned and dropped a shadow over his face so profound, that he seemed almost to blur right before the girls. He spat, "You'll change your mind! When you're old and wrinkly and your body is falling apart, you'll wish you had come with me!!" But Chad wasn't even listening to his own words, as true as they may have been, for if he had, he might have thought to be patient and objective. Instead, his dark mind turned over every possibility as to why Janet should wish to remain mortal. And every thought pathway returned to one idea – eliminate the competition!

He pounced on Mimi! Notwithstanding her physical strength and power, he held her from behind, one arm around her neck, and one hand held tightly across her mouth.

In that instant Janet screamed; but oddly enough, it was not for Mimi; it was for Chad! Walking toward them almost casually was a tall, thin man with longish white hair that stood up as if he was standing over a large vented fan. He was perhaps fifty paces away.

XV – Death with Dignity

Janet had an ominous feeling that this man must be the one that Tim the Schizophrenic had referred to as the wizard. Marcus had called him the Slayer!

Her scream brought the door of the club bursting open and Quince the bouncer charged out of it. He crossed the span of the parking lot with an amazing speed for someone that appeared to have tree trunks for legs. "OK, pal, let the girl go now!" he commanded with a bellow. With a *thwip-thwap-thwip*, Quince quickly removed his thick leather belt from around his tight denim pants; it made for a resourceful weapon in the absence of a gun. Unfortunately, he would have to wait until the little punk had released Mimi. He couldn't risk accidentally hitting her with it. Quince was a powerfully muscular bodybuilder, and he had no doubts in his mind that he could reduce this little punk to a puddle of goo.

Chad paid no heed to the bouncer, to Janet, or the approaching white-haired man. He held Mimi's head to the side and saw the two black puncture wounds like tiny opposing islands in a purple lake. (Mimi had concealed the mark during her show with a long feather boa). "I see you've been a meal for Marcus recently," he said with a malicious smile. "You know, it would be a dreadful shame for me to kill you before I had a chance to do this!" And with that he moved both of his hands lustily over her enormous breasts, fondling her perpetually erect nipples.

Quince the bouncer could not stand for such impertinence! His thick arms and hands moved to separate the accosted dancer from her attacker.

The young vampire had only a slight idea of where the strength came from, and for the moment he didn't care. He was just glad that he had it at his command. As the bouncer put a meaty hand on the side of Chad's face, attempting to pry him away from the busty girl, Chad's hand shot out, catching the bouncer's chin with enough force to spin the big man around while throwing him to the ground. The dazed Quince didn't even know what hit him!

Even as the bouncer fell, Janet was crying out, "Chad! Look out! He'll kill you!" But again, she was not referring to Quince. The strange white-haired man had closed the distance between them and was now only ten yards away. Janet could clearly see him fishing for something in the pocket of his windbreaker.

A strong feeling of invincibility swept over Chad. He had felt increasingly more powerful ever since his change, but nothing brought out the feelings of omnipotence like the opportunity to set his strength against someone who would have normally been much stronger. He was on top of the world, and it was in this state that he bit into Mimi's graceful neck, right into the same place that Marcus had the night before.

Mimi went rigid. If she had thought that last night's bite from the maddened Marcus had hurt, it was only because she hadn't yet been bitten by a complete novice. This bite, for whatever reason, was utterly excruciating!

Janet was no longer concerned about Chad's safety. If it came down to a choice between Mimi or Chad, Janet's mind was already made up. She was no longer monitoring the Slayer. In fact, if it was a slayer as Marcus thought, she was hoping that he would get to the chore before Chad had sucked Mimi dry. Despite a terrible powerless feeling, she moved against the vampire and his victim, bent on doing whatever she could to stop him. In her peripheral vision she caught a glimpse of a glow in the direction of the Slayer.

It was simply a sound that they all heard. It was like a high-pitched whine, or a whistle, or a dentist's drill, that continued to quickly rise in pitch until it was ultrasonic. There was a flash of light so quick that those present weren't even sure if it had actually happened.

Chad abruptly stopped sucking on Mimi's neck and released her. She fell against Janet's car and clamped a hand over the painful wound in her neck. Something had hit Chad, or shocked him; he couldn't be sure. He was aware of several sensations that had struck him with jolting suddenness. The first sensation was an intense pain in his left hand, the hand that had just struck the bouncer's chin, and he knew that his wrist was broken. It hurt like hell! The second sensation was that of severe nausea, and he promptly bent over and vomited a red geyser. The last sensation struck him after his stomach had completely ejected its contents – the sensation of vulnerability, weakness, sickness, aging, death. It felt to Chad for a moment as if he was wasting away, utterly.

But he wasn't wasting away at all. Physically he was fine; great, in fact, if you looked past the broken wrist. However, he was a vampire no more. There were still fangs in his mouth, but they no longer seemed to fit; they no longer had a purpose there.

Janet looked in the direction of the Slayer and saw that he was already walking away with the same casual pace. She realized that Chad had been so caught up in his feeding that he hadn't even noticed the strange man. However, Janet could only guess as to what had happened to Chad. She wanted to ask him if he was alright, but first she

XV – Death with Dignity

had to check on Mimi. Janet stepped gingerly around the spreading red lake and laid a tender hand on Mimi's back.

The former vampire was even more confused than Janet. Shaking, he reared against the glaring night sky and cried, "It's gone! IT'S GONE!!"

The entire affair had happened before Quince had been able to stop the ringing in his head. Now he rose, just a little unsteady, but quickly regaining his bearings. He wasn't sure how the little punk had been able to sucker punch him to the ground, but he'd be damned if he was going to let it happen again. It was now his moral imperative to pay the little shit back in kind.

Quince noticed the still spreading puddle of blood and then looked down at his blood-soaked pants. The regurgitated blood had covered his shoes and pants while he had been laid out face down on the blacktop. "That's it!" he growled, the rage growing in his voice. He moved toward Chad. "I'm going to break every bone in your body!"

Disoriented as he was, Chad was not so confused as to be unable to recognize the threat of the advancing bouncer. He deftly pulled out a large gun from inside his leather jacket; the gun that had once been carried by Officer Bruce Nader. Without thinking about it twice he pulled the trigger.

The sight of the gun had stopped Quince. He had been about to say something like "Hey! Be cool, man," when the gun cracked loudly. The report echoed endlessly between the buildings, and the humming sounds of the downtown night seemed to halt momentarily as if to ask, "Was that a gunshot?"

Quince felt a blow to his stomach that knocked the wind out of him. It took a second for the reality to sink in that he had actually been shot. After a moment of trying unsuccessfully to catch his breath, Quince fell to the pavement for the second time in one night, his own blood now a tributary to the red lake.

Janet was stunned by the sound of the gunshot but quickly slid into her best nurse mode. Reasonably sure that Mimi was pretty much alright, she got down on the ground next to the fallen bouncer and began to administer first aid. Mimi even straightened from the car, and knelt down to lend a hand.

Chad looked down with jealousy at the girls giving their attention to the injured man. This had turned out badly! Practically the exact opposite of what he had desired in coming back to the Bare Cage had somehow come to pass. Losing his shot at Janet stung him to the core, but worse than that was the apparent fact that he was no longer a vampire. His special powers were gone. He was just plain old Chad again. A plain old Chad, and still without a Janet.

His wrist was throbbing, and in a dark moment he had to stop and think of the last time that he had felt that kind of pain. The few weeks that he had been a vampire already felt like their own eternity; like a dream. Now he had awoken and learned that it had all been a dream. Now here he was back to his old life.

Except that it wasn't his old life. Chad really had died in the hospital. What was left was a dark, maniacally cynical, hateful, dismal creature that saw nothing but evil everywhere he looked. Chad was terminally tormented, and now heartbroken as well. He had failed to set in motion the causes that might bring about the effect of happiness, or the effect of a love interest, but he did not realize this. Instead, he simply felt deprived by life; short-changed by the universe.

At first he wasn't sure that he was going to be able to tolerate the terrible pain of his broken wrist, but then the old masochism surfaced in him like an oil spill on the ocean, and he slipped into the feeling of deriving pleasure from his pain. It was like putting on an old pair of Sunday shoes that never did fit just right.

Chad looked down one last time at Janet. He wanted to say something to her, but she was heavily engrossed in treating the bouncer. "That's just perfect!!" Chad nearly screamed and with a spring he bounded off.

Janet was torn about what to do – follow and care for the hurting Chad, or stay and treat the patient that she already had. Quince would no doubt die if he wasn't taken care of. "Can you go after him?" she asked of Mimi.

"I'll be fine," said Mimi rising, and holding her breasts to keep them from flopping too wildly, she jogged after Chad.

Several policemen patrolling various parts of downtown had heard the gunshot. It had been called in to dispatch, and within seconds they, and several more of their comrades, all responded to the alarm. One minute after Chad had bolted from the scene a patrol car arrived at the Bare Cage. Within another minute, the call went out from dispatch to be on the lookout for a male Caucasian, five feet ten inches tall, 21 years of age, wearing a black leather jacket and scullcap, and believed to armed and dangerous.

Chad had run as far as Pioneer Courthouse Square before police caught sight of him. He did not attempt to elude them. Two police cruisers skidded to a stop on Yamhill Street and four cops lit from the

XV – Death with Dignity

vehicles as if on fire. "Freeze! Police!" one of them barked. "Drop your weapon!"

Chad stopped halfway down the brick steps that also served as seating during events at the popular downtown square and raised his hands high. He still held the Glock. On the other side of the Square three more cop cars pulled up spilling out even more zealous keepers of the peace. Chad looked behind him, up at the four cops closest to him. The officer that had spoken before commanded again, "Drop you weapon or we will open fire!"

Chad grinned a twisted, maniacal grin. He did not drop the gun that he held in his gloved right hand. Instead, he lowered it slowly to his temple. "Not another step!" he cried, and the quaver in his voice was convincing. "Or I'll blow my brains out."

All of the uniforms abruptly looked as if they had been reduced to moving in slow motion. "Okay," said the cop. "Now is the time for you to be cool, okay? Let's all slow down, and be cool."

Even though it was in the middle of the night, there were still a few night-owl folk loitering around the area, mostly street people, but also a few other lost souls. Mimi had watched the scene erupt as she arrived at the square, and now Chad had the attention of everyone in the area. Five or six people could be heard chanting "Do it! Do it! Do it!" but it died out very quickly as one of the cops moved ominously toward the heart of the sound.

The cop spoke again, now in a much softer, mock-compassionate tone, "Okay, Mr. Reeves. Can I call you Chad? My name is Craig. Let's just have nice, friendly chat, shall we? Don't you want to put the gun down so we can just talk things over?"

Chad mused at the whole scene, and it should be said that the experience for him was surreal to the point that he did not truly comprehend his own peril. He smiled sickly at the idea that just a second ago these cops were ready to fire on him and now they were trying to 'talk him down,' to save his life. He wondered what it was in their 'cop training' that taught such a paradox. As if they really cared whether he killed himself or not! Perhaps they were just doing whatever was necessary for Chad to not fire his gun at all. So they were there actually to protect the innocent onlookers. As if Chad, in the effort to kill himself, would miss his own head and take out one of those people standing around waiting with morbid anticipation for him to deliver their entertainment for the week.

But on top of it all, Chad knew that the cops were just there to enforce the law. He knew that it was illegal to commit suicide. Because if it wasn't, why would there be silly laws on the books like the Death with Dignity Act? The self-righteous sympathy feigned by the cops was enough to sicken Chad, but, at the same time, he felt the power of being in control of the situation. He had the gun after all! He yelled, "I want to die!" and he could see the ripple of frustration through the gathering policemen.

In the distance, echoing a few blocks away was the wail of an ambulance siren, speeding Quince the bouncer to the hospital. Chorusing against the din were the voices of several of the onlookers, again engaging in their chanting, "Do it, Chad! Do it, Chad!"

"Chad! Think this one through with me, pal," said the cop named Craig. It was true that Officer Craig didn't really give a rat's ass whether this little mal-content lived or died, but talking down a suicidal was always worth bragging rights for a cop. He just hoped that he would be able to pull it off before someone else deployed one of the non-fatal incapacitating weapons.

Officer Craig Lewis was a fairly young cop. He was a handsome man but just starting to develop the upper-body paunch that is so common with policemen. Craig was the kind of ultra-hairy man that had a perpetual five-o'clock shadow, even right after he shaved.

Chad felt that power again now. He had control over these cops! Like it or not, they were compelled to respond to him. He would exercise that control. "Why don't you want me to die?"

"I don't want that for anyone," said Craig. He had to choose his words carefully; try to steer the conversation away from topics of death and pain. "But this is good, isn't it? Just us good buddies talking." The cop was less than twenty feet away from Chad now. He moved slowly, with an attempt at a non-invasive posture.

Chad wondered at what point they would try something. He remembered watching a bit on some TV magazine show about the non-fatal weapons that police were using now to incapacitate subjects. There were now twelve uniformed police officers surrounding Chad and gradually closing the distance. His left wrist throbbed, and the pain brought a dark smile to his lips.

Across the square on Sixth Avenue a KOIN news van stopped with an abrupt clatter and cameras were recording the drama only three seconds later. Chad watched the comedy and for a second thought of his family. They would be at home, perhaps, when this delightful news story aired. A twinge crossed his heart as he realized that they had watched AIDS kill him, and now they would have to watch this.

XV – Death with Dignity

This would end badly, Chad realized; it was inevitable. *Fuck it!* he thought. He had had his chance for revenge, and that had been all that he had originally wanted; the rest had all been a bonus. He had made pay those that he held responsible for his contracting AIDS; the cop, the judge, the drug dealer. The bastard that planted the needle was dead. The only person escaping justice would be Travis Noonan, and Chad found that he didn't really care about that. His dark mind was content with how it had come out.

An image of Janet entered his mind and Chad quickly banished it. *Lord, grant me serenity to accept the things I cannot change.*

The only thing left for Chad was to see how far he could push the cops; how much control one person might have by manipulating hypocrisy. Putting on his most pathetic air he said, "Nobody loves me."

"Lots of people love you, Chad," said Officer Craig.

"Do you love me, Craig?"

This was a loaded question here and Craig knew it. He could try to say 'yes' but if it wasn't convincing enough, it could seriously upset the subject and destroy any trust that he might have been able to establish. But if Craig tried to tell the truth it could be worse, because, as the old saying goes, the truth hurts. And the middle ground was just lukewarm enough to initiate the gag reflex. Craig said, "I love everyone, Chad. And everyone loves you," and he couldn't stop the visions of purple dinosaurs from dancing in his head.

"He's playing to the cameras; can't you see that?" came a harsh, commanding voice from far to the edge of the Square. "Get those newshounds outa here!" The ranking police officer had arrived; a tall, obese man with about two hairs left on his head, both of them coming out of his nostril. He held a peculiar twelve-gauge shotgun loaded with special bean-bag cartridges used for non-fatal incapacitation.

"Stop it!" Chad barked, addressing the two cops that had moved to restrict the cameraman access. "Let the cameras roll, or I swear to god I'll pull the trigger right now!!" The two cops froze, then backed away from the news van, stymied.

Chad dropped his pretenses of anxiety, curious to see how the cops would react. "Look, Craig; and rest of you," he said making an inclusive sweeping gesture with his swollen hand and he focused briefly on the big bald cop that would be ringmaster. "I appreciate your concern here, I really do, but I'm gonna kill myself and there's nothing you can do to stop it! I can do it anytime and you have no power to prevent it. Are you guys gonna try to stop me from growin' old and dyin' of old age, too? Now, I don't want to waste your time, so why don't you just get back to your donut shop or bustin' your traffic violators. And you can tell that fat bald guy up there with the goo-gun that it won't work. I've lashed this gun to my hand, so there is nothing you can do to make me drop it. If you try to incapacitate me I'll just shoot anyway and then you guys will have helped me to kill myself. Gosh! That's aiding and abetting; you'll have to arrest yourselves! So now go. Leave! Leave me alone!!"

Not one single police officer on the scene had any idea on what to make of that. Their job was to protect and serve. They had to do whatever they could to prevent this subject from harming himself and others; others first, himself second. But their powers did have a limit. Perhaps they really were powerless to stop someone hell-bent on suicide.

"What?!" Chad said trying to erupt. "You're still here?! You're not moving away! Go!!" His free hand, the broken hand, made an awkward, pain-filled shooing motion.

"C'mon, Chad," said Officer Craig. "Let's just keep cool. Let's just talk." He was only ten feet away.

Chad broke into a wide grin and laughed an amiable laugh. "Ha-ha. I'm just kiddin' fellas. I'm not gonna kill myself." His face went cold, slack, expressionless; the look of a man already dead. "You are." And he pointed his gun and fired nearly point blank into Officer Craig's head.

Time seemed again to stop for the young man, perhaps initiated by the crack of the weapon which echoed endlessly. For an eternity he studied the dark hole in Craig's forehead created by the bullet and the look of shock and fear frozen on the young cop's face. Somewhere, far in Tim's periphery, were the horror-struck faces of Mimi and Janet.

All of the training for rapid response in every one of the other police officers was stunned into temporary memory loss by this sudden reversal. In that one extra beat Chad fired on the blood-splattered cop that was just behind the slowly sinking Officer Craig. The bullet entered directly into the cop's eye and ripped unimpeded through the brain to back of the skull where it blasted away a generous portion of head upon exiting.

At that moment eleven guns fired as one, sounding more like a salute than a firing squad. The explosion seemed to swallow the decaying sound of Chad's two gunshots, echoing and reverberating around all of the shiny, electric lit buildings of downtown. The sound did not decay right away as it was continually added upon by crack

XV – Death with Dignity

after crack, report after report, squeezed trigger upon squeezed trigger, until there were no bullets left in the eleven guns.

Chad was pummeled from all directions, and so actually remained standing for a time, until a shot from somewhere finally hit him in the head, knocking him off balance. Red blood erupted from his body. True to his word, Chad did not drop the gun. Later, the police found a large patch of Velcro pasted to the gun's grip, and sewn to the palm of the black glove worn on Chad's hand.

Strangely, as Chad fell to the ground, he realized with some horror that he was still alive and coherent of what was happening. Where was the oblivion, or even the light? Where was Death? He lay there, on the red bricks of Pioneer Square, unable to move, his body permeated with pain and dread.

And time finally did stop… forever.

CHAPTER XVI

Marcus looked at the woman, looked into her eyes, and did nothing to disguise the feelings of desire that he had for her. Sure, he wanted to feed on her, but he also wanted her heart. She had become his choice.

Tina's disappointment had been brief when Marcus had told her that he was interested in another woman. As much as Tina also desired him, she could, as always, feel the strength and wisdom of the vampire. What he said was always sensible, and he would always be there for her. Listening to Marcus talk of his feelings for her mother, Tina had understood that it was the right thing, at least for this moment in eternity.

Now, at the very same moment that Chad was falling to the bricks of Pioneer Square, Marcus sat alone with Sarah for the first time. They were talking in hushed voices, like old friends, or co-conspirators, trying not to disturb the sleeping Tina.

Marcus was listening to Sarah talk more of her life. She had not been a strong woman in the past, and she was only now just learning how to take pro-active steps as an individual. Marcus had, however, been able to see Sarah's potential from the beginning.

First she would learn to take action, and make it a habit. Then she would learn to take power, and she would have total control over her own life for the first time. Finally, she would learn to use the special powers that nature had bestowed upon her as a creature of estrogen. In Sarah, Marcus saw bits and pieces of his beloved Maria, Shalimar, Ava, yes, and even Cyllia, and his second Maria.

To the unknowing onlooker it might have looked a little strange to see such a young looking man with a woman in her mid 30's. Every now and again, Sarah would notice it herself and have to pinch herself and wonder at Marcus's motivation.

He had not yet told her.

She asked, "What is it about you, Marcus, that intrigues me so?"

Though he was only holding her hand, the look in his eyes spoke volumes to her about the depths of his desires for more physical contact. He had not yet initiated more. For Marcus, this self-imposed restraint was exquisitely delightful – a mental and emotional frolic.

XVI – Marcus and Sarah

They talked as friends, rather intimate friends, with very little limiting to the topics.

Marcus smiled his perfectly crooked smile of centuries and said jokingly, "Could it be my stunning good looks?"

"Well, that's part of it certainly," said Sarah. "You make the little debutant in me swoon. But there's more. I'm an older woman. I reached a point years ago where young men simply stopped appealing to me. It didn't matter what they looked like, I just couldn't deal with the immaturity. But you seem more mature than any man I've ever met. And wise, and smart! I hope this is coming out right."

"It is," said the vampire. "I am so glad to hear of your perceptions. They do you credit."

"So what is it?" she asked again.

"I am a little bit older than I look."

"Really?"

"A lot."

"A lot older?" Sarah was just a little riled. "I thought you said you were twenty! How old are you, really?"

"I am sorry I lied," said Marcus looking directly into Sarah's deep brown eyes. "I only did it because I wanted you to be at ease. I greatly wish to tell you now something that may be difficult for you, but hopefully it will answer all of your questions about me and more. Are you ready?"

Sarah returned his intent gaze. Normally she probably would have been turned off by this sort of thing, and maybe even scared. But this was Marcus. She could see that his ageless eyes hid nothing. They told all, and now his lips and tongue would follow suit. She nodded.

The hormones flowed.

"First, I must start by telling you that you are a splendid woman. For what it's worth, you have nothing to fear from me. I trust you. This is a very serious secret, however, so if you think that you will have any problem keeping it, speak now."

Sarah nodded again, trancelike.

The vampire kissed her, like only a vampire can.

Sarah knew that she should have been alarmed, should have felt pain! But for some reason all she felt was incredible ecstasy. Even as she felt the blood being sucked from her veins she realized that she had never felt so alive; brimming with life. Death was the farthest thing from her mind. She had an abundance of life, and she would happily share that life.

Music, ethereal, sweeter and more passionate than anything she had ever heard, filled her head, vibrated in her entire body. Behind her tightly shut eyelids intense visions formed of... of what? Paradise?

She was dreaming. She knew that she had to be because she was flying, and she only flew in dreams. But never before had she been so lucid during a dream. It was strange that she couldn't remember what she had been doing just a minute ago. When had she gone to sleep?

Sarah looked down upon a richly beautiful landscape – intense, vivid colors of green grass, pink and blue flowers, magenta-blossomed trees. Even the bare patches of brown earth looked rich and life-giving.

The landscape was made up of lavishly colored rolling hills bejeweled with a sparkling river that would have been perfectly clear, except that it seemed to be reflecting the vibrant blue of the sky in which Sarah now soared. It would have been perfect, except... She looked over her shoulder and caught sight of Marcus. He was flying along with her, just a little behind her, but very close. Now it *was* perfect!

They chased through the fluffy, moistening clouds for a bit, then he caught her in midair; a soft, sensual grasp around her waist. Together the two of them turned, spun, as they flew through the air over the stunning landscape.

Sarah gradually became aware that the two of them were naked, and the sensation of her skin against his as they flew holding together on the breath of the wind was for Sarah beyond erotic. It seemed to her natural on the magnitude of a light spring rain dotting the large pedals of an iris with gems of precious moisture.

And then, somehow, they were copulating. He was in her, completely, filling every part of her it seemed. Sarah felt a vast cavernous space in her soul filled for the first time in her life, and she knew suddenly that Marcus was not to be credited with all of her amazing feelings of wholeness. Her intense, erotic, elation was actually a reflection, an indication of her healing and growth of late. She grasped concretely that she was responsible for her wonderful feeling, and that she could get it back whenever she wanted. And, like a pure, innocent child, she was aware that her growth and healing were only just beginning!

Sarah allowed herself to climax, and as the intensely wonderful and pleasureful full body spasm finally tapered down to just tingles and twitches, lovely little remembrances of the pleasure that she had just experienced, Marcus slowed his sucking; stopped.

XVI – Marcus and Sarah

The flight over the heavenly vision was beautiful, and Sarah was reluctant to open her eyes and take in the 'real world' once again. When she finally did open her eyes, however, she was deeply gratified to be looking into the deep brown eyes of Marcus, and reflected in those eyes was all of the beauty in the world. The real world suddenly seemed to carry that same paradisiacal radiance that had been present in her vision. Sarah realized that it was simply because she suddenly seemed aware of the true value of every thing around her; not just the dollar value, which was relatively low, but the value to her in her life! The worn furnishings in the room had seemed drab to her before, but now it seemed that the items served her. The room was cluttered and unclean, but Sarah knew that it was only time and effort away from godly, and she knew that she could do it. She marveled at the entire experience realizing that with enough hard work, she could duplicate almost all of it in the 'real world.'

The world and meaning of life all seemed so clear and apparent to her; she did not want to lose the feeling. However, Sarah knew that she needed to address with Marcus one very important item – the fact that he had just sucked her blood! Did she want to risk losing her epiphanous state to try to find out what Marcus had just done to her? The answer was 'yes,' but at the same time, she forced her mind to work over the mystery rationally.

Boldly, but with the tenderness of a lover, her fingers reached up to Marcus's face and lifted his upper lip, exposing his still extended, still blood-tinted, canines. She knew that she should have been horrified, or at least shocked; and maybe she was a little bit, but it did not show on her face. He had told her that she had nothing to fear from him, and she trusted that implicitly. As she watched the gleaming teeth contract back into the gums to take up their normal position, she wondered if she was only dreaming all of this. Lovely as it all had been, this was way too weird to be real. Slowly her finger left Marcus's lips and touched the hot burning bite on her neck. Applying a little pressure to the wound made it seem to sing loudly with a passionate sweet agony as if it had a mouth of its own intoning a beautiful, haunting song. Still, Sarah couldn't fully convince herself that she was not dreaming.

"It's real, Sarah," said Marcus in a firm whisper. "Somehow, due to a science that I am only beginning to understand, I am over 500 hundred years old. I am what folklore refers to as a vampire."

Still looking deep into his eyes, Sarah pondered for just a second over whether this could be true or not. It seemed extremely fantastic;

mind-bogglingly fanciful. But her experience had been undeniable...
"Am I dreaming?" she asked.

"If you were, I would still tell you that you were not. Deal with reality as you perceive it, my love, striving always to see it for what it truly is, and knowing that it is possible to do so."

"What if I can't trust my senses?"

"Do the best you can. You are not ready for the loony bin yet."

Sarah laughed delightedly; a vampire with a sense of humor! She decided that she would open her mind to the possibility. She believed (correctly) that Marcus would either convince her, or reveal his true self as a raving lunatic, or she would eventually wake up from this delicious nightmare. *Curious*, she thought; she wasn't in fear for her, or her daughter's life.

Sarah remembered how she had first met Marcus; she had seen the bullet wounds! Then later he had seemed fine; no sign of injury. As implausible as it was, his revelation could explain fantastically how he had recovered from seemingly fatal wounds the way he had.

"Does Tina know?" she asked.

"Yes," said Marcus. "I am sorry. I did not realize just how young the girl was when I first encountered her. She is quite mature beyond her years. Tina was very receptive to my secret, and has prudently maintained absolute discretion."

Sarah asked, "Why did you wish to tell me your secret?"

"Sarah, my love, I have felt a fondness for you ever since I first saw you. My fondness for you has grown as you have grown. It is particularly delightful for me to watch as a passionate woman discovers the beginnings of her potential."

The answer had been a little deeper than Sarah had expected, and she realized with some self-amusement that she should have known that Marcus's answer would exceed her expectations. Then she thought about the answer itself and, in spite of herself, felt touched. From any other young man she would have felt patronized, and Sarah was aware that she was having difficulty cramming the wizened mind and mature heart of a five-hundred year old man into the young body of a beautiful twenty-one year old. But Marcus had delivered the answer with such a lack of prejudice, such objectivity, that Sarah could not help but feel as though he should know what he was talking about. So what was he talking about? Her eyes grew damp as she asked, "Potential? For what?"

"Potential for anything you want; potential to live whatever life you choose to live with great passion, independence, love, and happiness."

XVI – Marcus and Sarah

Sarah had heard those words before and knew that women today were supposed to be able to experience them. Why hadn't she, she wondered? It had always seemed that those words applied to other women – married women with husbands that were strong, true, and handsome; not her. Even now she unconsciously regarded those qualities as gifts bestowed upon her by Marcus. Her eyes and the tone of her voice reflected that sentiment as she asked graciously, "Why me? I don't understand why you chose me."

"Nothing I can say to you will answer that question to your satisfaction. Everyone has the light inside of them, but not everyone can see their own light. When the time comes that you can see your light, you will know why I have strong feelings for you."

CHAPTER XVII

Hutchinson took some measures to keep the job separate from his life at home. He was determined that Melody, his wife, would not be another cop's wife. His efforts were largely successful and as a result his beautiful wife had very little notion of what he did on a daily basis to keep the city safe for her and their three children. Darrel loved his family dearly, and as far as he was concerned, everything he did on the job was to make the city safe for them.

Darrel liked the part of his job that was about bustin' the bad guys, but he was always careful to avoid situations that put his life at risk. For hazardous duties he was quick to delegate or pass the buck. He had not needed to put himself at risk to earn measured success as a detective. Darrel marveled at crime-drama TV shows and movies that showed police detectives putting their lives on the line and dodging bullets. Those situations were real, (for the most part), and he could be in them if he wanted to, but he didn't know a single cop that really wanted that. If his life as a detective had really been like a TV crime-drama he would have found another line of work.

But above all, he did not want his wife and family touched by the shit that he dealt with every day. Hence, his wife did not hang out with other cop's wives. They never attended police social functions. He had refused the standard police protections over his family, opting instead for an extremely sophisticated home security system covering their house in a gated neighborhood that he could hardly afford to live in. Darrel felt proud that he had done everything he could to keep his family safe without the involvement of the department.

Hutchinson had decreed that a call from anyone at the station to his home phone was a cardinal crime. He had his special cell phone for those purposes. And so it was that as Hutchinson answered the ringing 'SWAT' phone this morning, the voice of Captain Rahal on the other end answered snidely, "I hope I'm not interrupting family time."

The detective was just on his way out of the garage this morning. One minute earlier and the Cap'n would have been interrupting his long and sensuous good-bye kiss with Melody. He was in a pretty good mood and responded with sincere gratitude, "No, your timing is good. What's up?"

XVII – Henderson Works the Phone

"We had a very busy night. I take it you haven't heard?"

"Nope," answered Hutchinson with an aloofness that he was proud of. "What happened?"

"Well, first, we had a real messy suicide downtown at 2:30 in the morning. Are you acquainted with Officers Lewis and Tidwell?"

"Yeah, I know 'em."

"They were KLOD last night, trying to talk the suicidal down."

Hutchinson was aghast at the news. Talking down a suicidal seemed like an unlikely place to get killed in the line of duty. But he didn't really know either of them all that well, and the main thought that was running through his mind as he piloted his special-issue unmarked police automobile past the security gate at the entrance of his suburban neighborhood was not for the fallen men or their families left behind in mourning. He was thinking, *Sure am glad it was them and not me. I'll have to get the details on this later so I can avoid such a thing happening to me!* Only sensible.

Rahal interrupted the detective's thoughts. "But there's more, Darrel. Stan the Man was found about an hour ago in an alley behind the Bismarck Hotel cut into pieces."

"What?!!" Hutchinson almost screamed. "How?"

Rahal continued, "I called Stone in on it, since you were at home."

Hutchinson could only stammer, "But, Cap'n –"

"I'm sorry, but I didn't want to bother you with it at the time. Give Stone a call if you want the details."

"Thanks, Cap'n," Hutchinson said resignedly, and flipped his middle finger at the phone as he hung up.

This would be the kind of phone call that Hutchinson loathed to make. He was being forced to basically beg Detective Stone for information that was concerning the case that had belonged to Hutchinson since the beginning. Hutchinson realized that he didn't even know Detective Stone's cell number. He had to place a call to Miller, his virtually invisible partner at the station and have him look it up. At last he was dialing, and seconds later Detective Mike Stone was greeting him on the phone.

"What's up?" asked Hutchinson flatly.

"Nothin' much," answered Stone casually. "What's up with you?"

As if he didn't know!

Hutchinson wanted to reach through the phone and strangle the junior detective, but now more than ever, this situation called for a cool tack. He used a voice that was firm, without (hopefully) sounding too demanding. "What can you tell me about Manuel Stanley?"

"His mutilated remains were found scattered behind the Bismarck Hotel sometime around 6:10. We found traces of his blood and few other scraps on the roof, so we suspect that the doer killed him, and cut him up on the roof, and tossed the pieces over the side of the building. We also found a knife, also apparently tossed into the alley with the remains. We're pretty sure it's the knife that was used to cut Stanley up. I checked with Miller and it also looks like it might have also been the blade that was used on Jamie Thompson."

There was a slight pause as Hutchinson waited, hoping that Stone was just catching his breath and would continue presently. Finally he asked, "Is there a connection between the murder of Stan the Man and the suicide at Pioneer Square?"

"I doubt it," said Stone. "Just a full moon on a Halloween night."

Hutchinson knew that he had tapped out the other man for information, at least for the time being, so he graciously terminated the phone conversation. He needed to think about this latest development.

So, his eyewitness was dead! And the murder smelled a lot like the prime suspect grasping at straws to avoid getting nailed. Hutchinson mused at what an idiot Jensen must be if he thought he could get away with this latest move. The only question that remained was did Hutchinson have the balls to make the arrest with that predacious lawyer Lambert lurking in the shadows, waiting to pounce on him?

An idea came to Hutchinson; a very pro-active idea! He had an ally, someone in his corner who just might be able to pull the leash on Lambert. With a quick call to directory assistance, Hutchinson soon had the number to Judge Noonan's office.

The sweet voice of the young secretary answered the phone, and the detective was connected very quickly to the Judge upon identifying himself. Noonan's voice came bellowing across the digital microwave phone lines, compressed but still squawking loudly in the ear piece, "Darrel, it's good to hear from you! How goes the good fight?!"

"It's good, Judge. Thanks for asking. I have all but busted the case of the Psicko Killer wide open. But I do have a wrinkle."

"Oh?" said Noonan. "What is the matter?"

"I think I can pin at least one, maybe more of the dismemberment murders on one guy. I even had an eyewitness until this morning when the poor guy turned up dead! Guess what? Dismembered!"

"Oh my God!" Noonan exclaimed with genuine shock. Then, with his voice cloaked in nonchalant innocence, he added, "Who is your prime suspect?"

"The security guard from the Bancorp Tower – Dan Jensen."

XVII – Henderson Works the Phone

"Ah yes," said Noonan, sounding quite guru-ish. "Exactly who I thought, too. You know, he's working for Jimmy Bechard now."

"Yeah, I know," lamented Hutchinson. "That's the problem! Bechard's lawyer Lambert was at the station yesterday blowing legal smoke up my ass."

"Listen to me, Darrel. I trust your instincts! I know you've got the right man and I'd be willing to stake my reputation on it. What's more, I'm positive that Bechard paid Jensen to do it. Nobody profited more from the deaths of Preston, Goulier, and Stanley more than Bechard. I'll take care of Lambert, and then you can do your job and apprehend Jensen. Once you have him in custody, do what you gotta do to make him talk. He's not a strong man; I know you can break him. Get him to implicate Bechard, then you will be able to bring down the mastermind behind all of these terrible crimes!"

Something about Noonan's instructions sounded sleazy to Hutchinson. But, he reasoned, how would he even be able to carry them out if Bechard wasn't guilty? He felt strength and reassurance from the judge and his directives. "Okay, Judge. You got it. Just let me know as soon as you've got Lambert on ice."

"Well, things are very busy right now with the election, but I should have time to do what is needed to tie his hands."

"How soon?"

"Before the middle of next week," answered Noonan.

Carl and Audrey Reeves were faced with the second greatest heartbreaking task that a parent can have to do next to burying a child. And that particular task was not far off in the future. Now they had to identify the remains of their son Chad.

A perpetual chill seemed set into the halls of the building that housed the Coroner's offices and laboratories. The pale green walls seemed painted with solemnity and morbidity. The eeriness of the place could make the most hardened skeptic jump at the slightest movement in the corner of their eye, certain that some miraculously animated zomboid corpse was coming to eat their brain. Ghosts were everywhere!

The Reeves walked down the haunted hallway, escorted by the coroner, a Doctor David Breaux, an older man that was expanding slightly with age and had a couple of fuzzy caterpillars inching along the top of his tinted trifocals. They entered into an even colder room through a pair of swinging insulated double doors with little rounded rectangular windows. The largish room contained rows of tables, most of them covered completely with a mountainous sheet-scape that followed human corporeal contours. Audrey hesitated and Carl could not suppress a shudder.

"Believe me," said Dr. Breaux. "If there was any other way for us to get a positive identification on this one, we'd do it."

"Honey, you don't have to do this," said Carl taking her shoulders. "You can wait outside. I'll take care of it."

"It's okay," she breathed. "I want to do this." They were both numb. They had been anticipating Chad's death for so long that they were temporarily out of emotions. Naturally, the Reeves had been disturbed by the story that the police had given to them about the circumstances surrounding Chad's death. It seemed to them that there was definitely some strange mystery here that they could only hope to solve.

Dr. Breaux stopped at a particular table and paused after grabbing a corner of the thick, pale sheet. "Like I said before, we wouldn't normally need for family to make a positive ID in a case like this except that we're wholly unsure if this is Chad's body. This body does not match the medical records or the dental records that we received for your son. Are you ready?"

The Reeves stood in a half hug, both of them wondering just what it meant to have medical and dental records that didn't match a body, and hoping beyond hope that there had been some mistake and that Chad was not underneath this sheet; that he was in fact, out there in the city somewhere, enjoying his last days alive.

It didn't matter. If it wasn't Chad under this sheet, he'd be under another one soon enough. They all would be – life is too short! They nodded solemnly, and Dr. Breaux slowly pulled the sheet down just far enough to expose the head.

The corpse was pale, its face completely drained of blood. The eyes were closed and the corpse looked simply not alive. The stubble-covered head sat slightly tilted to the side; the ghastly wound from the bullet that had finally dropped Chad could have been seen if someone had turned the head, but the coroner wasn't about to do that.

As numbly prepared as they were, recognition still smacked the couple in the face. Tears sprang from Audrey's eyes as if under pressure and she buried her face into Carl's chest. Carl looked at the somber face of Dr. Breaux and nodded. "Are you sure?" asked the surprised coroner as if he had fully been expecting them to confirm the negative. His detachment lost its veil of solemnity. "Take another look. I need you to be positive."

XVII – Henderson Works the Phone

Carl erupted, "We are positive, goddamit!! What's your problem?! Jesus!!"

"I'm sorry," said the doctor. "It's just that these discrepancies in the medical and dental records are kind of strange."

"What the hell are you talking about?!" barked Carl.

Flustered and frustrated, Dr. Breaux rattled papers as he spoke, "It says here that Chad underwent a tonsillectomy at age eight. Is that true?"

"Yes, it is! So?!"

"Well, this guy has tonsils! Chad's dental records show caps on three of his molars, and this body has perfect teeth! Perfect!"

Carl was immediately quiet, though not calm by any stretch, and Audrey was sufficiently mystified to momentarily forget about crying.

"And there's one more thing," continued Dr. Breaux a little quieter now. "Chad had been diagnosed with HIV. After noting the other discrepancies, out of curiosity, I had some blood from this body tested. It came back absolutely negative for HIV!"

CHAPTER XVIII

Marcus listened with acute focus as the girls related to him all that they had seen transpire in the parking lot of the Bare Cage and at Pioneer Courthouse Square. Little deranged Timmy, who had accepted Marcus's invitation to stay at the house for a while, corroborated on their story relating numerous accounts of similar situations that he and Desperado had witnessed.

The group, consisting of Janet, Mimi, Tim, and the vampire, sat around the front room of the house. Desperado was also around, showing himself occasionally. The room was rather plain, furnished simply, with well-kept (hardly used) older furniture that was strong on quality but without any flash or luxury. The walls were practically bare; neither Marcus nor Gerald had ever been a collector of 'things.'

They had already had a moment of silence for Chad. But the mourning had been brief even for Janet. To her, Chad had died a long time before.

The group talked and surmised about whom the Slayer might be and what it was that he did to vampires. Marcus mostly brooded while the others theorized and speculated. Even though he didn't want to think about what the Slayer might be, he had a very good idea about what the Slayer might be doing to vampires, and it was calling his long-standing denial to the mat.

Marcus had always maintained that he, along with all of the other vampires, were the evil anomaly in the world, that they did not belong, that their existence upset the universal equipoise. To correct that he had killed nearly every vampire that he had ever encountered, partially in an attempt to right a little of the wrong that was his own existence, and partially in the hope that one day some vampire would get the best of him and end it for him. Marcus wanted to believe that if he had ever discovered a way to be cured of vampirism, or even a way to die, he would promptly exploit any such opportunity. Now, here he was, faced with such a possibility, and feeling hesitant. Was he really ready for the 'hell' to end, or had he simply been self-righteously fooling himself for five hundred years?! These thoughts he kept to himself.

"There's something I've been needing to tell you, Marcus," said Janet. "I performed a series of tests on your blood from last night. One of the things that I found was that it had absolutely no enzymatic activity. None at all! Normally blood should have at least some enzymatic activity due to the presence of metabolic enzymes. Keep in mind that metabolic enzymes are the catalyst for virtually every bodily function, and that the body can produce only a limited number of them.

"I think that it may be possible that whatever those little lobster thing-ies are, they may require human metabolic enzymes to function. This theory may explain why you need to drink fresh human blood; it would naturally be the most readily available source of metabolic enzymes. And it has to be metabolic enzymes apparently, because otherwise you would be able survive on stored blood, or perhaps even enzyme rich foods, and we know that is not the case!"

"That all makes sense," said Marcus, and he radiated his pride and respect for the clever nurse. "Do you have ideas on how I might be able to supplement on metabolic enzymes?"

"Unfortunately, no. If such supplementation were ever developed it could theoretically treat a myriad of illnesses associated with everything from allergies to organ failure. So far, the best thing that I have been able to come across is food enzyme supplements." Janet held up a plastic bottle full of non-descript capsules. "They're basically a supplement derived from plant foods that are extremely high in enzymatic activity. The theory proposed by their manufacturers is that the ideal diet should consist of foods that are rich in enzymes, to ensure proper breakdown and absorption of the food and its nutrients. They suggest that the modern day diet of the average person consists of too much cooked and processed food; enzymes die at temperatures above 117 degrees. In the absence of enzymes in the food, the body diverts its limited supplies of metabolic enzymes from other functions in order to aid in the digestion process. Supplementation with food enzyme capsules could help to make up for what is cooked out of the foods we eat, so they say!"

All eyes were upon Janet as she continued. "So! My theory is, if all that is true, that you would receive more of what you need from a donor that has a lot of metabolic enzymes in their system, as opposed to someone with only a few. Does your experience by some chance support this idea?"

Marcus was intrigued at the thought. He was also more than a little amused that the girl had given the subject so much thought and research. He had to admit that it sounded good. "Your ideas do make sense. And I can tell you that there is a difference between the blood of someone in good health as opposed to someone who is not."

"Good!" said Janet, brimming with satisfaction and excitement. "As an experiment, Miriam and I are taking huge doses of these food enzyme supplements to see if our blood becomes more satisfying to you. Perhaps less of our blood will be required to satisfy you, or maybe you will be able to go longer between feedings!"

The old vampire couldn't suppress a large, genuine smile. These were certainly exciting times. Sneakily, covertly, while he had been distracted by cynicism, hope had crept back into his heart. Now would be such a bad time to die. Now might even prove to be a very good time to be a vampire!

Marcus took charge of the meeting then. "Janet's news is indeed the most exciting news that I have heard since I first became a vampire. And so I feel a renewed desire to live. This Slayer menace must be neutralized. According to Tim, and Desperado, the Slayer is probably on his way here; probably on foot, but still relatively close nonetheless. I believe that since I spent my day-sleep in Hillsborough, he will be approaching my location from that general direction. I need some more intelligence on this fellow, but I will need your help to get it."

The vampire paused and waited for affirmation from all of those present. After everyone had chimed in with his or her willingness, Marcus laid out his plans.

Not even an hour later the group moved into action. Marcus, Tim, Janet, and Mimi piled into the SUV and traveled a short distance in the general direction of Hillsborough. They ended up stopping near Washington Park. There they waited, somewhat anxiously for the Slayer.

Tim had his handy night-vision goggles, and still wore his strong smelling band of garlic around his neck. His job was to hopefully spot the Slayer while he was still some distance away. Within another hour, he was successful! "He's comin'!" Tim said excitedly. "It's lucky we did this, 'cause he woulda gotcha if you had been at your house tonight. And if he hadn't gotcha then, he woulda gotcha tomorrow during the day."

Through the dim light of night, Marcus laid eyes upon the Slayer for the first time as he stepped under the stark illumination of a street light. Even in the distance, the old vampire recognized the strange man immediately. It was as John had said so many years ago – the Slayer was the beautiful blue-skinned being that had appeared in every one of Marcus's dreams, only without the blue skin.

Marcus recalled John's words the night that he had first told him of the Slayer. *"He looks like a man, naturally, but understand, you will*

XVIII – Marcus Gets Some Recon

never wish to lay your eyes upon him. If you are ever that close, he will already have you!"

Like hell! thought Marcus. *We did not have sport utility vehicles back in 1524!*

Phase two of the plan involved dropping off Mimi and getting Marcus the hell out of there, which didn't happen quite fast enough to suit the old vampire. Still the SUV got away before there were any bright flashes or high pitched sounds.

Mimi, dressed sexily in a tight, revealing top, mini-skirt, stockings and five inch stiletto heels, would be the one to attempt contact. Additionally, she would basically be checking for the presence of a penis on the Slayer. Marcus had instructed her as to what he wanted her to say.

The strange, white-haired man walked steadfastly in the direction in which the SUV had sped away, showing no signs of hurry or frustration; only, perhaps a deep, ancient grief that time had resolved into a simple sadness, like wind erosion that transforms a craggy rock over the millennia into a smooth stone.

Mimi approached him and said flirtatiously, "Hey, stranger." He regarded her for maybe one half of a second, and didn't even break his stride. The long-legged amazon took up pace with him and turned up her charm as much as she knew how. "Hey, handsome, you look lonely. Would you like someone to talk to?" He continued on, without a word or a glance.

At this point Mimi changed her approach. She looked at him closely, looking for any sign of comprehension. Surely, the man spoke English; had Tim spoken a lie when he told the story of giving the Slayer a ride to Detroit in his van? She noticed that in spite of the look of calm maturity, the man looked extremely young; as young as Marcus. And the man was more than handsome; he was beautiful! Mimi recited the words that Marcus asked her to say to the man. "I must warn you that the one you hunt has reason to fear you. That fear will compel him to continue to evade you, and to fight to the death if he should find himself trapped. Wouldn't you prefer a more reasonable resolution?"

At this the strange man did stop. He brought out from his pocket the bright blue smooth orb-shaped crystal and examined it. After a moment he regarded the busty girl with a cocked eyebrow while he returned the object to his pocket. Then he continued on his way, walking in the direction that the black vehicle had disappeared.

Marcus spent the next few hours leading the strange man on a merry chase. He never let the distance between them shrink to below one hundred feet. From that safe distance the vampire observed the strange hunter. The wizard behaved exactly as Tim had said he would. He walked, never ran, after his quarry, as if he had walked forever.

"How often does he have to buy new shoes?" Mimi asked of Tim, after they had circled around and picked her up. She had meant it as a quizzical jest, but Marcus was seriously curious.

Tim said, "When he needs shoes or clothes, he usually just goes to the store; pays with diamonds! He never says anything to the checkout person; just hands 'em a little diamond as he walks out of the store. I've seen him do it a few times. Once I bought one of 'em off a clerk for a hundred and fifty bucks. The stone appraised out at eight hundred dollars!"

"So you've never seen him steal for anything he needs?" asked Marcus.

"He might have stole those diamonds," said Tim.

Marcus doubted that, but he didn't voice that opinion. Instead he said, "Surely, we are dealing with an individual as immortal as I am. I have reason to believe that he has been traveling the earth on foot since at least the time of Jesus Christ. It may be reasonable to assume that whatever it is that keeps me alive keeps him alive as well. I imagine that he will be immensely wise, and strong. If he chose not to communicate with Miriam, then I am sure that in his superior wisdom that such a decision was made and executed with the utmost rationality and reason. Surely, I have been in such a place myself many times!"

"There's something else I forgot to tell you," said Tim. "He's a shape-shifter! I've seen him do it a couple of times." There was dead silence in the vehicle as this new information sunk in. Mimi's eyes were wide with amazement at the thought of it and Janet's generous mouth hung open. "It takes him a little while to do it," Tim continued. "Usually a day or two. But he can totally morph! And I'm pretty sure that's what he'll do now since you've got a make on him."

Marcus was thoughtful. Could this be true or simply more delusional hallucination from the schizophrenic? Marcus decided that it could be possible. He said, "I might have known that he could do something like that. I had heard rumors that certain vampires had acquired such skills, though I never saw anything firsthand. I had always dismissed it as utter rubbish, because the purveyors of such rumors always talked of magic and other mysticisms. However, morphing at a cellular level is at least theoretically possible."

XVIII – Marcus Gets Some Recon

"Yes," said Janet. "But it would require engineering cell reproduction, probably even altering the DNA."

"How could he do that?" asked Mimi.

Janet answered her with a satisfied smile. "With nano-machines."

"Perhaps," Marcus nodded. "If they existed. But I would consider that explanation only two steps higher than the 'magic hypothesis'. We must remain scientific."

"Do you have a simpler theory that explains all the data?" Janet asked. She was not defensive, but earnest.

"Well, no. Not yet. There is the 'virus theory' but it has as many holes in it as the 'nano-machine' theory. However, may I suggest that we not get too attached to any one theory lest we should become biased. The nano-machine theory is good, but the question 'where did they come from?' plagues me. Do you realize what that question implies? Such devices could only be other-worldly! I would need more evidence before I could accept such an explanation."

"Your evidence is walking toward us right now!" said Tim with alarm. "We'd better get moving!"

Dawn was only a few hours away. Marcus knew that he would not be able to bed down for the day at his house. He would need to put some distance between himself and the Slayer until he could decide what to do.

In the meantime, the Slayer would need to be monitored. It was decided that Tim and Desperado would be perfect for such a job, and they agreed to do it after Marcus offered them the modest consideration of one hundred thousand dollars. Janet would stay in touch with Tim by cell phone. Tim was then delivered to his van, where he set about immediately to carry out his charge.

Marcus and the girls sped west, out of town, trying in vain to outrun the dawn. The vampire took cover for the day at a hotel in Seaside.

CHAPTER XIX

How does a man admit to a crime that he didn't commit, and implicate along with himself another innocent man? The process is fairly simple.

First, he is presumed guilty.

Then, he is stripped of all hope.

Finally, he is offered a deal.

Could it be that the ever-dutiful officers of the law consciously or purposely play such a head-trip on a man? Let us give them the benefit of the doubt. They are, after all, only doing their jobs. And society needs that... don't we?

Dan Jensen found himself once again seated in a small interrogation room across a stainless steel table from Detective Darrel Hutchinson. He would not have been nervous like the other day, except that today there was something especially smug about the detective's demeanor. The detective moved with an air that suggested he had an ace up his sleeve, and Dan was uneasy wondering about what it might be.

Detective Hutchinson had received an informative phone call from Judge Noonan just over an hour before. Lambert's license to practice law was in suspension thanks to a complaint petition to the state bar review board. The news had given Hutchinson the courage to pick Dan Jensen up and bring him back down to the station. Noonan had conveniently forgotten to mention that the suspension was only temporary pending a hearing, but the Judge was pretty sure that he could keep Lambert out of action until Jensen and Bechard were safely out of the way. After that, Lambert could have his way with Hutchinson.

"Get Jensen to sing on Bechard!" Noonan had commanded. It struck Hutchinson that this didn't really seem much like detective work, let alone police work! But, Judge Noonan was a man to be respected. Hutchinson believed that good things would come from obeying the powerful politician. Besides, Hutchinson knew that Jensen was guilty of at least three of the murders, and if Noonan said that Bechard had conspired with Jensen, then that was good enough for the detective. He was ready for the big score that breaking the case of the

XIX – Jensen Sings

Psicko Killer was going to give him. This was going to look great on his resume.

"Where were ya' the night before last, Jensen?"

"I was working."

"Anyone with you?"

"No."

"My eyewitness, the guy that was ready to testify against you, Jensen, was found dead!" Hutchinson was careful not to use Stanley's name or how exactly he died. He was going to see if Jensen was foolish enough to let it slip.

Dan's confused mind raced. It seemed his life was spiraling out of control and there was nothing he could do to right it. He said nothing, waiting on the edge of his seat for the door to burst open again with Lambert, his savior. The sharp-talking lawyer had assured Dan the other day that everything would be alright. Lambert had believed that he was innocent! But where was the lawyer now?

Hutchinson continued, "I know it was you, Jensen. You've got means, motive, and we found enough forensic evidence at the scene tying you to the murder to make it stick like glue."

"Don't I get a phone call?" Dan asked. He wanted to be strong and sure like Lambert, but his voice broke with nervousness.

"Sure ya' do, and if you're lucky it might even do ya' some good," said Hutchinson. "But don't waste it trying to call Lambert, 'cause his license to practice law has been suspended! Seems that he doesn't have too many friends in the legal community right now."

Dan's bare scalp began to ooze and then to drip. The corners of his mouth dipped involuntarily and his lip shook. He was doing his best to hold himself together, but a breakdown was eminent. It would have happened the other day after the lineup if Lambert hadn't walked in and saved him at the last second before the emotional core breach. Now, the news of the lawyer's suspension was nearly the last straw for poor Dan Jensen.

Hutchinson continued on relentlessly. "Your ass is so mine, Jensen! You *will* be convicted! There is a cell at the pen with your name on it, and you'll never see the light of day again!! And there's a big hairy redneck waiting there with 'Danny Boy' tattooed on his johnson!! Three counts of murder one is all it takes to make sure you die in the joint."

Dan Jensen, a grown man, lowered his head onto the cool steel tabletop and cried like a child. His life was over! Why had he not killed himself when he'd had the chance? He should have known that it would come to this! Stupid! Stupid!! What had he done to deserve this? He was innocent, after all... wasn't he?

But it didn't matter if he was innocent or not. Somehow, the police believed that he was guilty; they had the evidence to prove it. That was all that mattered. Hutchinson was right – Dan would die in prison. Just when it seemed that his suckin' life couldn't get any worse, this happened! Dan Jensen realized that the most suckinest life as a free man would be better than the best life as a prisoner, and he suddenly wished that he could have his suckin' life back.

Hutchinson fell silent for a moment, giving Dan a little time to collect himself. Finally the detective spoke again in a low, confidential voice. "But you do have someone on your side."

Dan raised his head revealing red, wet eyes, runny nose, and a questioning face. From nowhere it seemed, Hutchinson produced a tissue, and handed it to him.

Hutchinson continued, "There is a certain person with the power to reduce your sentence. He could have you a free man in, oh, seven years. What do you think of that?"

A confused look twisted up Dan's grieving features. What game was this cop playing? Dan grasped desperately at the idea of hope. He had never really had any even before his life went to shit; the concept was foreign to him.

The detective had paused the necessary beat to allow Jensen a moment to ponder the possibilities; now he continued. "We know that you weren't acting on your own. You give me the name of your employer and this whole thing could be lot easier for you."

The look of confusion intensified on Dan's face. It had come back to this again! Why, he wondered, did this cop want so badly for him to point the finger at Mr. Bechard? Did it matter? The detective was offering him a way out... sort of.

Dan still couldn't bring himself to say anything, but Hutchinson could see that the man was at least not opposed to what he was proposing, so he continued sounding thoughtful. "Of course, you'd have to sign a confession... stating that you are the Psicko Killer... but you could say that you did it all for the money... you know... someone put you up to it. So! Who was it, Jensen?"

"Bechard," said Jensen in a quiet voice.

"Who?" asked Hutchinson, as if he hadn't quite heard.

"You'll get me a light sentence?" Jensen nearly choked on the words. He had never uttered such a phrase, and previous to this could never have imagined himself in a situation where he would need to.

XIX – Jensen Sings

The reality of his current state of affairs still seemed so unreal to him; more like a movie. It felt like he was reciting lines; but lines that he had to get just right.

"Sure!" said Hutchinson, and he immediately kicked himself for not sounding more convincing.

"You'll get me outa prison in seven years?" Dan verified. The thought of any time at all in prison filled his beating heart with a dark dread that was sent coursing out to his every extremity. But seven years was still better than a lifetime, and Dan would do anything to get out of spending the rest of his life in prison.

"At the very most!" said Hutchinson sounding too much like a used car dealer.

"Okay," said Dan. "Jimmy Bechard paid me to –" he choked; cleared his throat. "To kill all those people."

All over the Great State of Oregon registered voters were traveling in herds to the voting booths. It was Election Day!

Noonan had campaigned hard; had done all that he could to acquire voter support. Their support was all that he needed; he didn't really need their votes. He knew before all of the ballots were in that he already had the position; Bechard had seen to it. The situation had gotten a little out of control, but Noonan had managed to keep a lid on it, and now the situation had cleaned itself up quite nicely. Noonan simply wanted the gubernatorial position and the increased tax revenues! He was giddy at the thought of how he would spend all that money.

But Noonan knew that it would not be enough to simply 'assume the position.' It was understood that in exchange for his receiving the position, he would be expected to play ball. Bechard would have the politician more in his pocket than ever before. Somehow the old coot had the resources to put Noonan into the Governor's mansion, and it only made sense that Bechard could also replace Noonan as well, if he should feel so inclined; crush him; make him disappear!

Noonan despised the old man and his zany anti-political ideas. He did not wish to be obliged to Bechard, in Bechard's debt, or under Bechard's thumb! His only hope was to take Bechard down – in disgrace! Only then would his gubernatorial position be safe. Only then would he be free to attain to his own political objectives. As governor he would be able to take his shot at the presidency.

And it all finally started with today.

CHAPTER XX

The wheels of business turn, gratifyingly, much faster than the wheels of the 'justice' system. An agent of Bradley Holdings contacted Jimmy Bechard's personal secretary at Bechard Properties by phone. The agent was well received because of the long-standing business relationship between to the two companies. Was it possible, the agent wanted to know, for him to meet and have an audience with Jimmy Bechard?

"Of course," the secretary said. It was known without saying that such a meeting would be for the purpose of negotiating a large, probably complex, mutually profitable deal. It wasn't the first time that the secretary had seen it. The high priority appointment was set for later in the afternoon.

For more than one hundred years Bradley Holdings had operated and functioned as an actual corporation. It had come a long way from being the dummy corporation for a vampire. It was now a financial institution with subsidiaries and subsidiaries to the subsidiaries. Bradley Holdings had its roots from old European money, and even though it was a lender and depository, there was no way for anyone to invest in or own any piece of the old corporation. Throughout the years of economic boom and turmoil in the world, through two world wars and several smaller foreign and domestic conflicts, Bradley Holdings remained a financial rock, keeping a low profile at all times, quietly doing business around the world.

The company and its many numerous subsidiaries produced uncountable goods and services; everything from apples to zucchini, from car parts to computer parts, from home loans to legal services. The Ava Group owned large chunks of Oregon farmland and produced massive quantities of produce, never with the help or hindrance of government assistance, subsidy, or incentive.

Bradley Holdings operated with a board of executives; every person hand-picked by Marcus for his or her talents in making capital work. Marcus had instituted the fifteen member executive board in 1890, putting them in charge of assets at the time that amounted to more than ten million dollars. Each of the members, twelve men and three women originally, was paid a percentage of the profits that he or

XX – Marcus Confronts the Slayer

she generated using the leverage and power of the Bradley Holdings capital.

At first, Marcus had monitored them closely, making sure that every person on the board comported him or her self with honesty in all of their deals, but after a few years he relaxed and allowed the members of the board to operate with little guidance from him. In the last century Marcus had been compelled to terminate only four executives from the board. All the rest had either retired extremely wealthy, or worked productively and happily until the day that death caught up with them.

The members of the executive board had no idea that they worked for a vampire. They believed that Bradley Holdings was an old company owned for many generations by the same family. An annual report, a complex summary of all of Bradley Holdings activities for the year and the activities of all its subsidiaries, was prepared by the board members and delivered to a special post office box. Occasionally, every few years, a written mandate from the owner of Bradley Holdings would be delivered to the board for their prompt execution. The mandates were distinctive, written on fine parchment and bearing a distinguished seal, so that there could be no mistaking the origin of the written directive.

And today, as the executive board met for their morning conference, there had been one such mandate. The board was to obtain a lease on a particular plot of land currently owned by Bechard Properties, and the mandate instructed the board to pay any amount necessary to secure temporary control of the land along with its construction site. A lease agreement document had been included with the mandate. The document did not state what Bradley Holdings would be doing with the property.

The property in question happened to be the plot near Lloyd Center that Jimmy Bechard was currently building on. It was to be the future site of an illustrious mid-town hotel; perfect use for the land being so near the convention center. A four-story cement parking garage had already been erected.

"I've been authorized to pay 250,000 dollars to procure temporary use and control of the site," said Jeremiah Heinel later that day. Heinel was the agent from Bradley Holdings designated to meet with Jimmy Bechard, and also a member of the executive board. Heinel was accompanied by two members of his personal staff.

They met in a lavish conference room that was part of Bechard's suite of offices located in southeast Portland. Jimmy sat at the head of the table with one of his own aids to his right, reading over the lease agreement that had been slid to him across the table by Heinel. At hearing the money offer, Bechard could not suppress a thoughtful frown.

After a pause Bechard said, "That is a very generous offer considering I only paid a skosh more than that for lot to begin with. I see that this contract doesn't specify what you'll be using the land for. Of course, if I were to let my imagination run wild with my memory, I might be inclined to surmise that someone from your company was looking to clean up a mess before any more batches of bones turned up."

"I honestly know nothing about it," said Heinel, and Bechard believed him. "I am simply carrying out my instructions."

"I will need some assurances in writing that I'll be compensated for any damages to the property, its fixtures, and the equipment located upon it in the course of your stewardship, plus indemnification for any damages or loss that Bradley Holdings might incur. I assume that you won't be carrying insurance." Bechard knew that one of the many subsidiaries of Bradley Holdings happened to be an insurance underwriting company.

"Bradley Holdings will put up a deposit of 5,000,000 dollars, and the lease agreement states that Bradley Holdings will pay any and all damages and/or losses. The document also includes an indemnity clause."

"I get the feeling that you have your heart set on this. That is a bad position for you to be in to negotiate," said Bechard, and he turned to his aid. "Normally, if it were anyone else, I would exploit that, but I've had a long-standing business relationship with Bradley Holdings." Turning back to face Heinel, Bechard continued, "I'm sorry, Mr. Heinel. I do not mean to drive a hard bargain, but I gonna need for you to sweeten the pot just a little more."

"We'll pay a half a million dollars to secure the lease," said Heinel without pausing. "We're prepared to purchase the property if we have to."

Bechard blushed; he hadn't meant to take advantage of the negotiations to that extreme. "That won't be necessary. You've got a deal."

And just like that, Marcus the Vampire had acquired a suitable place where he would attempt to capture the great Vampire Slayer.

XX – Marcus Confronts the Slayer

It had been all that Hutchinson could do just to recruit six other policemen to accompany him to the large, modern home of Jimmy Bechard. Even though he had an arrest warrant, volunteers had been unenthusiastic for apprehending the feisty old man.

Hutchinson would have preferred to carry out the arrest a little later in the evening. It was always fun to shake up the subject just as they were getting comfy for the night on their couch. Following a hunch, however, that may have also been a lack of patience, Hutchinson decided to pick up Bechard just before the dinner hour.

A bitter disappointment came to Hutchinson and his cronies when they arrived at Bechard's domicile to find him not at home. Damn! He'd been so ready to bust the old coot right in his front room.

His impatience spiked as he got back to his official detective car and issued an APB on Jimmy Bechard. The old man was probably still at his office, or on one of his properties. They'd find him, and in no time.

In addition to procuring the lease on the Bechard property, the executive board had been instructed to make immediate purchase of an airplane refueling truck, complete with kerosene, and have it delivered to the site. Needless to say, the members of the executive board were confused and curious about the reasons for their bizarre instructions.

Janet had been asked to direct the rest of the preparations, and by the time Marcus had arisen in the evening the trap was nearly set. It lacked only the bait! The vampire had to admit that the timing for all of this was good. The season was well past the fall equinox. The nights were now gloriously long.

Marcus drove to the construction site and double-checked all of the preparations. Everything was indeed in readiness. A call from Tim informed him that the Slayer was closing, maybe two hours away. "Thank you, Tim. Please keep posted me on his approach."

The vampire had not told Tim exactly of his plans to capture the wizard. He wanted Tim to believe that he was simply carrying on with his reconnaissance. Marcus felt it was possible that Tim might feel some attachment to the strange being that he had been stalking for the last six years.

Marcus sat cross-legged on the cement floor of the second level of the empty parking garage. Next to him was a switch box with two round buttons on it. Running out of the control box was a long, thick cable that snaked across the short distance where it disappeared into an empty shaft still waiting for the installation of an elevator. Marcus would have preferred a smaller, more graceful control switch, but naturally he hadn't been able to oversee the daytime crew that had rigged the mechanism. No matter; it would serve.

The old vampire meditated as he waited. At long last, after five hundred years of nightmares, he would finally face the Slayer. He had always hoped that this day would come sooner; that the Slayer would come to him in his feverish day-sleep and end it mercifully.

Now Marcus was of a different mind. And he knew that deep down he always had been. Sure, he had all these years been basically suicidal, and there had always been the involuntary survival reflex that managed to keep the vampire from doing mortal harm to himself. But faced at long last with the opportunity, however painful or frightening, to finally bring it all to a conclusion, with oblivion or whatever might be waiting on the other side finally within reach, Marcus was reluctant, even unwilling, to embrace it. He would not cross blindly, ignorantly, over to whatever lay beyond. It was as John had always said – he had to live!

Even at the cost of innocent lives? Marcus didn't want to think about that. *Marcus, old boy, when did you cease your apathy? Is there really hope that you can improve things?*

One thing was certain, though – Janet's idea seemed to be working. With both of the girls taking mass quantities of food enzyme supplements, Marcus found their blood to be more satisfying, and he was able to go longer between feedings! Perhaps Janet's hair-brained scheme truly would allow Marcus to live for the first time without having to look for suitable victims.

A vibration in Marcus's pocket signaled a cell-phone call. It was Tim. "He is about ten minutes from the site," he said with some excitement. "And he's changed his appearance!"

"Dramatically?" asked Marcus.

"Not really. He's a little shorter now, with dark hair, thin face, big nose."

"Good. Thank you, Tim. And give my thanks to Desperado as well." It was a dismissal that Marcus hoped Tim would obey. The vampire had insisted that Janet and Mimi not accompany him on what might prove to be a very hazardous confrontation.

Marcus stood up and took the night in, sharpening his senses. From his location on the second level of the parking garage he could see the emerald lights of the glass spires of the convention center, and in the opposite direction was the glow from the illumination of the Lloyd Center Mall. The dominant sound was that of the incessant traffic;

XX – Marcus Confronts the Slayer

wheels on pavement, the growling engine of a bus accelerating from a stop, the squeal of a car's sudden stop, a car horn followed by two longer more belligerent blasts; city night sounds at their finest. The scent in the air seemed to be more of a temperature rather than a smell – cool, damp.

Across the street from the parking garage a car sat parked. The vampire's keen eyes picked out the shape of the person sitting in the driver's seat of the certified pre-owned Lexus. It was unmistakably Jimmy Bechard, no doubt keeping a worried eye on his asset in spite of all the financial protection that he had been given by Bradley Holdings. Marcus smiled thinking about his old friend. This was so like him. And even though Bechard would be powerless to prevent damage to his site, Marcus could find no fault in the businessman's curiosity and concern. The old vampire was rather proud of his protégé. Jimmy Bechard had made himself with out help from anyone; only words of objective wisdom from an old vampire.

It was regrettable that Bechard would be a witness to the trap that Marcus had planned for the Slayer, but it couldn't be helped now. Marcus knew that he would need all of his focus to carry off the task at hand. This was one of those rare instances when he would have to act, let the chips fall, and deal with the aftermath after the primary threat was neutralized.

Being tuned to his senses proved to be a fortunate stroke for Marcus, for he was totally aware when they suddenly failed him. In spite of the fact that both his head and the world was swimming, he could just make out the blurred figure walking up the ramp from the first level of the garage. Squinting in an effort to focus, Marcus finally managed to make out the form, and when he did his first impulse was to run and embrace the man striding toward him – it was John!

How long had it been this time? Nearly two hundred years! Two hundred years since they had parted in New Orleans, and even though Marcus had felt loathing for the vampire John, he could not deny that he loved the man, his friend. And here he was, still young, still a vampire without a doubt, but what stories they could share. It's funny, Marcus hadn't been feeling terribly lonely these past few months, but now, at the sight of his old friend, the time that he had missed with John stabbed at him with a bitter-sweet pain.

But something was wrong. It looked like John, but the man did not have John's walk. John had always walked fast, purposefully, as if he had no time left to get where he was going. This John moved methodically, closing the distance surely, but without vigor.

Like waking up from a deep, feverish sleep, Marcus came back to himself just as the being that would appear to be John was fifty feet away. He knew that it couldn't be John. It could only be the Slayer, that clever Slayer! Marcus held the control switch in his hand and immediately depressed the 'ON' button. A half a second later the fire control sprinkler system came to life, spraying nearly all of the second level with a noxious, pale pink liquid. The Slayer and a large area around him were quickly soaked. Marcus stood safely outside of the 'sprinkle zone,' and before the Slayer had even thought to try to escape the kerosene-soaked area, the vampire had pulled a flare-gun from his pocket.

"Don't move!" commanded Marcus. "I do not wish to torch you, but I will." His senses were returning gradually.

The Slayer did freeze, head bowed, fully aware of his peril. However, it was obvious by his wide-eyed look that he was surprised at having been bested. The sprinklers, originally designed to help to prevent a damaging fire, continued to drizzle with the flammable liquid. Even if you didn't know of kerosene or its properties, you could not mistake that the area simply smelled combustible. Normally, kerosene is not terribly offensive to the nose; however, it was enough in these amounts to be nigh overwhelming.

"I know about your crystal devices," said Marcus. "Pull them out slowly."

The Slayer hesitated.

"Do it, or burn!" said Marcus, and the Slayer complied. "Put them down and back away."

The Slayer started by producing the object that Marcus knew to be the tracking device – the blue orb. He bent at the knees and carefully laid the item on the cement surface. Next came the small crystalline dish, then another light blue orb identical to the first, and finally a crystalline cylinder about five inches long and one inch in diameter. Each piece caught the dim light and seemed to magnify it, stretch it; amplify it.

Marcus pressed the button on the control box that stopped the sprinklers from spraying out any more of the flammable liquid. "Now," said Marcus, unable to conceal his relief. "Now that you are no longer a danger to me, you and I are going to have a little chat. I want to know who you are, where you are from, and what you are doing!"

The Slayer bore the look of an ancient sadness. He slowly shook his head.

XX – Marcus Confronts the Slayer

Marcus shook the flare-gun as he spoke, "I do not wish to do this, but I will, so help me. I have no compunctions about roasting you alive. You must convince me that I should not!"

The Slayer finally spoke. "I dare not," was all he said.

The vampire hissed the question; "Your fate for telling me who you are will be worse than a fiery death?!"

"My fate, and that of your species," said the Slayer simply. "I dare not speak of it until you are cleansed."

"Cleansed? Is that what you do to vampires?"

The Slayer nodded.

"Why do they go mad?" asked Marcus suspiciously.

"When that happens, it is for the same reasons that you are disinclined to cease your vampirism," said the Slayer.

"You do not kill them?"

"It was you that killed so many of the vampires," said the Slayer solemnly. "My purpose was only to cleanse." It was strange, pondered Marcus, that the Slayer spoke of the other vampires in the past tense.

A commotion of flashing lights outside on the street caught the corner of Marcus's eye. Keeping the flare-gun trained in the direction of the kerosene-soaked Slayer, Marcus glanced out to see what was going on.

The scene was rather alarming! Several police vehicles had pulled up and boxed Bechard's Lexus in, as if in anticipation of his flight. Now they had the old man roughly out of his car, and Marcus heard the belligerent policeman in plain clothes announce that Jimmy Bechard was under arrest for the murders of Preston and Goulier!

Jimmy Bechard was as surprised and confrontational as he ever was. He had been busted many times before for everything from speeding to possession of a controlled substance, and it remained something that he simply could not adapt to. Bechard consistently lost his cool whenever someone threatened his personal freedom. A stout cop, additionally thick with a Kevlar vest under his blue uniform, barked, "Stop resisting!" and an elbow from somewhere suddenly caught Bechard on the side of the face.

"Get him down," yelled another uniformed cop as he moved into the fray in an attempt to get purchase on one of the old man's limbs. A second later the air was rife with the hot odor of pepper spray.

Bechard was really trying *not* to resist, but with four police officers pulling him in four different directions, it was impossible for him to physically comply with their barked orders, so it was several more jabs, punches and sprays before the cops had wrestled the old man down to the ground and pinioned his arms harshly behind his shoulder blades. Like a thief rifling over a corpse for valuables, a uniformed police officer searched the subdued man.

Marcus thought quickly. It simply would not do for his old friend to take the blame for the killings! He was compelled to intervene. Addressing the Slayer, he said, "We will have to continue this another time. You are free to go. Leave the devices! Stay close; I will come to you when I am ready."

Again the Slayer hesitated, and Marcus barked, "Go!" After a moment, the being that appeared as John backed out of the kerosene soaked area. Within moments he had disappeared down the ramp and into the shadows.

Marcus quickly sloshed through the wreaking area and retrieved the four objects. He did not have time to examine them just now. With a quick phone call to Janet, he instructed her to initiate the clean up and restoration of the construction site, then he hurried down to the street just as three policemen were stuffing Jimmy Bechard into the backseat of one of the patrol cars. The rest of the cops seemed to be milling around, talking on their radios, generally doing whatever it is policemen do whenever they seem to be doing nothing.

"I say!" said the old vampire to the nearest cop in his haughtiest manner. "What is going on here?"

"Who are you?!" asked the cop in a voice equally puffed.

"My name is Mark Lance, Esq. I am attorney for James Bechard." Marcus made a point of appearing to take note of the name badge on the policeman's uniform.

The young policeman could not suppress a little anxiety as he called over his shoulder, "Lieutenant! This guy says he's Bechard's attorney!"

Detective Hutchinson, wearing civilian attire, an expensive, casual tan suit to be exact, stepped up to the old vampire. "Is this some kinda joke?!" asked Hutchinson with all the belligerence he could muster.

Marcus gave him a hard smile while discreetly secreting a special mixture of hormones and brain chemicals to help calm the detective and keep him confused. "I assure you that it is not," he said, and he held out his hand in an amiable gesture.

Hutchinson pretended not to see the proffered hand. "Let's see some credentials."

Marcus reached into an inside pocket of his trench coat and groped elaborately for something that he knew was not there. This was one time when it wouldn't work for him to try to pull the wool over the

XX – Marcus Confronts the Slayer

other man's eyes and charm him into seeing something entirely different than what he was looking at. The vampire managed to look embarrassed without seeming like a con-artist. "I do not seem to have my bar association membership card with me. But no matter. I'll pick it up on my way down to the police station."

Hutchinson and the other cop looked at the attorney with newfound fear. The kid didn't sound like he was trying to pull a job on them.

Neither man spoke, so Marcus continued, "I assume that you will be transporting Mr. Bechard to the police station for your standard booking procedure!"

Hutchinson cleared his throat nervously, "Ahem! Yes! Of course."

"I will meet you there," said Marcus simply, "But first, would you mind if I talked briefly with my client?"

"Whatever," said Hutchinson. "Make it quick!"

"Thank you," said the vampire, thinking of the old Aesop's Fable about the sun, the wind, and the traveler.

Another uniformed cop opened the rear door of the patrol car and Marcus stuck his head inside, looking upon his old friend, beaten and red faced. The effects of the pepper spray prevented Bechard from getting a good look at Marcus, however the blurry visage before him was enough to bring rushing to his mind the memory of his child-hood friend. Marcus took the old man's leathery hand firmly and said, "It is alright, Jimmy. I am here. Everything will be fine."

Bechard felt a warm wave flow over him, the feeling of a rush that he was well acquainted with from working out at the gym for fifty years; a feeling that he commonly referred to as 'the endorphin rush.' He stammered. "What?! Who?"

"Mark Lance, Mister Bechard," said Marcus. "Your attorney." And he removed himself from the car leaving the old man speechless with confusion, and a mild euphoric disorientation.

The vampire turned back to Hutchinson and said 'Thank you' once again, then stepped past the grumbling detective quickly and strode off into the direction of his Cadillac SUV. Hutchinson was chiding himself intensely for allowing the young man to talk to the prisoner. It had obviously been for the purpose of corroboration. Stupid! Oh well, the damage was done…

The uniformed police officer mumbled, "We are gonna catch hell for this."

"No we're not!" said Hutchinson. "We've got the governor-elect on our side."

Paul Beach – The Angel's Final Charge

"Most of the initial tallies are in, and so far it's Noonan by a landslide!" announced a zealously patriotic young volunteer over a PA system at Noonan's campaign headquarters. "Von Raines has just conceded the race!"

Members of the press began crowding the area, trying to get closer to the big man. Travis Noonan gushed and smiled hugely, waving as the large hall erupted into cheers and applause.

Almost as an afterthought, he put an arm around his wife, who was looking about as pleased and beautiful as she ever had in all her forty years of life. Patricia Noonan had the look of a woman who had resigned herself to getting old, and so looked quite a bit older than she was. She was of the firm opinion that no woman over forty should try to wear long hair, an idea that she had heard her own grandmother profess, so hers was styled much like a matronly grandmother's might be, even though she was still a couple years away from being a grandmother herself. Any strong opinions that Patricia had were generally concerning the trivial; she was glad to ride on the 'intellectual' coattails of her husband. Patricia was proud of her outspoken husband and was as supportive of his politics as any wife. Her dull, brown eyes were those of a barnyard animal.

"Speech!! Speech!!" The faithful crowd would hear from their newly elected state leader.

Noonan stood not elevated, but framed from behind by a large 'Travis Noonan for Governor' billboard on the wall at the head of the great hall that served as his campaign headquarters. He was not quick to quiet the maelstrom coming from the exuberant crowd. Noonan held the microphone to the PA system, and in front of him were a dozen more mics held by aggressive news officials waiting to capture his victory speech. Camera flashes flickered incessantly like light catching the facets of a white gem, and the less obtrusive video cameras silently captured the entire scene for later re-viewing.

At length, Noonan mustered some emotion and spoke. "I just want to say 'thank you' to all of the great people that ran my campaign. Thanks to my beautiful wife Patricia for her love and support. And thanks to the people of this great state for choosing me to take up the reins in the capitol." This last line he had used on purpose as a subtle snub to his opponent; it had been part of the losing man's campaign slogan.

"I want to take a second and acknowledge my opponent, Von Raines. He is a great man, he was a worthy candidate, and he would have been a fine governor. I wish him the best." *Too bad he didn't*

XX – Marcus Confronts the Slayer

stand a chance, thought Noonan with a silent laugh, and his mind turned momentarily to Bechard who surely had somehow fixed the race in Noonan's favor. Hutchinson would be busting Bechard right about now.

Noonan focused back on his speaking. "As your governor I will have the security and prosperity of every Oregonian as my number one priority. I have worked hard in the past to fight the increasing crime rate. Now, as your governor, I will lead the forces of good against the minions of evil, and of course, you know I'm talking about the criminal element; everything from the two-bit drug dealers to sex offenders, and the Psicko Killer, who I am proud to announce was taken into custody just this morning!" Applause erupted like an explosion, and before it had even begun to taper off Noonan yelled triumphantly over the mic, distortion lining his voice as it issued from the PA speakers, "Together, we will fight the good fight!!"

The scene deteriorated into a pandemonium of shouting and cheering, handshakes, hugs, backslapping, and even dancing as music was piped over the PA system. After only a few minutes Noonan was trying to think of an excuse to leave.

Minutes later, amidst all the hand shaking and congratulations and toasting, Noonan felt his cell-phone vibrate. Checking the caller ID display, he saw that the call was from Detective Hutchinson and he decided to take it. "Give me the good news," said Noonan cheerfully as he answered.

"I picked up Bechard," said Hutchinson. "But there is a wrinkle. He's got another lawyer, some guy named Mark Lance, and I'm worried that this guy will be just as bad as Lambert. I don't want to get sued."

"Mark Lance, eh? Name doesn't ring a bell," said Noonan. "Actually, Darrel, I'm very glad you called. I wouldn't want to miss Bechard's booking for anything else in the world – not even my own victory party! I'll come right down to the station and keep this Lance fella under control."

"Thanks, Judge. Or I guess I should be calling you Governor!" said Hutchinson in a tone that was at once relieved and congratulatory.

"You can just call me Travis." The big man had changed his mind about Hutchinson completely. Now that his lead 'button-man' was dead, Noonan had his eye on Hutchinson for the job. The detective had proved his ability and his loyalty. A 'business' relationship with the police detective would be ideal for the politician's new job!

"Say, Darrel," said Noonan; he had thought of something else. "Try to keep both of them out of the way until I get there. Put them in a room without video surveillance. I want you to handle all of the processing, and do it discretely, you got that?"

"Yessir."

"We don't want the media and we don't want a lot of witnesses."

Noonan could hardly contain his excitement as he quietly left the party without explanation. "Business," was all he said to his wife and campaign manager when they pressed him for the reason. "Cover for me." Finally, after all this time, Jimmy Bechard would be getting his due.

This would be a perfect ending to an excellent day!

CHAPTER XXI

The small interrogation room would normally have been cool, but it was feeling fairly warm and moist from the five bodies seated in it. They were an odd collection of men, acquainted with each other, yes, but with such differing lives, differing opinions, differing values, and differing agendas. Where was the common ground?

Bechard sat at one end of the rectangular stainless steel table. He was still reeling from all of the night's strangities, still feeling the burn in his eyes and face from the pepper spray, and his head felt heavy from the blows it had received. Blessedly, the throbbing had subsided at some point. The bust for him had come out of the clear blue, and he kicked himself for not seeing it coming. He should have known something was up when Philip Lambert received a suspension from the state bar.

The old man was feeling rather shanghaied, and he hated that! He was accustomed to having a lot more control over his own situation. Jimmy wondered at what point he should just go off and physically resist. It was not a rational notion considering that such a fight would be against overwhelming odds. He remembered reading a recent news headline about some kid that had killed two cops right before being gunned down, and the thought of those two dead cops now warmed his heart. Being held in captivity made the old man's blood boil like nothing else!

At the same time however, seeing this young man that was such a striking resemblance to his old friend Marcus was enough to take Jimmy Bechard far into the surreal. Old memories, mostly good, had flooded the theatre of his mind all during the ride to the police station. His custodians had expected him to raise a ruckus all the way to the station and they snidely made remarks to that effect as they arrived. One of them had said, "I guess we knocked the fire outa the old dude."

So who was this Mark Lance? Maybe, thought Bechard, he was distant kin to his long lost friend. It couldn't be a coincidence that he should come walking up just when Bechard was needing a sharp lawyer so badly! Bechard was also extremely curious as to why Travis Noonan sat across from him. What in the world was *he* doing here? That could not be a coincidence either.

The politician filled his stainless steel chair, leaning back in it as if he had just finished a satisfying meal. Never before had he felt so in control of a situation. He thought of his victory party and smiled again. Hutchinson's timing for the arrest had been perfect!

Sitting on one side of the table, between the politician and the business man, was Detective Hutchinson, with a few bits of paperwork, Bechard's processing, before him. Hutchinson had followed Noonan's instructions to the letter, and virtually no one else in the building knew of their presence. It helped that it was 'after hours.'

Shackled to a chair that was bolted to the floor in the corner of the room was poor Dan Jensen, freshly retrieved from the lock-up according to Noonan's discreet instruction. He looked down, refusing to make eye contact with anyone and remained silent. Amazingly, it was easy for the others to forget about his presence, even in the small room.

And finally, Marcus the Vampire, though the other men knew him for the moment only as Mark Lance, Attorney at Law, sat seemingly disinterested across the narrow span of the table from the detective. He was, in contrast to his appearance, extremely alert. It had been a long time since the vampire had exposed himself to such risk, but after all that had happened earlier in the evening, he felt that this situation would be of little consequence as far as his secret was concerned.

Before he could release a strong hormone mixture he needed to try to ascertain the various moods of the other men. It was easier to detect each man's respective scent, and thereby discern his disposition while the air was still clear of the vampire's more potent secretion.

Bechard was mostly angry, with strong doses of upset and scared mixed in. He was also obviously a bit confused and frustrated as well. Every now and then he would go through a spell of nostalgia. Hutchinson was more nervous than he allowed to show, and Noonan's outward show of confidence was betrayed only by a subtle body odor that suggested his grasp of control was tightly held because he was seriously afraid of losing it! The vampire did not need heightened senses to see that Jensen was depressed, dejected, and without hope.

"I want to be examined by a forensic medical examiner," said Bechard.

"I am an FME," said Hutchinson without looking up. "You're fine." It was an egregious denial of rights, and Hutchinson fully expected to hear a strong protest from the lawyer, but to his surprise and relief none came. Still, the detective could not relax his tight grip on the pen that he held between white knuckles.

XXI – The Real Vampire

Bechard worked consciously to try to calm himself, then said strongly, "What the hell am I doing here?"

The question had been directed more at Noonan, but Hutchinson intercepted it casually, still not diverting his attention from the paperwork. "You're under arrest for murder, Mr. Bechard. Right, Jensen?"

Dan Jensen missed his cue from the detective.

"No," said Bechard. "I mean, what am I doing *here*, in this room?"

Hutchinson lifted his head finally and tried to appear indignant. "I thought you'd be a little more appreciative of the privacy and discretion that I am graciously affording you."

"You never graciously afforded me squat!"

"Fine!" spat Hutchinson. "If you'd rather we can just go out and I'll run you through the drill like every other –"

Noonan cut in, "Whoa! Whoa! Calm down here, men. Let's remain civil."

Bechard did calm down, but his words kept a very sharp edge. "And what the hell are *you* doin' here, Travis?"

Noonan tried so very hard not to sound like he was gloating, but it was difficult to disguise. "I am here at the request of Detective Hutchinson. Quite frankly, Jimmy, you and your lawyer are notoriously hard to handle. It's no secret that many officers of the law are afraid to carry out their duty in regards to you because of your strong influence with the powers that be. Now, you've been in some scrapes before, Jimmy, and I've been very quick to get behind you. But let's face it – this time you've gone too far. I can't let you get away with murder."

Bechard bit back rage. "Why you little –" He managed to stop himself from saying something really bad, then continued. "After all I've done! I can't believe this!" Turning to the detective he continued his controlled burn. "These trumped up charges are absurd! I don't see where –"

"It's actually quite simple, Mr. Bechard," Hutchinson interrupted. "I suspected you from the beginning because it was clear that your dealings with Preston were not above-board and you wouldn't cooperate with me in my investigation. I knew the job was a hit – a pro with some serious issues. I figure that Preston was probably fixin' to expose you on some sleazy proposition you had presented to him. When the IRS agent was found I learned that she was hot on your tail for tax evasion, and the pieces started coming together. But the clincher was when we picked up Dan Jensen for murdering Manuel Stanley and Jamie Thompson. Jensen is a clever man, great at playing the idiot. I have to admit he was the perfect man for your scheme, but he was careless about cleaning up his loose ends. He sang on you, Bechard; told us everything."

"You think I hired Dan Jensen to murder Greg Preston?!" Bechard exclaimed with sincere incredulity. In the corner Dan sat with his balding head bowed, his chin touching his chest. Bechard ranted on, "That's an insult to my intelligence! I've never had the desire to kill anyone! There would be no profit in such an action."

Noonan turned to the young man Mark Lance and said, "You may want to advise your client at this point. He is not under obligation to incriminate himself."

"You are not truly concerned with my client," Marcus said simply. These were the first words that he had uttered and they had a chilling effect on the room. Noonan found that he had no reply, and Hutchinson stopped his writing. He couldn't think of the next thing…

Bechard was the first to break the short silence. His tone was suddenly less harsh; more amiable. "Look. Hutchinson. Maybe you and I got off on the wrong foot, so let me tell you how it is. You've got to understand that I did not pay Jensen to kill anyone! I hired him as a security guard! That's it! Now, I'm sure that there are a few things you've been wanting to buy for yourself and your family. I can arrange a gift for you. How about a hundred and fifty thousand dollars?"

Hutchinson's eyes went wide and crimson crept up the back of his neck and around to his face! That sum was nearly three times his annual take-home salary. He'd been offered bribes before, even took a few when it looked safe, but this was far beyond any of that small time crap. He looked over at Noonan with an expression on his face that the politician was unable to read, and the big politician spoke quickly. "Bechard! You're going to try to bribe an officer of the law right in front of the governor?!"

"Oh, give me a break!" exclaimed Bechard. He was bound by his word to never speak of his previous graft deals with Noonan, so it was the most that he could say. However, the bond of that promise was definitely under some strain at the moment.

Noonan was sure that at some point Bechard would start talking fast about all of their 'business' deals; which was one of the primary reasons that he was very glad to be here. Not only could he sit and watch while Bechard took his big fall, Noonan could also act as a sort of buffer for Hutchinson. The detective was fixing to hear some pretty amazing and incriminating stuff and Noonan needed for Hutchinson to keep the big picture in sight. Turning once again to the lawyer he said,

XXI – The Real Vampire

"I really think you should say something to your client before he gets himself into trouble."

Marcus was cool. "Your concern for what my client says reveals your true desires – to have him not incriminate you with his words."

Again the chill.

Hutchinson could not focus his mind. He was boggled by the thought of what he might do with 150 G's, truly tempted by the offer. But it didn't seem real to him – impossible! The paperwork before him suddenly seemed written in another language. And just what exactly was this lawyer talking about?

Bechard was also finding it difficult to articulate his thoughts into words, but it seemed plain to him that the cop was entertaining the idea of his offer, so he did the only thing that came to his mind to help push Hutchinson over the edge. "Two hundred and fifty thousand!"

Noonan finally gathered his words again and spoke, rather stammered, in the direction of Bechard and Hutchinson. "Anyway, it's too late for that. Detective Hutchinson does not have the power to stop this process. You're going to stand before the grand jury my friend and –"

"That is not true," said Marcus, interrupting the powerful politician. He reached across the table and casually snatched up one of the pieces of paperwork that Hutchinson was feverishly trying to fill out. It was a criminal petition form. "Nothing happens until this document finds its way to the court administrator."

"Hey! Give that back!" Hutchinson said, sounding more like a whiner than he wanted to.

"Remarkable, is it not?" Marcus continued. "One little piece of paper that can set in motion tremendously damaging and costly effects for one particular individual and the rest of society. In essence, you, Detective, hold the fate of this man Bechard in your hands, at least as far as the next few months and perhaps years go. Whether he is truly guilty or indeed innocent, you decide if he is to undergo tremendous expense, damage, and loss. Do you understand how it is that you have such power?"

Hutchinson found himself actually able to think at last. This lawyer had engaged him with a question. Mark Lance had yet failed to show him anything that even suggested that he was really a lawyer, but that fact was now sitting idly towards the back of Hutchinson's mind and did not nag at him. The guy had to be a lawyer; he talked like a lawyer... sort of. But Hutchinson decided that he liked the guy. He didn't seem to be pulling any punches. He wasn't threatening to sue somebody with every other breath.

Before Hutchinson could fully organize his thoughts into an answer however, Noonan fired off a quick, easy response. "He gets his power from the public trust."

"I was not talking to you," said the lawyer in a bone-chilling tone. Then he smiled affably back at the detective.

"I – I do my job for the good of the public," said Hutchinson. "If I have power in my job then I suppose it would come from the public."

Marcus nodded his thoughtful nod. Bechard was very familiar with that gesture as the other men in the room soon would be. "Perhaps," said Marcus. "But, who physically stands behind you and the decisions you make in the capacity of your job as a law enforcement officer?"

Hutchinson had to think about that one for a minute. It wasn't the public per say; the civilians were the ones that he was commissioned to protect. The public stood behind him only with their collective support. His power, his muscle, came from the system itself. It came from the organization that was the police force. It came from his fellow officers, his colleagues, his brothers in arms. Hutchinson suddenly saw the poison in the question. He would have to avoid that minefield! "Look, I just do my job. I investigate the crimes, build the case, make the arrests, do the paperwork; from there its outa my hands."

The lawyer's tone remained even. "What you do in the course of doing your job is also a cause set in motion. The results may or may not be a benefit to society. The results to you personally are more likely to be negative rather than positive, believe me. Would you try to deny responsibility for your own actions?"

"Hey! When did this become about me and my job? Bechard is the bad guy here. Now gimme back that damn form!"

"Darrel," said Noonan. "Don't listen to him. He's just trying to mess with your mind. He's trying to set us against each other! Don't fall for it. You protect the city! The streets would go completely to hell without brave police officers like you."

Meanwhile, Bechard had been staring in disbelief at the young Mark Lance since he had started talking. Not only was this kid a dead-ringer for Marcus, his childhood friend and mentor, but he sounded like him as well. How could that be? He said almost in a mumble, "God! You remind me so much of someone I knew a long time ago."

Marcus said quietly, "For the moment we must remain focused on the present." And Bechard knew that that was exactly what his old friend Marcus would have said. Then, with a mischievous grin, the lawyer slid the paper across the table, back to Hutchinson. "So what about Bechard's generous offer? Enticing, is it not?"

Hutchinson paused only for a nano-second before he blurted, "I do not accept bribes. I'm an honest cop." He said it quickly knowing that if he stopped to think about it any more, he'd go the other way on the decision. Noonan glowed with gratification, and relief. But it was to be short-lived.

"YOU STUPID, SILLY NOTHING!" Bechard yelled. "Honest cop, HA! There is no such thing! Everyone has their price! Five hundred thousand!"

But Marcus was clapping. "Bravo! There is hope for you yet, Detective. Clearly you have some moral conscience about where your gold comes from. So now we get down to it – where do your wages come from?"

"Could we please stay focused on the issue at hand!" Noonan bellowed. "We are not here to discuss Detective Hutchinson's finances! We're here to get the wheels of justice moving."

The lawyer stood up quickly. "We shall get to justice soon enough!" he said sternly, and the statement had that chilling effect on the room. "But first, Detective, please tell me from where your payment originates."

"I – I don't feel inclined to discuss it," said Hutchinson. "It's late, and I would rather finish this up and get home to my family. I don't want this to take all night."

Marcus turned his back to the table, stood with his hands held behind his back, and gazed into the dark mirror that served as the one-way window from the adjacent observation room. A strange thought struck him and he mused to himself, *Its a good thing that that one bit of folklore about vampires not casting reflections in mirrors is false.* Then he focused his gaze on the reflection of Hutchinson in the mirror, still seated at the other side of the table. "Come now, Detective; work with me. You are obviously in good with Mr. Noonan; and his objective here tonight, clearly, is to make certain that Mr. Bechard is booked. He is committed to making sure that it is done before he leaves, and he most certainly expects the same commitment from you."

"Now wait just a minute!" Noonan was rising to his feet as well, but Marcus cut him off.

"Please, be silent!" said the lawyer. "Your words do nothing but convince me that there is no hope in trying to educate you."

Noonan's jaw dropped, and he huffed and stammered. "Huh! Fuh! Uh! You – you can't speak to me like that! I'm the governor! You can't just tell me to –"

"Shut up!" Marcus interrupted. "I pity you. In additional to your warped values it is plain that you cannot recall the last time that you talked to anyone who was not trying to get something from you. I do not seek favor from you, Mr. Noonan. You have no power over me."

It took a second for Noonan to realize what the lawyer had just said, and when he did finally get it he had to admit that the young kid was right! Everyone that ever came into the politician's orbit had an agenda. Everyone was hoping for some form of advancement through an association with the powerful politician. All of the people that helped with the campaign; they all wanted something from him. Many of them were undoubtedly political gunslingers waiting for their own rise to power. Even his plain-jane wife sucked him dry somehow. Did anybody really care to know who Travis Noonan was as a person? Did Travis Noonan?

Bechard had nearly the same situation. Most of the people that ever had the extreme good fortune to interact with him had hidden agendas. But like a good Mafia Don, Bechard listened to the hopes and desires of the people that came to him. Some of those people he helped; money, influence, connections. Then they were beholden to him, and Bechard would store their debt away, deeply out of sight, until he needed a favor. The old man had learned long ago that even the smallest, most lowly of men, could, in the right circumstances, provide a valuable service to him. Bechard did not care that few people knew who he was as a person. He kept the most important people in his life close to him, and everyone else were like birds that fed from his hand; only the most bold stepped forward to eat richly.

Hutchinson could only imagine such a status for himself. And right at this moment he was also sitting stunned that someone, even a hot-shot lawyer, would talk to someone like the judge – oops! The *Governor* in that way!

"Now, Mr. Hutchinson," Marcus continued. "It's a simple question – from where does your income originate?"

Hutchinson decided to comply with an answer. "Well, I guess it basically comes from the city budget."

Marcus seemed only slightly frustrated. "For the ease of explanation, shall we stipulate that you are paid essentially by the taxpayers?"

XXI – The Real Vampire

"Sure, if it'll make you happy." The reflection of Marcus in the mirror frowned at the detective, and Hutchinson got the distinct impression that now was not the time to be flippant. "Yes, I am paid by the taxpayers."

"The taxpayers!" Marcus echoed. "That includes everyone that lives or does business within the jurisdiction of the local government, right? They each pay, giving the government the necessary funds to continue its operation. In return, the government provides services such as police protection, emergency services, public education, certain utilities, roads, and even recreation. Do any of these people have the choice to not pay?"

"Why would they want to do that?" asked Hutchinson.

Marcus smiled a thin closed-mouth smile. "Suppose that a certain individual that was considered part of the public body did not desire or need a particular service being offered by the government. Should that individual still be compelled to pay for the unwanted service?"

"Hey, I don't make the rules. That's just the way the system works, you take the good with the bad."

"Of course, you are correct," said the lawyer. "But does that mean that you should be compelled to pay taxes by force and the threat of loss of private property and freedom?"

"It's not that bad, really!" said Hutchinson.

"So you don't believe that you should have the right to private property?"

"What the hell has this got to do with Bechard murdering Preston and Goulier?" asked the detective. "I don't know how you've done it but you've gotten us way off the track here!"

"It is really quite simple, my dear Detective. You refused Mr. Bechard's extraordinarily generous offer of cash to use your position as officer of the law to allow him to carry on with his life and business unfettered by these murder suspicions, yet you gratefully receive a trifling sum from the local governmental body; funds that were raised essentially at gunpoint."

"Well, the government doesn't commit murder!" exclaimed Hutchinson, quite frustrated. He wished that he could have accepted the half a million clams. But there was no way he could take that kind of money with the judge watching. It seemed now that calling Noonan had been a regrettable mistake.

Marcus laughed as if he had just heard an uproariously funny joke. He laughed almost too long; the sound of it turned sinister. "First, my dear detective, do not think of the government as some splendid, perfect, all-powerful organization that operates solely for the good of the public. The government on every level is nothing more than groups of individuals like yourself, most of them not even as conscientious as you are, and all of them highly fallible!" As he spoke he rounded the table and approached Hutchinson until he was nearly in the detective's face. "And yes," he continued. "They do commit murder, my friend – with alarming frequency." He continued his laughing.

Smack! came the flat of Noonan's hand down on the top of the table. "This has gone on long enough!" he yelled. "I have had it! Hutchinson, finish the paperwork on Bechard and let's get this over with!"

Marcus straightened and turned, heading casually back around table as he spoke. "Is it not curious, detective, how motivated Mr. Noonan is to see this booking business through? What do you suppose his motivation is, I wonder?"

"I'm just here to see justice served," said Noonan. "I am committed to the people to do all that I can to make the city –"

"Zip it!" said Marcus with a rather flamboyant dismissive hand gesture.

"Uh!" Noonan stammered, jaw open, stunned that he had once again been interrupted by this pissant lawyer. Tomorrow, the politician would fix things to make sure that this lawyer never practiced law again! Noonan recovered, "I will NOT zip it! I will not sit still for this! We are going to get back –"

"Shht!" Marcus hissed loudly. "Mr. Noonan, you forget; of the five men in this room, you are the one that least belongs. As the prisoner, Mr. Bechard has some rights; that explains my presence. As an officer of the law Mr. Hutchinson has some liberties; that might explain the presence of Mr. Jensen, but it does not adequately explain what *you* are doing here. Don't!" he held up his hand as Noonan tried to speak again. "We have already heard your explanation and we see through it like glass. But I would not dream of imposing upon you to leave. Indeed, I want you to take part in this discussion, but only as a listener. Please, do me the courtesy of raising your hand if you wish to speak."

Noonan was up in arms! He wanted to walk out just to show the little bastard up, but he needed to make sure that Hutchinson wasn't prevented from completing the paperwork on Bechard. Damn this lawyer was slick in an entirely different way! Noonan had to reestablish control. He said in a huff, "Why, I never! Where do –"

"Please!" Marcus cut him off again! "Your protests are wasting valuable time. Now, Detective, what do you think are Mr. Noonan's true motives here tonight?"

"I think he wants to see justice served."

"Be more specific."

"He wants Bechard booked for murder."

"Yes! Why?"

"Because Bechard is guilty as hell."

"How does he know that?" asked Marcus.

That stopped Hutchinson. He had been so caught up in his own suspicions of Bechard that he had not given a lot of consideration to that question before now. In the back of his mind he had always assumed that Noonan knew something, some secret that he had been privy to by virtue of his position. "Look! I've got a signed confession from Jensen stating that he was hired by Bechard to carry out the murders."

"OK," said Marcus. "Let us discuss Mr. Jensen for just a moment. Now, I understand that you have some very compelling evidence suggesting that he physically carried out the murders, and you even have the statement of a particular eyewitness that has since been murdered himself. Which murder was it that finally put you definitively on Jensen's tail?"

"It was the murder of Jamie Thompson, no question," answered Hutchinson. "That was the job where my eyewitness stepped forward."

"What was the motive?"

"I've got the statement of an eyewitness. The prosecutor wouldn't need to establish motive to get a jury to convict."

"That might be true, if your eyewitness was credible. But your eyewitness was, in fact, a two-bit drug dealer. His statement before a jury would carry some weight, but it would not carry the conviction by itself. To guarantee a conviction, the prosecutor would need more from you, do you not agree?"

Hutchinson knew this was true. "So?"

"So what was Jensen's motive?"

"Maybe he was acting on his own on the Jamie Thompson job. Maybe Jensen was so turned on by chopping up his victims for Bechard that he had to go out and engage in some extracurricular dicing. We found evidence to suggest that Thompson had been planting AIDS infected needles around town. Maybe Jensen was playing vigilante."

"Ah yes, the dreaded AIDS needle scare. It would seem that all of the pieces of the puzzle fit together quite nicely. So what about the police officer killing from a couple of weeks ago; what was his name?"

"Bruce Nader," answered Hutchinson.

"And you can tie Bechard to that one as well?"

"Bechard hates cops; it's a well-known fact! Do the math! Look, if you know something why not just spill it? Why are you leading me like this?"

"What I know I cannot simply tell you; you would find it too incredible. No, my dear Detective, this is a conundrum the answer to which you must arrive at on your own. It brings to my mind that age old riddle; I am sure that you have heard it. It is the brainteaser where you are faced before two identical doors – one which leads to freedom and the other leading to instant death, final; and you do not know which one is which. Standing before each of the doors is a sentry – one of them speaks nothing but the truth, and the other speaks only lies, and again you do not know which one is which. You are permitted one 'yes-or-no' question to either one of the sentries, and then you must choose a door and pass through it, to whatever awaits. Have you heard this one?"

"What the hell has this to do with anything?!" Noonan bellowed.

But Marcus simply held up his hand and leveled a glaring eye at the politician. "It is not your turn to speak!" he said through clenched teeth. "Raise your hand and wait for me to acknowledge you."

Hutchinson could not believe the trouncing that Noonan was taking from this young lawyer. He was grateful that he was not the target of Mark Lance's cutting mockery. The detective decided that he would continue to try to maintain good rapport with the unusual attorney. "I do remember that one from when I was a kid," he said. "The answer is you ask one of the guards something like, uh, 'if I was to ask the other guard if this was the right door would he say 'yes'?'"

"That is pretty much correct," said Marcus. "But do you know why asking such a question works?"

"I never really thought about it," admitted the detective.

"It works because it is a 'yes-or-no' question that will elicit the same response concerning the particular door in question regardless of which sentry you ask," said the lawyer. "This is significant because you are now faced with collecting facts from two men. You will try to get the truth out of both of them, but you have no good reason to believe anything that either one of them has to say. The obstinate Jimmy Bechard will more than likely continue to be unwilling to cooperate

XXI – The Real Vampire

with you as an 'authority figure,' not even to save himself from the gallows, and the motivated Travis Noonan walked in here this night with a distinct purpose. You do not have to determine who is lying and who might be telling the truth, but you do have to uncover the truth about what happened. That is, as you say, your job. Or would you prefer, perhaps, to simply quit right now? Take the money that Mr. Bechard offered you and do something productive with it?"

Hutchinson let out a long breath. The bribe money again! Jesus!! And this time from the god dam attorney! He stole a quick glance at Noonan who seemed itching to say something steadfast and self-righteous but not willing at the moment to take another of the young lawyer's rebukes. "Look!" said the detective. "There's no way I'm gonna take money –"

"Not even a million?!" Bechard interrupted. What was he if not persistent?

"Not even a billion, if you had that much," Hutchinson affirmed, and Noonan relaxed perceptibly.

"That's fine," said Marcus. "Just fine. I have high hopes for you, Darrel." And everyone there sensed the significance of Marcus addressing the detective by his first name. "We have a lot of ground to cover and not a lot of night. Are you ready?"

"Ready for what?" asked Hutchinson, and noticed that his mind was clearing for the first time since they had arrived. He suddenly felt very mentally alert.

"Good," said Marcus. "Why don't we start with the two kinds of people in the world – Bechard?"

The old man smiled broadly, not missing his cue. "There are two kinds of people in the world – those that take care of business by producing more than they consume, and those that don't take of business by consuming more than they produce."

Noonan's eyes went wide. "What the hell is going on here?!"

But Marcus cut him off with a severe gesture.

Hutchinson was also a bit confused as to what exactly was happening even though he felt better. "What *are* you doing?" he asked of Bechard.

Marcus grinned slyly and answered, "Mr. Bechard is officially issuing his statement. Please continue, Mr. Bechard."

"Right!" said the old man. It was just like old times! "Producing more than one consumes is a relatively easy endeavor. One must simply devise some kind of product or service, and then market that product or service competitively. By doing this the person improves the quality of life for himself and everyone else in society. The person of course must be committed to never causing a damage to anyone or anything. He must deal honestly at all times, remembering the laws of cause and effect."

Noonan rolled his eyes. If he had a dollar for every time he had heard Bechard rant and rave about capitalism, he'd be a billionaire himself.

Hutchinson took advantage of the pause. He was still only half listening. "Is that all?" he asked.

"Not even close," said Bechard. "Then there are those lazy and dishonest individuals who consume more than they produce. They expect the rest of society to take up their slack. The world truly is this simple – black and white! You are either taking care of business or you're not. So detective, which is it?"

"Whoa, whoa! You're not sucking *me* into this," said Hutchinson.

Marcus spoke gently, "Darrel, if you really care where your gold comes from you'll answer the question. Either that, or you should just accept the bribe. If it is that you are hesitant to take a bribe in front of Mr. Noonan, please allow me to assuage your fears. He will say nothing."

"Goddammitt!" said Hutchinson, the voice permeated with frustration. "I'm trying really hard to do the right thing here!"

"Then answer the question," said Marcus.

"Okay, fine. What's the question again?"

"Are you taking care of business or not?" asked Bechard. "Do you produce more than you consume?"

Hutchinson pondered for a minute. He had always felt like a hardworking productive American, but something about the way they had worded it made him think that this was another poison question. Why did it feel like he was on trial here in this little interrogation room? What was keeping him from finishing the processing paperwork? At last Hutchinson said, "Of course I do. I work damn hard for the public. I have money in the bank and money tied up in investments. In my own small way, I'm moving America forward!" And Noonan stood up and clapped!

Marcus waved a dismissive hand at the politician and said, "So, you provide a valuable service; that is true. But there is one problem – you do not market your service competitively. Instead, your services are foisted upon the public literally by force, whether they desire them or not, and they are forced to pay for them along with all other government services, whether they use the services or not."

XXI – The Real Vampire

Hutchinson's face screwed up into a contortion that reflected his confusion and inner-conflict. "I can not begin to comprehend all of the implications of what you are saying to me!"

"I know you mean well, Darrel," said Bechard. "All you ever wanted to do was make an honest living and provide for your family. But you have to ask the question 'does my employer honestly market valuable goods or services' and in the case of the government the answer is 'no'."

"Darrel, don't fall for this hogwash!" exclaimed Noonan. "They're just trying to confuse the issue!"

Marcus said, "And remember that the organization that you call the government is simply a group of individuals. They are not superior to you. The governmental body gets sustained life by duping more and more mis-educated recruits and adding them to the bureaucracy."

Noonan was sounding a little frantic. "Darrel, don't listen to them. Sure, there are some problems in government right now, but we can fix them. I am very committed to my good, honest policemen! And the city needs you!"

"It sure *sounds* good, doesn't it Hutchinson?" said Bechard. "Everything that Noonan says. The amazing thing is that we all know its malarkey. We joke about how politicians lie and cheat, do whatever it takes to get into office and then never do anything that the public wants, but come Election Day, we're still down at the hall, puttin' in our useless vote."

"How do *you* take care of business, Mr. Bechard?" asked Hutchinson.

"That's a fair question," said the old man. "And I'm glad you asked it. Basically, I improve real estate; by giving it higher and better use, I increase its value and functionality. To make that happen I put my own capital at risk, and I employ my knowledge and skills to solve problems and bring certain parties together. It's true that sometimes I manipulate the governmental system as a means to meet my objectives, but it's always for the purpose of increasing the real value of property."

Hutchinson noticed that Noonan had become oddly quiet for the moment. He had a sneaking hunch that Bechard and Noonan had been in a lot of deals that involved that exchange of money for political favors, and the thought of that along with everything that had just been told to him began to overwhelm him. His brain was trying hard to process all of the insights that had just been put before him. He said, "Is this your way of beatin' the rap? You come in here and lay all of this deep philosophical shit on me?"

Bechard said, "Well, Darrel, I'd be lying if I said that wasn't part of my desired objective. But the big reason we are telling you all of this is a little thing I like to call 'drop-in-the-bucket economics,' which basically says that all of the little things eventually add up. In talking about the progress of mankind we, that is all of us in society, either add our drop to the bucket or take a drop from the bucket. Which one would you prefer to be remembered for? As for my endeavors to educate, well, that's just 'drop-in-the-bucket economics' again. Every little bit helps! Every person that becomes more productive from my encouragement is just one more drop in the bucket for the progress of mankind."

Hutchinson smiled, for the first that night – for the first time since… "It's like the Jimmy Bechard School of Anarchy." He was genuinely amused at the idea.

"More of a church," said Bechard. "I like to call it Jimmy Bechard's Hip and Jive Church of What's Happening Now. But don't confuse a free market capitalist society with anarchy. If the world was full of individuals that all took care of business, there would be no chaos, no crime, no war, no poverty! Those maladies are always caused by someone or some group trying to get somethin' for nothin', or trying to steal or destroy."

Noonan finally cut in with mild sarcasm. "I'll bet you didn't know that Bechard was such an idealist." Marcus let the interjection slide.

"If I'm an idealist it's only because I've seen the profound effects that just one individual can have on everyone's quality of life. And I've also seen the amazing effects that capitalism can have on quality of life. Everything so fine about your quality of life, from your house in the suburbs to the fruit you ate at breakfast this morning is the result of capitalism. But I have an example that I like even better than that! Darrel, Travis, both of you are old enough to remember when we didn't have computers and the internet. I remember the first computers! They were amazing machines, big! Noisy! Expensive!! But they were marvelous. Over the decades they got smaller and smaller, until finally, they were small enough to fit on a desktop. I'm sure that you can remember some of those earlier computers. By today's standards they were slow as molasses, and for most people prohibitively expensive. But here's the strange thing – the development of computer technology was not regulated by the government! Government regulation is the polar opposite of a free-market economy, and by some strange quirk of fate, computer technology was allowed to develop unfettered by government regulation. And we all know what happened. The rate of technological progress in the computer industry took off like a rocket. The price of computers dropped while their speed and performance increased off the charts. Today, even low-income households can afford a computer and have the benefit of the internet in their homes. For less than a thousand bucks you can buy what I couldn't buy for a million dollars twenty-five years ago. That's a dramatic increase in quality of life my friends, and we all watched it happen within our lifetimes. That is what gives me hope that someday, everyone in the world will commit to taking care of business!"

"That's a beautiful story, but it doesn't matter," said Noonan. "The people will always need government. They will always need to follow leaders!" He was finally going to have it out with Jimmy Bechard. The politician had listened to too many of Bechard's ranting anti-government sermons. He had dreamt of the day when he could sit Bechard down in a room and tell him that his ideas were stupid, destructive, and nothing more than a rationalization for all of his sleazy, underhanded deals. Noonan continued, "Capitalism doesn't work because the companies that supposedly provide the public with all these fabulous products tend to get out of control. They will do anything, pollute anything, advertise anything, and forget about quality control just to get more profits. Without government regulation we'd end up with monopolies, and they don't do anything to increase the quality of life. There is too much corruption in big business."

"Travis, you make it sound as though businesses out there are just lookin' for any way to screw their customers to make a fast buck. It's simply not true."

"Oh, but it is!" said Noonan. "Do you think the big oil companies give a damn about the environment that they leave for their customers? Then there's the pharmaceutical companies pedaling band-aids for broken bones. Masking the symptoms is much more profitable that marketing the cure! The agricultural industry using hormones and irradiation to make their food products grow faster and larger, and last longer, but who knows what all of that is doing to our health! And don't forget your precious Bill Gates! He may have brought us Windows, but how many programmers did he steal ideas from to deliver that bug-filled behemoth of an operating system?! Not to mention his other crimes against society. Only government can keep the big business in line.

"There's also the issue of petty crimes! It's sad but true, poverty and other conditions drive certain people to commit burglary, rape, even murder. The government with its fine police force is the only thing standing between order and chaos!"

Bechard said, "There would be only favorable conditions and no poverty to speak of if everyone just took care of business, produced more than they consume! And that goes for every government employee."

"Wait a minute!" Hutchinson's head was starting to spin with all of the contrasting opinions. How had they gotten to this point on a simple book processing? "This is too much for me to take."

Noonan was quick to come to his aid. "You don't have to sit there and listen to this murderer and his crooked lawyer try to tell you that you are not a productive member of society. They're the non-productive ones. They're the ones causing all the destruction. I know you wanna do the right thing, Darrel, so book him! Get it done, so we can go home. And I'll take care of the lawyer first thing in the morning."

"No, Judge," said Hutchinson resolutely. "I don't believe you. I think you've been passing only half-truths to me this entire time, to say nothing of the general public. It seems that you try to keep my attention from the real point by raising issues that don't really matter. Clearly, you've been playing me since our first interview, feeding my ego, steering me in the direction that served your purpose. I knew you were doing it but I ignored it because I wanted to believe that you were doing the right thing. I can see now that you were just using this serial killer crisis to get votes; nothing like a good crisis to get people to follow the leader! And you were using me. I don't know what the truth is, but I believe Bechard speaks it better than you do."

From the corner of the room came the weak sound of Dan Jensen clearing a large amount of phlegm from his throat. "I – I wanna change my statement."

Travis Noonan stood up. "Okay! I can see I'm going to have to take control of this situation. Hutchinson, I'm calling in the booking sergeant." The big man stepped over to a phone hanging on the wall near the door, but before he could lift the receiver Marcus was there firmly preventing him. Noonan protested, "What are you doing?!"

"You will not call," said the vampire.

Noonan made a swift move for the door but Marcus's smooth hand reached out, covering the big man's hand on the doorknob. Try as he might Noonan could not turn the knob against the strength of Marcus's hand.

XXI – The Real Vampire

"You let me out of here!" cried Noonan, and he pounded the door with his free hand. But it was to no avail. If there was anyone within earshot outside the room, they would have been quite accustomed to the sound of pounding from inside.

Noonan got a hold of himself very quickly. A cool head would be needed to salvage things here. He said, "You are holding me prisoner?!" He wanted to hear a statement of admission, but none was forthcoming. "Help me, Darrel! Get this punk off me!"

The detective rose a little slowly, confused. He wasn't sure what was happening. His only reassurance was his sidearm held safely in his shoulder holster. The thought of pulling it out made him queasy, however. He rarely ever put himself into a situation where use of deadly force was necessary.

Noonan was bellowing loudly. "Call for help, Darrel! They're gonna kill us!" The big man was wrestling against the young looking lawyer, but he was unable to free himself from Marcus's firm grasp.

Obediently, Hutchinson reached for his cell phone. It would be safer, for the moment, than trying to physically confront the young lawyer. Even though the young man was not physically intimidating, there was something in the way that he moved that was indeed very intimidating. Best to keep him occupied with preventing Noonan from leaving or using the phone. Hutchinson hoped that the scene would not escalate any further. Shaking he tried to dial the number to the desk. Why had he never taken the time to program in the damn speed-dial numbers?!

Marcus finally got a hand over the fat man's big mouth. "Relax, Darrel. I am not going to kill anyone… yet. I simply did not wish to have Mr. Noonan involving anyone else in on our little discussion. I think you can see the wisdom of that. Somebody started out with the desire to keep this private; it was either you or Mr. Noonan here, and I am putting my wager on Mr. Noonan. Be all that as it may, I think you will agree that we should continue our exclusivity."

Hutchinson let out a breath of relief. Damn, but this lawyer was smooth! "I agree," he said. He replaced his phone, and pulled out instead a key ring. He spoke as he stepped over to the corner where Dan Jensen sat shackled to his chair. "I am sorry about this, Dan. I hope that I can do something to fix the damage I've caused you. You are free to go; I'll fix the paperwork at lock-up. You will still have an arraignment date, and the court will issue a bench warrant if you don't show, but I'm pretty sure that I can fix things so the prosecutor won't have a case. If you plead 'not guilty' they may just drop the charges.

Maybe Mr. Lance will represent you and take care of it. Either way you shouldn't have to go through a trial."

He continued as he unlocked the handcuffs binding Bechard's wrists. "Mr. Bechard, I don't know what to say. I thought you were the biggest ass on the planet, but I can see now that you are without a doubt a remarkable man. I am truly sorry, and I sense that you do not hold a grudge against me, which I truly appreciate. But now I don't know what to do!"

"You mean with your career, your life?" asked Bechard.

"Yeah. I mean, how can I go on being a cop after all of this?"

"This sure has changed the way I look at things," Dan Jensen inserted.

"Do you enjoy detective work?" asked Bechard.

"Yeah, I do. A lot. It's challenging."

"Detective work can be a valuable service. All you have to do is market your service competitively. I have a feeling that you'll be more successful at it than most."

"You make it sound it so easy," Hutchinson said. "But I have a wife and kids to think about."

"It is easy," said the old man with a wink toward Marcus. "But I got my start with a good bit of help, and I'm willing to pass the favor on to you."

Hutchinson also looked at Marcus who still stood holding Noonan immobile and silenced. "What am I going to do about him?" he asked gesturing toward the politician. "He's governor now and after this he's probably going to squash my nuts into oblivion."

Noonan glowered at the 'former' police detective. Damn right he was gonna squash his nuts! Noonan felt confident that with only a modest amount of damage control he could salvage the situation. Maybe Bechard wasn't going to get sent up the river just yet, but Noonan was too powerful now for Bechard to simply crush out of spite. *Besides*, he thought, *Bechard has too much invested in me to remove me from my position*. All Noonan would have to do is demonstrate his renewed willingness to play ball and he'd be right back on Bechard's A-list, or at least his B-list.

"You don't need to worry about Noonan," said Bechard. "I hate to admit this but he's my creation. I own him. Hell, I've been throwing money at Noonan for years! I've been putting him into powerful positions in exchange for political favors. That's why he was so gung-ho to see me sent to the gallows. He must be thinking that if he can get rid of me then he won't have to make good on his part of the deal. Now

XXI – The Real Vampire

that I've made him governor, he's become a little too big for his britches."

Hutchinson narrowed his eyes and asked, "How did you 'make' him governor?"

Bechard smiled broadly. "Remember how you said 'that's the way the system works?' Well, I didn't make the rules either, I'm just doing the best I can to be productive with the system given to me."

Marcus finally spoke again, "Perhaps Mr. Noonan should be made to pay for his crimes." And Marcus could feel the big man go rigid with fear.

"What crimes?" asked Hutchinson. "He might be a liar and a politician but that's not all that bad."

"He was fixin' to ruin the lives of two innocent men," said Bechard pointedly.

"He is much worse than even all of that, my friends," said Marcus. "He is responsible for many deaths and many ruined lives." Marcus walked the big man back over to his chair and firmly set him down in it. "Have a seat, my corpulent friend. Please, try to refrain from anymore outbursts." The politician remained quiet, planning, as if trying to decide the best possible moment to bolt for the door.

Hutchinson was inquisitive. "What exactly is he guilty of? Why didn't you say something earlier?"

Marcus knew that if he came right out with what he knew about Noonan, the big man would become even more desperate than he already was. He might remain somewhat subdued however, if he didn't know just how truly busted he was, so Marcus concluded that he would have to skirt a few of the facts before dropping the bomb. "Last week a police officer was killed in his home. Does anyone know who killed him?"

Hutchinson had no idea, even after having investigated the crime scene himself. Without the erroneous Bechard and Jensen conspiracy he was back at square one, not that he had ever truly been off of square one at any time throughout this ordeal.

Marcus continued, "The other night a young man named Chad Reeves killed two police officers at Pioneer Square right before being gunned down by the police. Does anyone know the origin of the gun he carried?"

Noonan relaxed somewhat. Obviously this young lawyer knew nothing. He was grasping for answers to obscure questions. How could he know anyway? The only way he could know was if he had talked to Manuel Stanley. The name Chad Reeves rang in the back of Noonan's brain however. It seemed he had heard the name before, but it could just as easily have been his imagination. For now, he just needed to stay focused on damage control.

Hutchinson remembered that he had not found Bruce Nader's firearm at the scene of his murder. He asked, "Are you telling me that this Chad Reeves kid had Bruce Nader's gun?"

"Chad Reeves had a vendetta of sorts against Officer Nader," said Marcus. "There was also a judge and his family found dead in their home at around the same time, was there not?"

"Yeah!" exclaimed Hutchinson. "They were done by Reeves, as well?"

"Yes," said Marcus. "The judge was part of Chad's vendetta."

"How? Why?"

Suddenly Noonan remembered where he had heard the name of Chad Reeves. The kid had been in the papers about a year and a half ago – the first of several people that had contracted AIDS from infected needles that had been planted around town in places where someone might accidentally get pricked. The politician broke into a cold sweat. Surely this pissant lawyer hadn't made the connection back to him. There would be no damage control able to help the situation if Lance had! It was impossible; he had been way too careful. And Stan the Man was dead! There was no way Lance could have found out. It was inconceivable!

Marcus continued, "Chad Reeves, if you will recall, was in the news before. Some time ago when he was diagnosed with AIDS. Do you remember the story?"

"Oh yes!" exclaimed Hutchinson. "Chad Reeves, the poor kid that got stuck by the heroin needle that someone had taped under a stair rail at the court house." And suddenly the vendetta made some kind of twisted sense to the Detective. The blood drained from his face at the realization.

Noonan eyed the door, then eyed the slight bulge under Hutchinson's jacket. If this got any worse he would have to go for the detective's gun. It would not be difficult. With the gun he would be able to regain control of the situation. The body count might have to increase for the sake of damage control, but Noonan knew that he could still work it out.

"Yes," said Marcus. "Whether or not they truly shared in the blame did not affect their outcomes – the police officer and the judge, and all that they loved were destroyed by Chad's hand. He made good his revenge on them. But that is only part of the story."

XXI – The Real Vampire

With a sudden movement that seemed in contrast to his size, Noonan heaved forward, grabbing Hutchinson's wrist, holding his arm and reaching for the Slim-Nine before Hutchinson could even comprehend what he was doing. Once Noonan had his fat hand around the grip of the gun, he gave Hutchinson a hard shove with his other hand and the detective fell from his chair, minus his sidearm.

Noonan was quickly on his feet and moving around the table, flicking the gun in every direction to show the other four men how close to death they might be if they made that one false move. Finally, once in the far corner, putting as much distance as possible between every other man in the small room, Noonan exclaimed, "Now you're the one who's gonna shut up, Lance! Not another word!!" His fat thumb disengaged the safety on the firearm. It was now all set to kill!

Marcus looked calmly at Hutchinson as the man slowly climbed back into his seat. "And now you see how it is, Detective. If you think about it, the puzzle pieces that make up the true picture should be falling into place."

"I said not another word!" cried Noonan. "Hands up!"

Everyone complied, except Marcus, who continued talking. "Jamie Thompson was the man who physically planted each of the needles; that much is correct. Stan the Man kept him supplied, and called the police anonymously every time there was another needle planted so that hopefully the needle could be located before anyone accidentally got stuck. The scheme was designed only to insight a panic in the public, and additionally to subtly turn public opinion against AIDS victims and drugs."

"Shut up!!"

"The whole thing came to a head when Jamie Thompson did not die quietly of 'natural causes.' At that point Stan the Man killed Jamie Thompson and skillfully framed Dan Jensen for the murder. Shortly after, Chad Reeves learned of the entire scheme and killed Stan the Man."

"SHUT UP!!"

"And the man that benefited the most from the crisis was the mastermind behind the whole thing!" Marcus continued, now talking directly to Noonan. "It was not even really all that clever; I have seen much more devious schemes in my time. Chad was probably on his way to kill you when he got himself into trouble and –"

BLAMM!! The gun sounded, then all sound was momentarily gone from the small room. Marcus dropped, a tiny hole directly in the middle of his throat issuing crimson. On the wall directly behind where he had been standing was a red Rorschach shaped blotch. He lay motionless on the floor. Noonan had been aiming for his head.

The politician quickly trained the gun back in the direction of Bechard and Hutchinson. "I'm sorry Darrel, but you're gonna have to take one for the team. How could you lose your temper and shoot Jimmy Bechard and his lawyer?" And with that Noonan aimed the gun at Bechard's broad chest and fired again. The old man fell from his chair to the floor, groaning.

Noonan then trained the gun on Dan Jensen. "I would prefer to not have to explain three deaths here tonight. So you will live only if I have your word to tell this story how it happened – Detective Hutchinson went ballistic and killed Jimmy Bechard and his lawyer!"

Jensen saw the detective turn toward him with a look that reflected only horror, but Noonan was pointing a gun him! Jensen nodded at the politician, almost enthusiastically. He would like to have asked if this still meant that he was off the hook for the other murders, but with Noonan pointing a gun at him he felt that it might be a bad time. Jensen made a mental note to ask about that later.

"And now, Detective," said Noonan lowering the gun. The big man paused to wipe the gun down with handy a handkerchief from his suit pocket. "You're going to put your fingerprints on this gun. Then we're all going to go face the music!" He placed the gun on the table in front of the detective.

Hutchinson quickly snatched the gun, engaged the safety, and stowed it back in its holster. Now that the present danger had passed, the detective got down where Jimmy Bechard lay gasping and groaning. The old man was going to die! "Judge," said Hutchinson, as he applied direct pressure to the wound. "You're outa your goddam mind if you think I'm gonna go along with this." Then he barked an order to Jensen. "Check on Lance!"

Jensen hesitated only for a second with a glance at Noonan, then he moved across the room to the fallen lawyer. Noonan just looked on with apathy. "Give it up, Hutchinson. You have to do this my way now! Don't worry about it. We'll tell everyone that it was self-defense. We'll make it look like Lance attacked me, and you saved my life. Then Bechard went crazy and you had to put him down, too."

Dan Jensen looked down at the lifeless form of the young lawyer. There wasn't a lot of blood, but there wasn't much left of his throat either. He was clearly deceased! Jensen was sad for the death, mostly because now the poor, life-buffeted security guard would be back in hot water. At least now he knew who had shattered his already pathetic life.

XXI – The Real Vampire

Now he knew that it hadn't been fate conspiring against him at all; it had been a man that he hardly knew, using him like a lab rat to achieve his political objectives.

Suddenly, Marcus heaved and coughed a wretched sound through destroyed vocal cords. Jensen shrieked and nearly jumped up on the table in shock and fright.

Marcus knew that his spinal cord had been severely damaged, but somehow he was still able to move; a bit slower, yes, but it would be fast enough. He sat up stiffly, then rose to his feet unsteadily. Jensen and Noonan stared, stunned, as Marcus lurched around the table.

"Oh shit!" Noonan was finally able to say through his shock. He wasn't sure how in the hell anyone could live through such an injury, but he could see by the dead look in the young man's eyes that he was going to need Hutchinson's gun again. He cried, "Hutchinson!!"

The detective had been rather intent on the injured Bechard; now he looked up, his jaw dropping slack in spite of himself. Even Bechard quieted his groaning. All eyes were on Marcus as he staggered toward Noonan, arms reaching out, eyes murderous.

Marcus's breath rasped through a shattered voice box, his words came out in a hoarse, guttural whisper. "You have shown to us what you really are! Now I shall show you what I am!" And all of the men watched the fangs extend.

Noonan raised his arms in a feeble attempt to defend against the vampire, but he found that his strength had abandoned him. As weak as Marcus was from having been shot, he still had the power necessary to subdue his victim and feed.

As the fangs pierced the sweaty skin of Noonan's neck and entered his carotid artery, the big man froze even more rigid than he had been, his eyes wide. The severe, concentrated pain was like nothing he had ever experienced. Travis Noonan had had the good fortune of a life with very little pain; his tolerance was low. A low, abbreviated, guttural scream that sounded more like a gargle used the last of the air in his lungs. Through the unfathomable pain, it seemed to Noonan that he had no power, even to draw in another breath. He wanted so badly to scream his pain, but without air in the lungs the scream only sounded in his head. The source of the scream was his mind, or perhaps his soul, and it filled his head until the only things real to Noonan was the pain of the bite, that now permeated his body, and the scream that resounded through his core, joining the pain like raging mountain runoff into a pulsing river.

His life was meaningless now it seemed. It flowed out of him, and he had neither the power nor the inclination to stop it. It wasn't his life anymore; it belonged to this creature that was in the process of sucking it out!

All of the power and riches that the politician had accumulated in his very short life – none of it mattered anymore. It surely did nothing for him now! Perhaps it would benefit his wife and children – his children! He truly had loved them, but what would become of them in his absence? They would be devastated.

Noonan had left many families devastated by his actions. The politician had left a lot of damage in his wake. Oh, the things he had done in his efforts to acquire power – the sacrifices! His family had paid a part of that price. The realization of his destructive life came to him only in the form of intense grief; regret that his life had never been his own.

The pain was ungodly, the noise in his head stripping him of his last remnants of sanity. And even through all this madness, he stayed strangely lucid, as if this creature that continued to drain his life away wanted him to get a good look at the end right before it came! It seemed that the sucking force on his neck was the only thing holding his eyeballs in their sockets. And the life kept flowing from him… flowing… flowing…

Marcus the Vampire sucked until there was nothing coming from Noonan's obese body. Only then did he stop the flow of adrenaline that had kept the politician's brain somewhat functioning even after it had become severely oxygen starved. The heart had stopped shortly after Marcus had bitten the fat man's neck, but Marcus was not about to let the politician off so easy! And, besides, the vampire needed every drop of that greasy blood.

The vampire turned stiffly; Hutchinson and Jensen might have been the mannequins at a Halloween specialty shop. Marcus looked down at Bechard, then bent and inspected the lifeless man. The pulse was faint; a lot of blood had leaked from the wound onto the floor. It would be sad for the world to lose the hardworking businessman. The vampire made a snap decision.

"Jimmy!!" yelled Marcus, as loud as he could, though it sounded like a terrible whisper. "Jimmy!!" He touched the old man's face and let loose a potent cocktail of adrenaline and other stimulants, then smacked it. The old man finally groaned.

XXI – The Real Vampire

The vampire bit severely into his own wrist, then held it bleeding tightly to Bechard's mouth. "Drink!" he commanded in a hoarse, windy growl. "Quickly!!"

It was not delicious to the old man, but the blood seemed to contain life! He could feel energy seeping back into his body; the pain subsided, faded! No, it was not delicious, but his body seemed to like it, crave it; like drinking nasty powdered protein mix after an extremely heavy workout; it doesn't taste good at all, but it sure goes down smooth!

Hutchinson and Jensen were utterly fixated by the grotesque activities. It was the stuff of Hollywood movies! Here, however, it seemed like a dream. More like a nightmare. Had the men just spent an evening with a real vampire? Hutchinson was more curious while Jensen seemed more apt to run for his life. The only thing that stopped him from such a panic was Hutchinson's relatively calm, controlled demeanor.

Suddenly Marcus wrenched his wounded wrist away from Jimmy Bechard's mouth. The movement had been totally involuntary, but Jimmy had had enough, Marcus decided. Jimmy would live, would survive the fatal bullet wound, would survive old age! Marcus bowed his head. He had just willfully created his first vampire.

The old man's head fell back. He had energy, life, yes, but now he suddenly felt overwhelmingly drowsy. He mumbled something completely unintelligible as he drifted into unconsciousness.

Darrel decided that he had no reason to fear for his life. He remembered the lawyer's words, the vampire's words, 'there is hope for you yet, Detective,' and concluded that the nightmarish creature probably did not want to kill him. Darrel looked at the fatal wound in the young looking man's throat. The bullet had obviously not been stopped even after impacting the spinal column. Darrel could see where the tiny projectile had blown away a chunk from the back of Marcus's neck. "Oh my God!" he whispered, in an attitude of reverence. He had never been a very religious man, but it suddenly seemed appropriate to acknowledge the Almighty.

At the other end of the room Dan Jensen started to shake, and emit a disturbed moan. He was at the end of his control and terror was beginning to take over. He moved drunkenly toward the door.

In a raspy voice Marcus said imploringly to Darrel, "Please, stop him, and calm him down. Neither of you is in any danger. But he needs to be calm before he exits this room."

Darrel was already rising to his feet before Marcus finished. He hurried over and put a firm hand on Dan Jensen's shoulder. "Dan!" he said. "Dan, it's alright! We are safe. He's doesn't want to hurt us." It took a full minute of coaxing before Dan Jensen finally calmed down and took a seat at the table.

"What are you going to do to us?" asked Dan, still just on the edge of hysteria.

"It is not my intention to hold either of you any longer," croaked Marcus. "However, I would appreciate just one last word with both of you before you go."

Both men nodded slowly, and Darrel could not keep himself from asking, "Is this white magic or... the other kind?"

"Neither," Marcus rasped through a smile. "It is science – a marvelous and terrible science; one that hopefully will soon be made without flaw to be a benefit to mankind. Until then, it would be advantageous if you both could protect this secret. I promise that you will find few who believe you, anyway. Only pathetic individuals blinded by mysticism would ever believe such a story. I urge you both to leave here tonight, and take power in your lives. Follow no one; you both have sufficient intellect inside yourselves to be your own authority. Commit yourselves to being honest producers, and you will both lead full and rich lives."

"Is that it?" asked Dan. He was still shaking with anxiety and apprehension.

"Would you like more?" responded Marcus quietly.

"I would," said Darrel matter-of-factly. He was adapting to the idea that vampires were real. "What's gonna happen to Bechard?"

Marcus nodded. "He will be fine."

"Will he be a vampire?"

"Yes," said Marcus.

"What about Noonan?" asked Darrel.

"Noonan is dead," said Marcus. "And it is good. He and others like him that endeavor to get their livelihoods by an unproductive means are the real vampires of society. As individuals they may not live forever, but they suck the life out of society."

Dan Jensen overcame some of his fear. "Do you live forever?" he asked.

"I do not know," said Marcus. "But I would recommend it."

After some minor planning, the four men left the interrogation room. Hutchinson escorted Dan Jensen to the front door of the police

XXI – The Real Vampire

station and released him, then walked down to lock-up and fudged the necessary paperwork to affect Jensen's release.

Marcus, meanwhile, carried Jimmy Bechard out of the building as inconspicuously as possible and drove to the safety of his house in the west hills. The vampire had done nothing to disguise the fate the politician. "Let the 'authorities' draw their own conclusions."

And on his way out of the police station, Ex-Police Detective Darrel Hutchinson stopped at a small room that housed the building's video surveillance control equipment. The equipment was not monitored by a person, just taped on eight different video tapes in case it was necessary to review them later. For those eight tapes, there would not be a 'later.' Then Ex-Police Detective Darrel Hutchinson exited the police station for the last time. He did not tell anyone of his resignation. He didn't even leave a note!

Darrel did send a short e-mail to Lori Conner at the county prosecutor's office. It told her that evidence had been found destroying the case against Dan Jensen and that he had been released from lock-up. "There is no case," the note read. "The charges are false and should be dropped."

Many hours later, police found the exsanguinated body of Governor-elect Travis Noonan. Concerning the details surrounding his death they were baffled, and horrified. Could it be possible that an honest-to-god vampire had done it?

CHAPTER XXII

The strange, white-haired man, the wizard, the Slayer, had, for a time, stopped walking. There was nothing for him to do but to fabricate once again the tools that he needed for his mission; tools that he had once again lost to another vampire. It had only happened one time before, and that had been quite accidental. What is life but a series of mistakes and learning experiences?

But this last time had been no accident, and even more of a learning experience. The vampire had anticipated his coming, had prepared a clever trap! The vampire now had the means, if he so chose, to destroy the strange, beautiful Slayer. For the first time ever he feared for his life. And there was nothing to do but to continue trying to carry out his just mission.

The strange man was seated on the ground amongst the thick foliage in the forest not far from Crown Pointe. He no longer had the appearance of Giovanni, John Locke, John the Revelator! With his beautiful serene face and shock of gravity-defying brilliant hair, he looked as if he belonged there in the dark among the ferns and nettles, the moss covered trees, the night-birds, the possums and slugs. He did not stand out, and he left no visible impact.

In his hands he held a small branch from an alder tree. Bit by painstaking bit, with immeasurable slowness, from the branch he grew a crystal. It would not take too long to grow the necessary crystal for the tool he needed – only about 75 cycles of the seasons. The second tool would take only a little longer to make.

The crickets had ended their communications; the moon was setting. It was the darkest part of this cool night. Nocturnal animals followed their instinctual wanderings heedless of the man that sat on the forest floor.

The tranquility of the scene was invaded by the growing sound of footfalls crashing through the forest. The sounds grew louder; someone was approaching, but the stranger stayed intent upon his task. Presently, the sound stopped as the approaching person at last entered the proximity of the white-haired man, but he still did not look up from his alder branch. He already knew without looking that the intruder was the young peerless man that had followed him for the last little while.

XXII – A New Day

"Hey," said Tim. "Marcus will see you now."

The strange, white-haired man did look up then. He could see that the visitor was wearing his trademark low-light vision-enhancement apparatus and was carrying one of the tracking devices. Gracefully, without a word, the beautiful being stood and walked toward Tim.

Tim was only a little nervous. "C'mon," he said. "This way."

The pair walked back through the dark forest, the strange, white-haired man moving without difficulty through the unlit undergrowth, and Tim faring with considerable less ease. Tim had to stay attentive on making his way, so he was unable to try to engage the wizard in conversation. He knew better anyway.

At length they emerged from the thick forest on a rutted secondary road. After some distance on the road, they finally came to the place where Tim's van sat parked. In the dark it appeared only as a terrible black shadowy shape next to the edge of a foreboding wood, unless you happened to be wearing infrared night-vision goggles, or unless your vision happened to abnormally acute and able to be tuned to be more sensitive at low light levels.

"Get in," Tim instructed, though he didn't need to. "And don't try anything funny!" he added in warning, though he really didn't need to do that either.

Tim maneuvered the van down the secondary road for a short distance before it let out into the curving mountainous highway. Within minutes, they were approaching Crown Pointe, overlooking the dark gulf of the Columbia River gorge. In the absence of light it appeared only as an abyss, a dark void powerful enough to suck in all light, even the glare from the metro thirty miles away. As Tim parked the van, the vehicle headlights passed over a group of people standing at the stone rail, looking out at the dark chasm as if there might be something there to see.

All but one, that is, looked out from the rail. Marcus the Vampire was fixed on something else – the small blue orb in his hands. He had been monitoring the approach of the Slayer. Marcus was focused on the center of the orb, just as John had instructed him that night nearly two hundred years ago on the outskirts of New Orleans. The first time he had looked inside that orb there had been many, many red dots representing vampires. Now he was contemplative and maybe even a little reassured to see that there were only three! One for the Slayer, one for Jimmy, and one for himself. He had been the last vampire in the world!

That thought filled him with a profound loneliness, even though he hated vampires and had been instrumental in their extinction. He knew it wasn't rational or logical, but he was not about to route the emotion. Was this truly the order of the universe? Were vampires truly the evil anomaly as he had always thought? Would their extinction bring about balance in the world? How?

For this momentous occasion, Marcus had invited a few special friends. Janet and Miriam stood ready to witness whatever was about to occur. Standing next to Marcus was Sarah. Tim exited his van and stood a little way off to the side. And Jimmy Bechard, now dramatically transformed, stood waiting to take part in the proceedings.

It had been three days since the shooting, and Jimmy Bechard was now fully restored, not just from his mortal wound, but also from old age as well. He now had the face and body of when he was twenty years old. Only his hair had yet to regain its youthful appearance, but Marcus had said that it would. Being a vampire does not speed up the growth rate of one's hair, and thank god for it! Jimmy's hair would grow in thick and blonde, just as it had when he was twenty. The old man decided that he could get used to this; he had more strength than ever, and he felt invincible!

But alas! Apparently he and Marcus were here this night to 'get cured.' Marcus had told him of the terrible complications of vampirism, and Jimmy had to agree that getting cured was the rational course of action. Being a vampire even for this short period had been the greatest adventure of Jimmy Bechard's life.

Janet radiated with an inner beauty that seemed to light up the night. She had lost weight, and was now very much in touch with her feelings. If it should be that she should ever suffer from depression again, she would know it, and take conscious steps to get better. She now had plenty of self-interest, and she paid particular attention to her choices and actions, and was careful to identify her motivations.

Miriam had all of the energy and joy of someone that was finally free of a heavy burden. She knew that life would have for her many more trials and hardships, but she was ready for the growth. She felt as though there was nothing that she couldn't accomplish.

Sarah moved with the confidence and grace of a woman no longer struggling with internal conflict. She was standing a little taller these days. She had quit smoking, lost all of the excess weight, and was in the process of learning about what was necessary to lead a healthy lifestyle. She was committed to living in a way that promoted

XXII – A New Day

longevity. And she was dedicated to improving her mind, and becoming an individual that produces a real value.

Tim wasn't sure what he was going to do with himself now that it seemed that his vampire slaying quest was over. Now that Tim was in no more danger Desperado was going to leave and go back down to Colombia or someplace and fight against slave-labor. Tim supposed that he could go back to being an accountant, but before he could do that, he would have some mourning to do – real mourning, the right way.

The strange and beautiful man alighted from the van and approached the closely spaced group. He stopped his slow advance when Marcus raised his hand. The cold stars made just enough light for Marcus to see that the face of the Slayer was utterly unreadable.

Marcus spoke slowly, "At last the evil of five centuries is to end. I have chosen the time and place where I shall cease to exist as a vampire." Marcus held up the dish-shaped crystal device, but did not hold it out to the stranger. The old vampire continued, speaking slowly enough and pausing between phrases to allow the beautiful stranger every opportunity to speak, but the white-haired man remained silent.

"Would that I could have figured out how to work this device," Marcus said. "I am pretty sure that this is the one you use to do it – to 'cure' vampires. I have studied my vampirism long, and now, at long last, only at the end do I feel that I am beginning to understand how it works. And if I had been able to learn the secret of this device, I would never have sought you out. I would have used what I know of vampirism and this device to bring to society a way to live virtually forever!" Marcus paused, trying to read the strange man's reaction to his words, but saw none.

"Imagine it!" said Marcus. "An enterprise where the sick and the dying could be turned into vampires and cured of their ills. Healthy donors could supply the blood necessary for the vampires to regenerate. Once the person was fully regenerated we could use this device to cure them of their vampirism, once again free to live a full life. No one ever need die; not from aging, sickness, or at the hand of a vampire!"

Again Marcus paused, and again no reaction from the Slayer.

"Speak up," said Marcus. "Tell me why I should not continue to try to discover the secret of this device and do as I have just outlined."

If the stranger felt any distress over Marcus's veiled threat he did not show it. He remained solidly impassive. But Marcus was not finished. "You will speak, sir! I will not relinquish this device to you until I am satisfied! Natural order be damned!"

The silence following the demand was palpable. Even the sound of the unseen river from the gorge below seemed suspended, waiting for the strange white-haired man to end his long silence.

In the dim starlight Sarah and the other three mortals could just see the faint smile cross the stranger's lips. It was an ancient smile, wise, objective, amused, but with notable sorrow and regret. The beautiful being spoke. "The one called John told me that you would be my most difficult charge."

Every question that Marcus had for the strange man was temporarily forgotten with the mention of John. Before he could collect his thoughts the man continued. "I speak only that I might more quickly end my mission to restore this society back to an uninfected state, and return to my own place. The responsibility for the infected condition of this world rests solely upon me and actions that I did take seven thousand, four hundred and seventy-two cycles of the seasons prior to the current cycle. I unleashed into this world the contaminant that resulted in nothing less than the retardation of and the deviation from the normal evolutionary course of this society."

Jimmy spoke up, "Whoa, now! That's being a little hard on yourself, doncha think?"

But the beautiful stranger shook his head solemnly. "I tell you this not for your sympathy, but only that you might understand my motivations. To help you to understand I shall begin at the beginning.

"I came to this world with three others of my kind, my teachers, seven thousand, six hundred and twelve seasonal cycles prior to the current cycle. Our purpose was only to examine, perhaps a little too closely, the current evolutionary status of your species, and for me to see some of the universe. My teachers had visited this beautiful world many times before."

"You're from another planet?!" The question came from Janet even though Sarah had been just about to ask the same thing. Mimi had been stunned into silence.

"Yes, my friend. At the time, the people of your species were just awaking to individual consciousness. Not all of them did. But I happened upon one that had not only awoken to her self-awareness, but she was also beautiful and strong. She, along with those other members of her settlement had acquired some agricultural skills. I first saw her in a large beautiful garden. She was exquisite, and I was instantly entranced.

"Although my teachers said that it could have catastrophic results, I engaged her in communication and I found her passing very fair. She

XXII – A New Day

had a far quicker mind than most others of her species, and she was very strong physically and personally. But what held me most fascinated was her passion! She was full of love and beauty! By virtue of our genetic makeup, passion is a quality that beings of my species do not inherently have or even understand. To learn more about it I stayed with my new love, while my teachers proceeded on without me.

"Her name was Lillith, and for one hundred and forty cycles of the seasons we lived together, and with the others of her family and settlement. Knowing that the budding society would have to discover new technology for itself in order for growth and progress to occur in the correct measure, I kept my knowledge of certain technologies to myself.

"But as my beloved Lillith began to grow old, it became clear to me that she would die before certain life-preserving technology was developed. From my education, I had some idea of how long it takes for an emerging civilization to progress to the point where certain technologies are developed, and my Lillith would not live long enough to benefit.

"I could not stand the thought of my beloved dying, her passion, her love, her consciousness forever snuffed out, leaving only the beautiful memory of her in my heart. So I made the fateful decision to give to her the life-preserving technology that worked so well in my own body. I had no reason to think that it would not work the same for her.

"But, it did not. The technology did not work in her body as I had desired, and her mind could not make the adjustment. Since then I have discovered the reason for the error. I now know that genetic differences allow the technology to work perfectly in my body while functioning with error in your bodies. The technology runs on a fuel which my body produces in abundance, while your bodies do not produce the fuel in sufficient quantity. Further, the technology should convert light energy to other sources of energy for its life-preserving purposes, but due to your genetics, the technology in your body becomes prohibitively light sensitive. And that was how my beloved Lillith died. After a feverish night of madness in which she inadvertently passed the technology onto a few others of her kind, she walked out into the morning sun and was forever lost to me. If I had the ability to better feel and express my passion, you might begin to understand the depths of my wretchedness and regret.

"Her death was inevitable. I could not change that with the technology. But I knew that it was my responsibility to remove the technology from those with whom Lillith had unintentionally shared it. I spent the next one hundred and fifty seasonal cycles fabricating the tools I would need to un-infect those with the technology. It took a little longer than I had –"

"A little longer!" Jimmy interrupted. "Seven thousand years!"

Marcus explained, "Time is relative to the individual. I am sure that for you, the years seem to fly by. For me, the decades fly by. Perhaps the Slayer is at such a tremendous age that the centuries or the even millennia fly by."

The strange white-haired man continued. "I worked as quickly as I could, and I almost had the task completed after only two thousand, nine hundred and fifty cycles of the seasons, when a rather clever charge managed to appropriate one of my tools. It was not until only six cycles of the season prior to the current cycle that I was, with the aid of this man and his transport," the Slayer gestured to Tim, "finally able to catch him and take my tool back."

"That was John!" whispered Marcus in excitement and awe.

"Yes, that was the one called John, though he had many other names as well. And after I had cured him I had to convince him to not seek you out, as I know he would have done, in order to re-infect, as he had done so many times before."

Marcus was stunned as he calculated John's age. His old friend had been immensely old; over five thousand years! And this strange man before him, this apparent interstellar traveler, was even older. How old must his teachers have been? And yet, Marcus surmised, not even that much older, in the vast relativity of space and time. Marcus thought of his old friend and his last words to him, *"We must live!"* and Marcus knew that John must be somewhere right now, working feverishly on the question of immortality. "How did you convince him to not seek me out?" asked Marcus, masking guilt.

"It was quite an undertaking, I must confess. He was very motivated to remain alive; but such motivation is necessary for the development of life-preserving technology. However, like a young bird must peck its own way out its egg and learn to fly on its own, a civilization must develop such technology for itself – a lesson that I have finally learned at immeasurable cost to your world.

"Mastery over natural aging and death is the chief accomplishment of an emerging civilization, not the development of nuclear technology, high-speed interstellar travel, cold fusion, or even worldwide peace. Once a form of life-preserving technology is developed to insure that not one conscious individual ever need be lost to death, the civilization

XXII – A New Day

has the rest of time to solve those other problems, and it surely does not take forever to work out any of those aforementioned trivialities.

"But herein lays the great damage of my terrible mistake. The contaminating influence of our life-preserving technology in your species complicated the normal progress of your society. It introduced a concept that budding societies usually eliminate early in their development – deceit! Because of the nature of a vampire's existence, my woefully infected charges found it convenient to exercise dominion over the rest of society. They found that it was all too easy to establish authority, a concept quite foreign to me, and surreptitious organizations that allowed them to live in secrecy, while enjoying the benefits of the resources of others. Now, even with nearly all of the vampires gone, the hulking husks of those detrimental organizations remain, operated by the conceptual descendents of the original deceivers; blind, indolent, dishonest."

"What are we to do about that?" asked Sarah.

"As I said before, develop first life-preserving technology; then you will have forever to solve the infinite mysteries of the universe. I think that with some form of biological immortality achieved and available to every member of society you will find that dishonest organizations like governments and religions will simply dissolve."

To everyone in the group except Marcus, that undertaking seemed daunting. "Can you tell me anything of the technology? Anything at all?"

The beautiful man smiled. "What I know of the technology, which is not any great amount, I must not tell. You will discover it for yourself soon enough."

The sky to the east was beginning to lighten. The shape of the gorge was forming beyond the edge of Crown Pointe. Soon, with the increasing light, it would slowly bloom with color. Marcus stepped forward and extended the three crystal devices that he was carrying. He signaled for Tim to do the same. The old vampire let out a long breath. "I do not know your name."

"I am Sonsenoi," answered the beautiful, white-haired man.

"Is it going to hurt, Sonsenoi?" Marcus asked.

"You should feel nothing if you are without injury. You will sense the absence of the technology," said Sonsenoi.

"Let's do it then," said Marcus; the devices changed hands.

Marcus and Jimmy stood next to each other at the edge overlooking the great gorge. Jimmy said, "Thanks for savin' my life."

"You deserve it, my friend."

"Are we gonna be able to figure out this 'technology' thing before we grow old and die?"

Marcus tried to hide his sly smile. "I do not know. All we can do is give it our best shot."

"Well," said Jimmy, returning Marcus's smile with a nod. "We have about eighty years to figure it out. What's the first thing you're gonna do as a mortal?"

Marcus sighed with a slight quaver to his breath. "Watch a sunrise with my dearest loved-ones."

Jimmy noted the rim of wet lining Marcus's hazel eyes, and nodded again. There was much, much more that he was going to learn from his old mentor. He said, "That does sound very nice. It's been years since I took the time to watch a sunrise." There was a pause, then he added, "But after that I've got to go in for a little procedure. I could never get used to having this damn foreskin!"

"Never?" said Marcus, grinning. He turned serious. "Are you ready?"

"No." Jimmy smiled nervously. The others looked on from the side, equally anxious, or more so.

"Good." Marcus turned to Sonsenoi. "Hit it!"

The high pitched tone began its glissando-ing rise into the ultrasonic followed by the barely perceptible flash. Marcus felt a mild disorientation that might have almost felt like the blow from a sudden gust of wind. Then, the invincibility was gone. The hunger was gone, and he felt for an instant as if he was dying. A fog seemed to settle over his head, and Marcus knew that his brain function was lessening. He would miss that the most, he knew. Memories, that only moments before were clear as cinema, suddenly took on the quality of dreams; indeed, Marcus felt a grogginess, as if he had just been awaken from a deep but restless, vivid dream-filled sleep. His mind scrambled to hold on to the most precious of those fleeting images. He wouldn't lose all of his memories, certainly not. The lessons of life learned over five hundred years were all still intact. But the absolute recall was no longer available.

For Jimmy, being such a young vampire and therefore not so thoroughly acclimated to the feelings accompanying vampirism, the sensation of being cured was less profound. Presently, both of them had recovered their bearings and smiled at the others who were waiting anxiously, expectantly for the two of them to say that they were alright.

As the sky lightened there was tearful rejoicing among the small group. Hugs and kisses were exchanged all around, and even Little

XXII – A New Day

Timmy felt like a part of this family. At some point during the jubilation, the strange and beautiful white-haired man, Sonsenoi, quietly receded into the forest. Only Tim noticed him leave.

Marcus knew as the blue spread across the sky to the west that he would not have to be concerned with the possibility of dropping into spasms, tearing violently to find protection from the sun. And he knew that he had nothing to fear from the sun itself. He was truly cured; only it was strange getting used to the idea. It wasn't quite real to him yet. He still had his fangs after all, and he wondered if they would ever go away. Perhaps he could have them pulled…

Sarah joined Marcus at his side. His arm fell about her waist as they looked to the east. She said, "It's so beautiful; I wish I could stare at it."

"Stare," said Marcus, "at life."

The sun dawned bright and beautiful, seeming to rise directly from the head of the Columbia River gorge itself. It's rays caught Marcus for the first time in over five hundred years, and he knew that it was going to be a great day!

THE END

About the Author

Paul Beach was born in Oregon and went to school in Portland. He spent the greater chunk of his adult life on the road as a professional musician. Paul now lives in Florida with Beverly, his soulmate, in a house full of teenagers and animals. He still plays music in a band.

In addition to The Real Vampires Trilogy, Paul has also written an action novel featuring a flying machine, The Flitbike.

Paul enjoys riding his tandem bicycles along the beach with Beverly, living a totally healthy lifestyle, and thinking about living forever.

3042005

Made in the USA